LEGACY

Kevin Boreen

Copyright © 2023 Kevin Boreen

All rights reserved

The characters and events portrayed in this book are fictitious. Any similarity to real persons, living or dead, is coincidental and not intended by the author.

No part of this book may be reproduced, or stored in a retrieval system, or transmitted in any form or by any means, electronic, mechanical, photocopying, recording, or otherwise, without express written permission of the publisher.

ISBN: 9798373657136

Cover design by: Ammad Zulfiqar

Printed in the United States of America

To Catherine

v

PROLOGUE

Deborah Fiske held her sedated son's hand as she stood beside his hospital bed. Padded restraints bound his arms and legs. The empty socket where his right eye should have been was heavily bandaged. Clear plastic strips closed deep gashes in his forehead where the tormented teenager had clawed his own face. A bag of clear fluid was suspended from a hook mounted on the head of the bed, a plastic tube running down to the intravenous needle in his arm.

A doctor passing in the hall noticed her and stepped quickly into the room. "Mrs. Fiske, I didn't know you were here."

She didn't look up from her son. His face, despite its fresh wounds, was so precious to her. He seemed at peace now, even angelic, despite the terrible demons that tormented him.

"How could you have let this happen?" she asked.

Deborah had brought Paul to the McAllister Hospital Psychiatric Treatment Center the day before. After a violent episode at home, one in which two male nurses had barely been able to restrain him, the doctors had wanted to keep him under observation at the hospital as they adjusted the mix of drugs that sought to control his extreme schizophrenia.

"We had him in a padded cell under continuous observation, Mrs. Fiske. He appeared to be asleep, but he suddenly jumped up and… did this to himself."

She closed her eyes, feeling the warmth of her son's skin on her fingertips.

"What kind of a life is this?" she asked quietly. "What am I going to do?"

The doctor stood beside her in silence for what seemed a long time. "I don't know what to say, Mrs. Fiske. Paul is one of the most severe cases I've ever treated. We've tried aripiprazole, clozapine, ziprasidone, lurasidone, asenapine, risperidone, paliperidone--"

"I know the names of the drugs, Doctor." Her voice took on a harder edge. "I asked you, what am I going to *do*?"

"For now, we'll keep him here under sedation. We'll have to make arrangements for the missing eye. The original is…irreparable."

"But is this *it*? Does he live out the rest of his life as a…some sort of… vegetable?"

"We don't like to use that term here. He's sedated now for his own protection. The new mix of medications may help. Once he's stabilized you can bring him home. With the facilities you have, your nursing staff can do as much for him as we can."

"Is there anything else in the pipeline? Any cause for hope?"

"There's always reason to hope. Recent antipsychotics haven't met expectations, sadly, but this is a heavily researched field with several new drugs under development. Please don't give up, Mrs. Fiske."

"This is my child. I'm his mother. I'll never give up. The question is: have you?"

"No, of course not." He shifted uncomfortably. "I'm very sorry that we haven't been able to improve his condition. I wish I had better answers for you."

"So do I."

The doctor shook his head. "I know you're frustrated. We don't want you to feel trapped here. There are other hospitals: Massachusetts General, Johns Hopkins—"

"We've been."

Deborah Fiske had so many regrets. She regretted marrying Paul's father, an absent billionaire thirty years older than her who no longer wanted anything to do with his afflicted family. He'd wanted a son, a legacy. They'd both known the risks. She regretted agreeing to undergo the special fertility treatments. She blamed God. She blamed herself.

But above all, she blamed Claude Dumont.

1

Tom Wright was in a mood to celebrate. A tall, broad-shouldered man with curly gray hair and soft brown eyes, he was a senior writer for *Future* magazine, one of the world's most prestigious periodicals. He had recently been named a finalist for a Pulitzer Prize in investigative reporting for a series of articles published the previous year. His date tonight was Britt Nielsen, at fifty-plus still one of the world's most beautiful and photographed women. They'd been friends and more for nearly a decade. He'd jumped at her invitation to attend the Art Basel international art fair. The timing couldn't have been better. Success in investigative journalism was a cruel taskmaster, and his publisher had recently questioned whether he was growing stale. Tom needed a new story, sometime big to follow his last triumph and maintain the trajectory of his career. Perhaps Art Basel would spark an idea.

They pulled up to the front of the Miami Convention Center. Tom suppressed a grin as he noticed the valet try not to look at Britt's long legs as she rose from the driver's seat of her Bentley. She looked sensational in her black Fendi dress and five-inch heels. She and Tom walked arm-in-arm past the long line of ticket holders waiting outside, cameras flashing all the way to the VIP entrance. This year's show featured work by David Hockney, Andy Warhol, Richard Serra, Jeff Koons, and Vija Celmins, but the highlight was the two Picassos on offer, sure to attract leading art collectors and dealers from around the world. While the fine art was exciting, Tom especially looked forward to the people-watching. It was one of many things that had drawn him to journalism, and to Britt herself. Indeed, she seemed to know everyone.

Once inside the vast building, they strolled past creations spanning the full spectrum of human imagination. There were impossibly large abstract metal sculptures, pop-culture balloon animals made of stainless steel, the most meticulous of drawings, and, of course, paintings of every size, subject, and medium.

"This is incredible," Tom said, stopping to pick up two glasses of Krug champagne.

"Two hundred galleries," she said, clinking glasses, "over four thousand artists. It doesn't get any bigger than this."

Tom smiled into her big blue eyes, which had a quality of color he had only seen in glaciers and icebergs. She was classically Nordic: tall, blond, and statuesque. She spoke at least six languages fluently and was completely at ease in any group or situation. For reasons he still didn't fully understand, they had formed an instant and lasting rapport. She genuinely seemed to enjoy his company, and he certainly enjoyed hers.

They wandered deeper into the exhibition. The crowd was eclectic, some casually dressed, some elegantly. The air buzzed with talent, hustle, and money.

"Ah!" she said. "The Picassos."

She led Tom toward a lively crowd standing around two cubist paintings, earlier works of the great genius. As they drew closer, Tom saw that most of the well-dressed men were elderly, evidently in their seventies or eighties. They were gathered around a tall, handsome man with a full head of silver hair and a carefully trimmed mustache.

"Is that Claude Dumont?" Tom asked Britt.

"In the flesh."

Dumont seemed to be having a marvelous time, smiling and laughing as if he were the father-of-the-bride at a wedding reception. Dumont moved with the graceful ease of an athlete as he organized everyone around the two Picassos for a photograph. When Dumont waved in a dozen or so younger people who had been standing to the side, Tom was immediately struck. It took him a moment to realize why. He had never seen such a beautiful collection of youth. He was instantly intrigued.

"Are those the grandchildren?" he asked into Britt's ear.

She laughed. "You're off by a generation."

"Great grandchildren?"

"Colder."

Tom glanced at her and laughed. "How is that possible?"

She squeezed his arm, whispering, "That's what everybody wants to know."

Tom saw the parents' pride in their offspring, the mutual glances, smiles, and caresses. He should have had that himself, but he didn't. He thought of the last time he'd seen his wife, the sheet being pulled over her face. He pushed the thought away.

Cameras were flashing all around them, so Tom didn't think twice about reaching for his cell phone. As he took a few photos of the crowd, Dumont seemed to recognize someone and emphatically gestured for him to get into the picture.

"Who's that?" Tom asked.

Britt wrinkled her nose in thought. "Oh, that's Scott Fiske. Private banker. Spends most of his time in Europe now."

Tom grinned at her. "How do you do that?"

"Do what?" She grinned and shrugged. "It's a gift."

She took Tom's hand and drew closer to get a better look at the Picassos. The paintings really were extraordinary, much more interesting and beautiful than could be appreciated in any photograph. If Tom had overheard correctly, Dumont had just purchased both. Tom couldn't imagine what they must have cost.

But his attention was drawn more to the purchaser than to the canvases. Dumont was even more impressive in person than in the magazines and television news stories Tom had seen. He had an aura of vitality and goodwill that drew people to him. Everyone seemed to want to speak with him. Tom felt the magnetic pull too and Dumont was within reach, so why not? He was about to introduce himself when another man put his hand on Dumont's arm and whispered something into his ear. Tom noted Dumont's concerned reaction and heard him say, "I'm back in the city tomorrow. Stop by and we'll talk about it." As Tom took another photo, Dumont gave the man a warm pat on the shoulder, made meaningful eye contact, and turned away, giving the next person his undivided attention. Tom's opportunity to meet the great man had passed, but not his newfound fascination.

"Well," Britt said, slipping her arm inside his, "you said you wanted to see people. We're off to a great start."

"I'd love to know who's in these photos."

"Have you got a story in mind?"

Tom hesitated to answer, partly because he didn't know himself. Sometimes his best ideas started with a calamity from which he methodically worked backwards, seeking insights into root causes. This felt the opposite. A chance meeting. A hunch. Perhaps a grain of sand that might grow into a pearl?

"I won't know until I do a little more digging."

She smiled at him. "You've caught a scent."

"Perhaps." He grinned back at her. "Anyway, what's next?"

"I'd like to see the Hockneys and Vija's work. Then there's the oyster bar, and I've got a nice after-party to take you to, unless you want to go straight to my place."

Tom smiled. "Tonight, I'm all yours."

She pressed her free hand gently against his chest. "That's what I like about you."

2

The next morning, Tom boarded a Delta flight bound for New York. He had a window seat in First Class and was grateful for the extra space to stretch out. Britt had kept him up until dawn, and he hoped his headache would pass before he landed at LaGuardia. As awful as he felt now, it had been a very enjoyable trip, and, on top of it all, he now had that grain of sand.

His visit with Britt had rekindled memories of his life's great tragedy, the loss of his wife and newborn son nearly two decades ago. It had been an apparently healthy pregnancy. He recalled rushing to the hospital full of hope and happy expectations. But things had gone wrong in the delivery room, and then misjudgments were made in the operating theater. Waiting nervously in the antiseptic hallway, Tom had looked up at the approaching doctor, and knew. Struggling against his own tears, the physician had delivered news that no man should ever have to hear. His wife and son were dead, and in that moment a part of Tom had died too.

A couple stepped into the aisle and stopped at his row. The man appeared to be in his late sixties, stout but vigorous, and she was younger and quite attractive, well-dressed with shoulder length blonde hair. The husband put their bags in the overhead compartment as she sat across the aisle.

"Would you two like to sit together?" Tom offered.

"That would be very nice, thank you," the man replied.

They exchanged seats, the man taking the aisle across from Tom. In the process, it occurred to Tom that he'd seen him before, but he couldn't place it at first. On a hunch, he took out his phone and checked his photos from the night before, and there he was: the one who had whispered in Dumont's ear.

Never one to hesitate on a potential lead, Tom extended his phone. "Excuse me, but is this you?"

The man was a little surprised at first, but took the phone, looked at the photo, and, smiling, said, "Yes, that's me all right."

Tom explained that he was a journalist and that he'd been invited to the art fair by an old friend. He said he'd been deeply impressed by the exhibits.

"Yes, it's an annual event for us. Have you been to any of the others?"

"I didn't know there were."

"Yeah, there are three big shows every year. There's Miami, and then Hong Kong and Basel."

"Are you a collector?"

"A bit, but nothing serious. I'm more of a car buff. A lot of our friends show up, though, so for us it's mostly social." The man leaned closer, discreetly pointing to his wife. "It makes up for all the horse races I drag her to."

"What do you do, if you don't mind my asking?"

"Don't mind at all. I own car dealerships in New York City, Miami, and Los Angeles. High end stuff: Lamborghini, Ferrari, Maclaren, that sort of thing. Name's Rick Miller." He extended his hand. Tom shook it. "And you?"

"Tom Wright. I'm a writer for *Future* magazine."

"Really? We subscribe. Have for years." He turned to his wife. "Sue, this is Tom. He writes for *Future*."

"It's a wonderful publication," she said. "It's nice to read positive news."

"I'm sure it wasn't me you were taking pictures of," Rick said with a grin. "Do you know Claude?"

"Only by reputation. I was going to introduce myself, but a lot of people seemed to want his attention."

Rick laughed. "You can't imagine. That guy. He's got so many irons in the fire, I don't know how he keeps track of them. I mean, the wine, the art, the horses, his estate in France. The man's got it all."

"And don't forget those kids," Sue said, leaning forward. "They're an absolutely amazing family."

"I was struck by that," Tom said. "I mean, the whole group. I don't think I've ever seen such a perfect collection of young people."

"Yes, it's remarkable," Rick said, lowering his eyes briefly. "Do you have children?"

"No," Tom said, feeling the deep stab of pain that always followed that question, an old scar that would never heal. "Married twice, but no kids. And you?"

"No," Rick said, taking his wife's hand. "Married ten years, but it hasn't happened for us yet."

Tom and Sue exchanged glances, and he sensed an intense longing in her before she looked away. He hoped he hadn't struck a raw nerve, but he couldn't shake the feeling that he had. The cabin door closed, the flight attendants gave the safety briefing, and the plane taxied to the runway. The Millers said little for the rest of the flight. Tom hoped he hadn't offended them. They seemed like nice people.

3

The next day, Rick Miller's limousine dropped him off at the 56th street entrance to 432 Park Avenue. As was his habit, he was a few minutes early for his 10:00 a.m. appointment. Rick had known Claude for years. Sue and Claude's wife, Nadine, were on a few charitable boards together, and Claude had purchased several cars from him over the years. Rick was both nervous and excited about his visit. He'd had made hundreds of millions of dollars in the car business over the past four decades, and the stock market had been kind to him along the way. Even so, his fortune was nowhere near Claude's league. Aside from the automobiles and some special service requests over the years, their relationship had been entirely social. Rick had never asked Claude for anything, until now, and he was about to ask for something he wasn't even supposed to know about. Not knowing whether the great man was going to make his dreams come true or throw him out onto the street, he took a deep breath and entered the building.

432 Park Avenue was one of the most iconic skyscrapers in Manhattan. At 1,396 feet in height, it had until recently been the tallest residential structure in the Western Hemisphere. Rick had never been inside. The lobby was sleek, minimalist, and impressive. A uniformed concierge greeted Rick and escorted him to the elevator that directly served Penthouse 95, which Rick had heard occupied an entire floor of the building. The ride up was smooth and surprisingly rapid. The doors hushed open and he stepped into a marble vestibule.

"Rick!" Nadine greeted him warmly. He had met her many times, but the sight of her still took his breath away. Thirty years younger than Claude and a former Miss France, she had shoulder-length auburn hair, bright brown eyes, full lips, and perfect skin. She wore beige chinos and a light cashmere sweater accented with a Hermes scarf. She gave him a hug. "Where's Sue?"

"At home, and she sends her best. Claude and I just had a quick matter to discuss."

"Of course. I'll take you to him."

They walked through the expansive living room. The views of Manhattan through the ten-by-ten-foot windows were stunning. A Brahms intermezzo was playing in another room and grew louder as they approached. They entered a large wood-paneled study and Claude stood up at the piano, smiling broadly. "Rick! It's good to see you!"

"I wish you hadn't stopped. That was beautiful."

"Oh," Claude said, waving dismissively at the piano. "I'm as rusty as a shipwreck." He grasped Rick's arm, his grip powerful. "I'm so glad we're both in the city today."

"I'll leave you two," Nadine said. "Rick, can I get you anything?"

"No, thanks, Nadine." Rick's palms were sweating. He hoped Claude hadn't noticed. "I'm fine."

Claude gestured to a leather chair and took one opposite.

"Thank you for seeing me, Claude."

"I sensed some emotion in you last night, my friend." Claude gazed across at him. "What can I do to help?"

Rick took a deep breath, collecting himself. He was accustomed to selling expensive cars to professional athletes, rock stars, and Hollywood actors, but Claude was easily the most impressive person he'd ever met. It wasn't just his wealth, his homes, his robust health, his beautiful wife, his accomplished children, and his thriving businesses. Whenever he was with Claude, Rick felt like he was the best possible version of himself, that literally anything was possible. To have this great man looking at him so intently, literally on the edge of his chair in his desire to be of assistance, was almost overwhelming.

"I'll get right to it, I guess." Rick looked down at his clasped hands for a moment, and then raised his eyes to meet Claude's steady gaze. "Sue and I've been married for about ten years now. We haven't been able to have children. We've tried everything, and I do mean everything." Rick looked down at his hands again, pressing them together to stop them from shaking. The silence between them stretched out.

"Please," Claude encouraged gently. "We're old friends, Rick. You can tell me anything."

"Sue really wants to have a baby. Our baby."

Claude nodded. "She's still young. What is she, late forties?"

"Forty-seven. I'm turning seventy next month." He paused again. "The fertility doctors have been warning us of the risks of a pregnancy at this stage in our lives, both to her and to the baby."

"Is your sperm viable?" Claude asked the question as if it were the most natural thing in the world, and then he chuckled at himself. "Listen to me, the old horse breeder."

"I'm told it's fine, but I know the chances of defects are higher for a man my age. Sue wants to keep trying. She wants that baby as much as I do."

Claude opened his hands. "You could adopt."

"That's a wonderful thing and we have friends that have taken that path, but we want the child to be *our* child. Claude, I haven't done the things in the world that you have…"

Claude waved away the compliment. "Don't be ridiculous."

"…but I want to leave…a legacy," Rick continued, "someone to follow in my footsteps. I want a son. I want my line to continue. I want that more than anything else in the world."

After a pause, Claude asked, "And you've come to me because?"

This, Rick knew, was the moment of highest risk, but he had come this far. "I'm told by mutual friends that you've been able to help them…with similar problems." Rick held up his hands and added quickly, "I don't know anything more than that. Whatever your secret is, it's very well kept. I came here today to ask you to help Sue and me have a baby." Rick took a long, slow breath. "Can you do that?"

Claude looked back at him for what seemed a long time. He seemed to be making a decision. Then he said, "Yes, I believe I can. It'll be expensive, and the process has some, well, highly sensitive aspects." Claude stopped, waiting.

Rick felt a deep excitement rising within

him. *So, it was true. It is possible.* "Money won't be problem."

"I'm sure it won't be." Claude rubbed his temples, a concerned expression clouding his face. He took a quick breath, as if to emphasize that what he was about to say was important. He leaned forward, lowering his voice. "What we're about to discuss must stay strictly between us. No exceptions, not even Sue. Can you do that?"

Rick hadn't expected to have to keep this from his wife. "I'll have to tell her *something*."

Claude considered that for a moment. "Fair enough. Only Sue, but less is better, okay? You'll soon understand why."

Rick nodded.

Claude raised his index finger. "No one else."

"You have my word."

"Good." Claude leaned back and crossed his ankles. "How much do you know about gene editing?"

4

Eight blocks away, Tom Wright looked down on Broadway from a height of twenty-one stories. Befitting the journal's name, his spacious office gleamed with polished steel and glass. Visitors to the magazine's headquarters likened it to a cross between an art gallery and a space station. One door led to a hallway and his assistant's desk, and another to a private conference room that could accommodate six people. Amy Klar, his intern, was hard at work there, cell phone, pens, legal pads, and laptop spread out on the table. On a whiteboard Tom had taped enlarged prints of his Art Basel photos. Penned arrows connected each of the elderly men to index cards bearing background information.

Ten years ago, Tom had selected three graduate students from top journalism schools to work with him for a semester as unpaid interns. It had been the best idea he'd ever had. Word had spread to other campuses and over the years the selection process had become highly competitive. Eventually he had determined that one intern always stood out, either due to talent

20

and desire or, perhaps more likely, because Tom worked most effectively with just one person. Accordingly, he had downsized his program to a single intern, and this semester's was Amy Klar. She was a tenacious, thoughtful journalist pursuing her master's degree at NYU. Blonde and fit, her morning five-mile jogs around Central Park did nothing to lessen her energy when she came to work. She had performed brilliantly these past four months. He intended to get as much as he could from her before the new intern joined him in January, and he knew he was going to miss her. He could already tell Amy was warming up to the Art Basel story.

"How's it coming along," he asked as he stepped into the conference room, not at all surprised to see her hard at work on a Saturday morning.

She smiled up at him as she removed her ear pods, a bag of cut carrots and a cup of coffee beside her laptop, her ubiquitous large water bottle within reach. "We're down to the last two."

"Already?" Tom, pleased, had asked her to identify the men in his Art Base photos. Standing at the whiteboard, Tom reviewed the current state of their research. Three of the men in the photographs were Arabs: Abbad Abdallah, Omar Baghdadi, and Khalil Darwish. Of these, one was a billionaire oil merchant, one was a Saudi royal, and one was a real-estate developer from the United Arab Emirates. All three were closely tied to the Dubai World Cup, one of the world's premier Thoroughbred horse races. John Hastings was an English lord, also prominent in racing circles. Joshua Cohen and Scott Fiske were American bankers. Abhay Nayak and Pratul Mukerjee were Indian billionaires, one a steel magnate and the other the founder of an information-technology outsourcing company. Lucas Montez was a rancher from Argentina. Apparently, his estancia included over 500,000 contiguous acres of land, a factoid that had made it onto his index card. Paul Ferriera owned a company in Brazil that made aircraft components. Rick Miller, the auto dealership owner, he'd met personally. And Claude Dumont stood in the center, proudly pointing to his newly acquired Picassos. Two men still lacked an index card.

"I've checked with anyone I could find," Amy said, pushing a strand of hair behind her ear.

Tom grinned. "This sounds like a case for Britt."

"Who's she?"

"An old friend." Tom took out his cell phone and tapped Britt's name on his favorites list.

After several rings, she answered. "What's up, Tom?" It sounded like she was in a crowded restaurant.

KEVIN BOREEN

"Am I interrupting anything?"

"Just out for brunch with friends. What's going on?"

"Remember that photo I took of the Picassos? My intern, Amy, has identified all the older guys but two. If I text you the photo, would you take a look?"

"Sure!"

Tom sent the photo.

"Ah," Britt said a moment later, "the lovely teenagers from this weekend."

"For now, I'm more interested in the fathers. Back row, second and fourth from the left."

"Okay," Britt said, "you caught me at the perfect time. I'm here with my brain trust." He heard conversation on the other end. Britt was obviously showing the photo around her table. He heard some laughter, and then a pleasant cry of recognition. Britt came back on the line. "The Japanese man is Yuma Sugimoto. He's an art collector. Lots of money. Very private. The other is Adrik Dorokhin."

"Can you spell that last one?"

She did. "Russian oligarch. Some kind of metal…nickel, copper, or something. Also lots of money."

"You're amazing," Tom said, waving Amy over and handing her his hastily scribbled notes.

"Is this going to be the big story you were hoping for?"

"Too early to tell. We're just trying to figure out who's who and doing a little brainstorming at this point." Tom walked to the whiteboard and touched the group photograph. "I can't stop thinking about it. Men their age with such young kids."

"Well, if you ever want to bounce some ideas off me…"

"I'm sure I will. In any case, Amy and I owe you a drink."

"Tell me about this Amy?" Britt said, her tone teasing. "Should I be jealous?"

Tom winked at Amy, who was watching him intently as she listened to his side of the conversation. "I could almost be her grandfather."

Britt laughed. "Then I most definitely *am* jealous. Anyway, I'm ignoring my friends. Call me later? I'd like to hear more."

"I will."

"Promise?"

"Promise." Tom hung up.

As Amy added index cards for Sugimoto and Dorkhin to the whiteboard, she raised an eyebrow. "Old friend, huh? Sounds like more than that to me."

Tom grinned and shrugged. "No comment." He stepped back from the board, his chin in his hand. Thirteen men, most of them in their eighties. All but Scott Fiske seemed to have a son or daughter pictured with them.

"What's your hypothesis?" she asked, returning to her chair.

"Maybe that people are having children much later in life?" Tom suggested.

"Particularly successful people? That might be the angle for the magazine."

"The wealth aspect is interesting," Tom agreed. "Maybe they're getting better health care than the rest of us."

"Or maybe," Amy said, "there's more advanced health care that makes it possible for them to have kids in the first place."

"Or maybe people who have devoted their lives to making money are waking up to the realization that they've missed the blessings of family life."

"Or," said Amy, "they've realized that they bungled things with past families and now have the time and resources to do it right."

"It could be any or all of those things," Tom said, enjoying her quick mind and enthusiasm. "It might amount to an interesting feature story. Let's start to include information about the children. See if there's something there."

As she reopened her laptop, she said, "I think this might appeal to Mr. Summers."

Tom had had the same idea. In fact, he was counting on it.

5

"I'm afraid I know very little," Rick Miller admitted in response to Claude's question. "Is it like cloning?"

Claude made a steeple with his fingers. "We're living in a time of enormous change, Rick. I don't need to tell you that. Look at everything that's happened in aerospace, information technology, finance, and manufacturing. But I think the most profound, far-reaching developments are now taking place in the biosciences. It's been a passion of mine for decades. Initially I wanted to improve my grapes and horses, but I found we knew so little about genes and how they work that I started to invest heavily in basic research. Over the years I'm sure I've spent hundreds of millions of dollars on this. The payoff has been, frankly, spectacular."

Rick looked back at him. This was not at all what he had expected.

Claude seemed to sense his confusion. "Genes contain the instructions that make us who we are. They determine our physical structure and guide the processes of life.

Those instructions are written in a long linear molecule."

"DNA."

"Precisely," Claude replied, his finger raised. "Your DNA is coiled up in string-like structures called chromosomes. When you and Sue conceive a child, the DNA from your sperm combines with the DNA in Sue's egg. Your child's instruction manual will be a unique combination of those letters strung together like beads on a string.

"Understanding those beads and how they fit together and interact with each other has been at the center of my life's work. I've learned how to make better wines, horses, dogs, and even people by correcting problems with faulty or misplaced beads, or by making small adjustments to bring about desired characteristics."

"That seems really important. Why haven't I heard anything about this?"

Claude frowned, nodding thoughtfully. "Let me tell you a little story. In 1975, Paul Berg, who later won a Nobel Prize, invited me to a conference he was organizing at Asimolar. About 150 people attended, mostly researchers, but also some lawyers and other professionals. The purpose of the meeting was to set voluntary guidelines to ensure that DNA research was conducted in accordance with the highest ethical and safety standards. It was a hot topic at the time. We'd just been through Watergate. There was a strong feeling that everything should be open, transparent, and in the public domain, including science."

"Sounds reasonable."

"It did, yes, but as I observed the deep, bitter disagreements among the attendees, I became convinced that the inevitable regulatory and ethical quagmire would impede progress." Claude leaned forward, his elbows on his knees. "Imagine you've figured out how to cut and insert DNA at particular points in a laboratory mouse's chromosome. But if you wanted to test it on human cells, think of the time it would take to get such an experiment approved, if you could get permission at all. You'd be second-guessed by everyone: academics, activists, lawyers, religious leaders, philosophers, politicians, and the press." Claude looked up at Rick, waiting for his reaction.

"So, what did you do?"

"I decided then and there to follow my own path. My own labs. My own scientists. The world had been kind to me. I had the resources and the connections to make it happen." Claude smiled. "We raced ahead, reaching out when we needed to, incorporating new tools and research wherever we found it. It was an exciting time for everyone in the field. Progress was being made. And then something terrible happened."

"What?"

"Do you remember the story of Jesse Gelsinger?"

"I'm afraid not."

"He was a young man who had a rare liver disease caused by a faulty gene. It was understood even then that viruses could introduce genetic material into living cells. A researcher tried to treat his condition by introducing functioning genes into his liver using an adenovirus as a vector. Many errors were made and, tragically, Jesse died of multiple organ failures. In the scandal that followed, the FDA practically shut down gene therapy research on humans."

"Did that affect you?"

"It reduced what was available to us from the outside, but fortunately we were independent and private, so we kept moving forward. *Discreetly*. Twenty years later, we find ourselves where we are today, light years ahead of everyone else."

"Is this prohibition on human research the sensitive issue that you mentioned?"

"It's part of it, yes. Human gene editing is now tied up in even more red tape and controversy than I imagined in '75. My lab and I would be in considerable trouble if our capabilities and applications were publicly known. I'm not at all embarrassed by what we've done. On the contrary, I'm extraordinarily proud of what we've accomplished."

"You should be."

"At the same time, Rick, I don't want to become a modern-day Galileo."

"The astronomer?"

"For his great crime of arguing that the sun was the center of the solar system, the Inquisition charged him with heresy. He spent the rest of his life under house arrest!"

"I assure you your science will be safe with me."

"I'm sure of it." Claude paused, and when he resumed eye contact, Rick saw a spark there that he hadn't perceived before. Claude continued, "You've come to me as a friend. You want to have a healthy child, and I have it in my power to help you. But I have a question for you, something you should consider carefully."

"Yes?"

"You say you want to have a child, but if your true desire is to create your legacy, maybe the real question should be: what *kind* of child do you want to have?"

6

Deborah Fiske sat alone in the great hall of their Westchester County mansion, embers glowing red in the big stone fireplace. Her two boys were asleep. A glass of red wine rested on the table, and a table lamp cast a soft cone of light on a thick family photo album open in her lap. Her husband, Scott, was somewhere in Europe. He'd texted only twice in the past week. As much as she loved her sons, on nights such as this she felt like a trapped indentured servant, dependent and alone.

The photo album was her refuge and comfort, a record of a time when she'd been happy. Over the years she'd carefully curated photographs that captured the times of joy she'd experienced: her pleasant, simple childhood in upstate New York as the daughter of a carpenter and a nurse; her pets and friends; an unexpected admission to Yale made possible by generous grants; earning a Master of Fine Arts degree while she worked three jobs; her early career as a curator at the Museum of Modern Art in Manhattan; and then, the early days with Scott.

At the time, it had never occurred to her that he was older. He was a handsome man, lean and tall with the silvered hair of a senator and bright, intelligent eyes. They'd met at a benefit at the Metropolitan Club. The attraction had been immediate and mutual. He'd asked her to dine with him the following evening. His French was superb and the evening had flashed by as they shared their appreciation of artists ranging from Berthe Morisot to Francis Picabia. He was an avid collector. He'd worked hard all his life, still putting in seventy hours a week. Now that he was established, he wanted to start a family. Until that evening, she'd never dreamt of being wealthy. The prospect of sharing Scott's lifestyle was intoxicating. Deborah was charmed. Six months later they married.

She immediately found herself in a strange, uncomfortable world. She learned that the rich truly were different. Yes, her days of merely window-shopping were over, but the glamour soon faded. Expectations were often superficial and unkind. Her days of hopeful striving had been replaced with a life that felt empty and unwholesome. Scott's work took him away frequently and unpredictably, so she was often lonely. They both thought a child would fulfill her. After years of trying, she eagerly accepted Scott's suggestion that they see an exclusive and highly recommended fertility specialist.

She turned the page and saw a younger version of herself, cheeks mottled, holding two newborns, Edward and Paul. At the time it had seemed a miracle. They had been so happy. She'd first taken maternity leave from the museum, and then a leave of absence, and then resigned altogether to spend more time with her twins. Scott had been busy and travelling, but he had helped when he could. It didn't matter. Deborah loved being the mother of her two boys. They filled her life with happiness and meaning.

She turned the page. The photo showed her in shorts and a tee-shirt on a park bench, Edward and Paul laughing on her lap. She smiled and sipped her wine, a velvet-smooth cabernet. She remembered that day so vividly. They'd gone to the Central Park Zoo to see the bears. A happy, normal day.

As she had done countless times before, she closely examined the faces of the two young boys, seeking any signs of things to come, seeing none. Edward had been the first to show signs of trouble. He became increasingly moody, alternating between periods of intense activity and times where it was hard to get him out of bed. She had taken him to their family doctor, then to a pediatrician, and then to psychiatrists. They diagnosed him with early onset bipolar disorder. The medicine they prescribed had considerably improved his symptoms and slowed his mental deterioration.

His bouts of depression grieved her, but he would live a somewhat normal life.

She wished she could say the same of Paul. Both the boys had been clingy as children. Scott was away so often she had actually welcomed the attention. It made her feel loved, and she had initially dismissed any suggestion that the attachments were excessive as the envy of friends. Over time, though, she began to worry that their behaviors were unnatural, hoping they'd grow out of them.

The next page showed the boys with a cocker spaniel, a wonderful family pet they had named Whiskers. She took a deep breath, remembering the night when Paul had crawled into her bed in the middle of the night to say that Whiskers wanted to hurt him. She assured him that the gentle dog loved him and would never do such a thing. When she asked why he was afraid, he said the dog had threatened him.

It was a silly, childish thing to say, perhaps a dream he'd had, but she found it hard to sleep that night. In the morning, Paul was in the kitchen having cereal, the dog barking from the pantry, where he'd locked it away. Paul wasn't wearing any pants, and when she brought him to his room to get properly dressed, she saw that he had soiled his bed.

That same afternoon, returning from a tennis match with her friends, Deborah had been rear-ended by a truck on the highway. An ambulance had brought her to the hospital with a badly broken arm that required immediate surgery. When she finally returned home, her son was almost unrecognizable.

She'd found him in his room, sitting with his knees folded beneath him, staring at nothing. No one knew what had happened to Whiskers. Paul said he'd seen the dog fly into the sky. He'd soiled his bed again.

Scott had flown back from Europe to attend meetings with Paul's psychiatrists, vowing to pay any amount to heal his son. He wanted answers, plans, and timetables. As the meeting progressed and the magnitude of Paul's problems became evident, however, Deborah saw resignation dawning on Scott's face, as if this were a deal that had gone wrong, a write-off. Soon thereafter, he returned to France on urgent business.

The doctors feared her abrupt absence at a time when Paul was highly vulnerable might have pushed him over the edge of sanity. They explained that, while the causes of schizophrenia were not precisely known, a combination of environmental factors and the genes from both parents played a role. She explained that neither side of the family had ever shown signs of excessive moodiness or psychosis. It was hard to believe that Paul's disease had any genetic basis, though his symptoms suggested otherwise.

Still recovering from her operation and

painful physical therapy, she entered a new life of doctors, social workers, psychiatrists, counselors, and support groups. They told her that Paul's schizophrenia was a serious, chronic mental illness. Deeply concerned, she read everything she could about the disease, consulted every expert that would speak with her. She worried through every phase of his treatment. They started him on haloperidol, but after a short, partial remission he had to be hospitalized. A subsequent course of lorazepam failed, as did the anti-psychotic agent amisulpride. The next therapy was clozapine, which they started at 12.5 milligrams per day, ultimately increasing it to 200. It helped at first, giving her hope, but the inevitable relapse followed, leaving him worse than ever.

She set the album beside her on the sofa and gathered a soft blanket around her. She loved her sons fiercely. They were her life, but it was a hard one. Scott had essentially abandoned them. She struggled every month to get him to pay their bills, which were considerable. The rumors of his affairs in Europe pained her, but after so many years of neglect any feelings of jealousy had calcified into the deepest resentment.

Her cell phone rang, a light chime. A woman's face appeared below the caller identification: SUE MILLER. Deborah reached for the phone.

"Hi, Deb," said her concerned friend. "How are you holding up?"

"Fine. No further crises, thank God."

"I'm so sorry about Paul. I heard this afternoon. I can't imagine how you must be feeling."

Deborah pursed her lips, fighting against welling tears. "I'm okay. I just worry about what life's going to be like for him. I can't...." She stopped herself. She didn't want to burden Sue with her troubles. "But thank you. How've you been? How's Rick?"

"He's fine. We saw Scott down at Art Basel. We were sorry we missed you."

Deborah felt a stab of anger. She hadn't known that her husband was in the country, much less with their friends. "Well," she said as calmly as she could, "I've had my hands full up here. How was it?"

"Fun." After a short pause, Sue said, "There's something I need to talk to you about. Rick's been talking to...Claude."

"Not about..."

"Yes."

Deborah closed her eyes and slowly shook her head. "You know how I feel about that."

"We really want to have a baby. Claude says he can help us."

Deborah's voice caught. "Like he helped me?"

A moment passed. "I know you blame

him, but…it was so long ago. Are you sure?"

"Oh, I'm sure," Deborah said. "Your real question is: can I prove it? And you know the answer to that."

7

Beneath a full moon on a clear night, Dr. Renard Bergeron drove his Aston Martin through the entrance to *Les Champs*, Claude Dumont's world-famous horse farm. Located fifty miles south of Lexington, Kentucky, its white rail fences surrounded a thousand acres of forest and rolling green pastures. He followed a long tree-lined drive that wound its way up a low hill topped by a long stone chateau that looked like it had been plucked out of the Loire Valley. The majestic stables, softly illuminated, housed Dumont's legendary Thoroughbreds. He didn't stop there, however, but continued for a mile until he reached a heavy gate. The guard recognized him and the gate rolled to the side. Bergeron pulled through and stopped. When the barrier was shut behind him, another opened, allowing him to proceed deeper into the compound.

Unlike the gentrified parts of the farm that tourists, trainers, and buyers could see, the fencing here was of steel chain link, built as much to keep people out as to keep animals in. Many more trees grew here. The giant oaks, maples, hemlocks, and pines prevented observation from the air. He passed beneath unseen cameras that continuously monitored this restricted area of the farm, part of the protective infrastructure put in place by Maxim Fedorov, Dumont's global head of security, a man that Bergeron did everything in his power to avoid. Just visible in the side spill of his headlights, enormous dogs ran silently beside his car on both sides of the fence. He passed some empty paddocks and then pulled into a covered garage that connected to a low brick building with a steeply pitched roof.

No sooner had he turned off his engine than his phone rang. Claude's name appeared on the screen. He swore under his breath and answered. "Yes, Claude?" Renard adjusted the rearview mirror so he could watch himself as they talked. Claude, always free with advice, had recently told Renard he might come across as more pleasant over the phone if he smiled more. The face that looked back at him now was lean and handsome, his black hair streaked with silver brushed back from his forehead. He forced himself to smile, but it felt ridiculous. He rubbed his hand over his short salt and pepper beard, wishing he hadn't picked up.

"How was your day?" Claude asked. He sounded like he was in a good mood, but he nearly always did. Renard found it irritating.

"Fine." He looked down at his briefcase, which contained a vial of semen from a racehorse that had caught Claude's attention at the last Kentucky Derby.

"So, do you have it?"

"Yes. I just pulled into the lab. Let's make this quick. I need to get it into the freezer."

"Fine, fine. Renard, I called because I have another favor to ask you."

"Claude, I really am very busy."

"I know, I know. If we need to move some things around, we can. But a man, an old friend, came to see me—"

"Now's not a good—"

"--and I told him that you'd speak with him."

"You know I'm leaving on vacation in a few days."

"Yes, of course, and you need it, but this will work out perfectly. He'll meet you there, you answer his questions, and we proceed. Totally discreet. No one will ever know."

Renard let his head fall back against the car's headrest. "What's the situation?"

"Like the others. He's not well versed in this. I figured you'd be better at the details."

"Thirty minutes."

"That should be more than enough. His name's Rick Miller. I'll send you his photo."

"I'm flying down late Monday night."

"Yes, I know. Shall we say 1 p.m. on

Tuesday? Eden Rock, just down the hill from the villa? A cocktail, or perhaps a short walk on the beach?"

Renard noted that Claude had characteristically thought through every detail. "Can this be the last one for a while?"

Claude laughed over the line. "Renard, I'm eighty-eight years old. I don't have too many whiles left." Claude ended the call.

Renard sighed. He loved Claude like a father, and Claude irritated him in ways that only a father could. As for his life expectancy, he had recently reviewed the results of Claude's latest annual physical. He was sure he'd be doing Claude favors for many years to come.

8

Tom worked late that night. Amy had wanted to stay, but he wanted time to think. He sent her home to get a good night's sleep, insisting she take Sunday off. The whiteboard was now completely covered with photos, index cards, and post-it notes. Thick files were spread across the conference table. A printer and a desktop computer had been brought in. Tom wasn't precisely sure where this story was going, but he was increasingly convinced he was onto something.

Future magazine had been founded thirty-seven years ago by Henry "Hank" Summers, then a young journalist who had inherited a small fortune from his socialite parents. An admirer of *The Atlantic*, he'd sought to create a periodical of that quality but primarily oriented to the interests of the wealthy and successful. He had succeeded beyond his dreams, proving himself an excellent marketer, administrator, and judge of talent, if also a demanding and relentless taskmaster. The magazine's features varied widely, ranging across medical advances, philanthropy, food, wine, music, art, and, of course, profiles of the successful. Today there were few elite social events in the world where *Future* wasn't welcomed.

Consequently, the magazine had an extensive archive of articles and photography to draw upon. They had made good use of it. In fact, the volume in this case was so large that Tom had had to enlist several people from his department to supplement Amy's search efforts. Their requests for information on the distinguished men in his Art Basel photograph had already yielded thousands of photos and articles.

These men were heavy hitters. The photo archive showed them at the World Economic Forum in Davos, the Sundance Film Festival in Park City, Super Bowls, The Masters in Augusta, Wimbledon, the Olympics, and the Monaco Yacht Show, to name but a few. As Tom examined one photograph after another, it was uncanny how often the handsome face of Claude Dumont centered the frame.

It was clear to Tom that Dumont had ties to each of these men, but not how or why. They were all fabulously rich, of course, but there was nothing unusual about wealth seeking to be with wealth. They were all elderly, but again, it wasn't odd that people of the same age would want to associate with one another. All their wives appeared to be decades younger, but again, that was not hard to understand. What Tom could not explain was how each of these men had fathered healthy offspring at such an advanced age.

His curiosity had been vastly increased as he'd learned more about Dumont's life. If there had ever been a more charmed existence, Tom had never come across one.

Claude Dumont was born in Paris in 1937 to a wealthy family. His father was a prominent French surgeon, his mother the daughter of an American banker. As war loomed in Europe, Claude, an only child, and his mother traveled to the relative safety of the United States. They spent the war years on her aunt's horse farm in Kentucky, where the young Claude developed an early passion for Thoroughbreds. His father had served in the French resistance, saving many lives and emerging from the war a hero. The family reunited in France, where Claude excelled as a student and athlete, returning to Kentucky every summer. His acceptance to Harvard had surprised no one. His life was then marked by one success after another: an Olympic gold medal in rowing, Harvard Business School, and a meteoric rise to partner in a preeminent investment banking firm.

Tragedy stuck in 1967 when both of his parents were simultaneously killed as two Formula One cars collided and spun into the crowd at the Monaco Grand Prix. At the age of thirty, Claude inherited their estate in France and $800 million in investments, a staggering sum at the time. A year later, his great aunt passed, leaving him a thousand acres of prime Kentucky land and the horse farm he had loved since childhood.

It wasn't long after that, Tom saw, that Dumont began to routinely appear in photographs with the rich, famous, and talented. And while he posed with kings, presidents, actors, athletes, senators, CEOs, writers, and artists, his businesses flourished.

Several articles from the archives touted his remarkable stock-picking skills. One described how he'd purchased millions in Coca-Cola stock in 1980 for 73 cents per share and sold it all in May of 1997 at $33, nearly a 5000% gain. In that same year, 1980, he'd purchased a sizeable position in the tobacco company that became Altria at $1.43 per share. He'd sold that position in 1999 at $55. *Fortune Magazine* estimated his current net worth to be over $40 billion.

That was a huge sum, but as Tom read more, he learned that that Dumont possessed treasures that one simply couldn't put a value on. At the age of 62, he'd married the reigning Miss France, and by all accounts they had enjoyed a happy, storybook marriage without the slightest hint of scandal. Fifteen years ago, they'd purchased Vaux-le-Vicomte, the fabulous French estate that had provoked the jealously of King Louis XIV and inspired Versailles. The vineyards of Chateau Dumont were among the best in the world, his wines ranking among such legends as Petrus and Romanee-Conti. His fabled art collection was a frequent topic of conversation at top galleries and museums. His two children, twins aged nineteen, showed every sign of being as exceptional as their parents.

Tom set down a recent photo of their family. His own first marriage had been rocky from the beginning. They'd both been young and hot-headed. She wanted to travel the world, while he was burning with ambition. They divorced after two years. He'd married Julia ten years later, and they had been truly happy. He kept her photo on his desk, her smile still melting his heart whenever he gazed upon it. Her death had been the cruelest loss, the result of careless errors that somehow fell outside the edges of malpractice. Their son would have been eighteen next month.

Tom shook his head and returned to Dumont's dossier. As if the man didn't possess enough for a hundred successful lives, he absolutely dominated the world of Thoroughbred horse racing. His Kentucky stables had produced dozens of champions. Dumont's horses had triumphed at the Kentucky Derby, the Dubai World Cup, the Royal Ascot, and the Melbourne Cup many times over the past two decades. He was widely acclaimed as the leading breeder of racehorses in the past century...

Tom stopped abruptly to reexamine the group photograph he had taken at Art Basel. Rich old men. Gorgeous kids. Claude Dumont, the world-famous *breeder*. Tom stared at the photo. Could there be a connection? Amy had included an article from years ago about how Chateau Dumont had genetically modified grapes to create some of the world's best wines. How much farther had Dumont taken that science since then? It was an outrageous idea, but the more Tom thought about it, the more it made sense. If it were true, it explained so many things. He felt a jolt of excitement as he typed an e-mail to his assistant, asking her to schedule what he hoped would be the first of many interviews with Claude Dumont.

9

Dr. Renard Bergeron activated a retinal scanner beside the lab entrance and heard the lock click open. He passed through a softly lit reception area into a large, open space where Claude displayed his eclectic and, in Renard's opinion, boring equine collections. He walked by the double doors that opened to a suite of offices for Claude and himself and then descended two flights of stairs to the basement.

"Evening, Doctor Bergeron," said the armed guard stationed at the bottom.

"Hi, George."

Another retinal scan opened a steel door that led to the laboratory itself. It was a large space built at a time when equipment and computers were much larger and when biochemical processing was more manual, thus requiring more hands. He walked to a microscope and opened his bag, removing the vial he had collected from a local veterinarian that afternoon. He took a small drop from the sample and deposited it on a slide. He set the scope to six hundred times magnification and adjusted knobs to bring the slide into focus. The semen's concentration looked fine, as did the motility and morphology. He transferred the full sample into a tube, sealed it, and put it in a centrifuge that he set to run at 500 G's. He set the timer for 15 minutes and climbed back upstairs.

Claude had long insisted on having 24/7 administrative coverage. Susanne, one of several executive assistants, was at her desk, earphones in place, typing on her keyboard. It was a pleasant space with a television, a couch, a small kitchen area, and a large picture window overlooking a pasture, now dark. Some minor masterpieces from Claude's collection graced the walls.

"Hi, Renard," she said, smiling. "When did you get in?"

"Just now. I'm processing a sample."

"How romantic."

He forced a grin. "I need to get something from Claude's office."

"Let me know if you need help finding anything."

Renard opened a heavy oak door and entered Claude's inner sanctum. The expansive room was paneled with dark wood. Oriental carpets covered the floor. The light was dim except for a spotlight that drew one's eyes to a painting of Jesus Christ by Leonardo de Vinci: the famed *Salvator Mundi*, 'Savior of the World.' Claude had purchased it in 2017 at a Christi's auction for \$430 million, making him the only private individual in the world to own a painting by the great artist. The auction had taken place over the phone, utterly confidential. Only Renard and a handful of others knew it was here.

Renard went to a side table, poured himself a generous snifter of Claude's private-label cognac, and sank back into the leather desk chair, admiring the painting as the liquor slowly warmed his throat. Da Vinci had a unique understanding of how the eye and the brain perceive light, a gift for seeing things in ways that others couldn't, and he'd fully incorporated that subtle complexity into his art. Claude was like that, Renard mused, seeing possibilities that others overlooked, and then acting on them decisively. Renard thought the same of himself. The things they'd accomplished in basic and applied genetic science were historic and far-reaching. While he agreed with Claude that it was too early to reveal that knowledge to a world deeply divided across politics and religion, the day was coming when human biology would enter its next phase. That would be *his* legacy.

He finished his cognac and checked his watch. The centrifuge run would finish in a few minutes. He left the empty glass with Susanne on his way out.

"Have fun in St. Barts," she said. "The jet's all set."

"I will. I need a break."

"Take me with you?" she called after him.

Back in his lab, the sample had separated into a soft sperm pellet that he easily removed from the remaining seminal plasma. He added an extender consisting of a cryoprotectant, mostly glycerol, and a lipoprotein to create a protective coating during freezing. He transferred the treated sperm into .5 mL straws and recorded the horse's name and the collection date. He placed the straws into a programmable freezer and hit run, commencing a process of slow cooling to 5 degrees centigrade that would prevent cold shock before freezing it in liquid nitrogen.

He was a meticulous scientist and did most things by the book. In this case, he wouldn't be storing the sample long. When he returned from his vacation, he would cut out the MSTN or myostatin gene, a segment consisting of 6,172 base pairs on chromosome 18, make a few base-pair amendments, and replace that segment in the DNA of First Love, one of Claude's favorite horses. The resulting growth of musculature could result in a superior Thoroughbred, a horse with the optimal combination of fast and slow twitch muscles for speed and endurance. First Love already carried the genetic package that gave it the oversized heart that won it the Triple Crown. Renard smiled to himself. When the newly created champion won, Claude would laugh and pour champagne, accepting the congratulations of his friends, admirers, and rivals. The jockey would pump his fist in the air as he rode around the track, garlanded with roses. But on that day, Renard would know that it was he and he alone that had produced the winner, and the only applause that would matter to him was his own.

Walking to his car, he reflected, as he often did, on how fortunate he had been three decades ago when Claude had hired him after he was censured by Harvard University and essentially banned from the life sciences industry. Had it been mere happenstance that horses had roughly the same amount of DNA as humans, about 3 billion base pairs, and that their DNA was more like that of humans than mice, the standard genetic research animal? Renard had learned more about human DNA by working on horses than he ever could have in academic or pharmaceutical research. He was rich beyond his dreams and, though nobody but Claude and himself knew it, the leader in his field.

It was almost as if it had been meant to be.

10

At 9:30 a.m. Monday morning Tom arrived at his office and went straight to his new Miele PureLine coffee machine, a recent gift from his co-workers to celebrate his Pulitzer nomination. Tom had always been a night owl, which hadn't been an impediment in his profession, but it did put a premium on good espresso. As he sat as his desk, he was pleased to learn that his assistant had already heard back from Dumont's office. He was invited for coffee at Dumont's condo that afternoon.

Amy must have come in early, because manila folders for each of the families were neatly stacked on his desk. The left side of each had biographies and photographs of the parents, and the right had similar information for the children.

Tom started with the top file, labeled DUMONT. He flipped quickly through the left side. He was familiar with the contents: the investment success, the horses, his wines and estates, and the beautiful, accomplished wife. On the right, separated by tabs, were dossiers for his two children.

Tom stopped to look at the photos. There were many, thanks not just to social media but to several publications that had featured the talented twins over the years. They were beautiful children, though Tom noted they were now nineteen years old. He could see both their father and mother in their features. There was no question that these were their natural children, though Tom now wondered just *how* natural.

The son, Chase, and his sister, Audrey, were both born in Kentucky. Home-schooled by tutors and trainers, they'd traveled around the world with their parents until the age of eight when they matriculated at the Institute Le Rosey, more commonly called Le Rosey or simply Rosey, the so-called "school of kings" in Rolle, Switzerland.

Chase, academically brilliant, was now the top varsity tennis player at Harvard in his sophomore year. He was also an exceptionally accomplished pianist. He had recently won third place at the International Chopin Piano Competition, a remarkable achievement for someone so young. Music critics compared him to the legendary Martha Argerich, who won first place at that competition in 1965 at the age of 24.

Audrey was even more impressive. She excelled in mathematics, downhill skiing, horseback riding, and philanthropy. As a senior, she had won first place in the Concours General, the most prestigious high school math competition in France. She was an Olympic level dressage rider, helping France win a first-place medal at the Eventing World Championships. She had also led a highly successful effort to provide clean water to tribes in Mali, for which she had been publicly praised by no less than the Secretary General of the United Nations. She was currently in her second year at Oxford University studying mathematics.

Amy had included a short profile on Audrey that had appeared in *Future* a year ago. Tom was surprised he hadn't remembered it, but he knew the author well and picked up his phone.

"If it isn't Tom Wright of Pulitzer fame," a lively voice answered.

"Fingers crossed, Joe. Just nominated."

"Congrats all the same. What can I do for you?"

"I'm poking around a potential story, and I noticed your piece about the Dumont girl, Audrey."

"Yeah, that's mine."

"I just reread it and wanted to know if there was anything else, anything you might not have put into the article."

Tom heard the tapping of keys. "Give me a minute. Okay, here it is." Seconds later, Joe said, "I think it's all there. Nothing else comes to mind."

"Any personal impressions?"

Joe paused. "What I remember most was that she was just a great kid in every way. Warm. Kind. Thoughtful. Respectful. Just a perfect young human. She wasn't my daughter, but I couldn't help but be proud of her."

Tom nodded his head slowly. "Yeah, I get that. Thanks, Joe."

Tom hung up and gazed at the photos of the Dumont children. With their extraordinary and wide-ranging talents, good looks, unlimited wealth, credentials, and network of contacts from Rosey and some of the finest universities in the world, not to mention those of their parents, there seemed to be no limit to what these two could achieve in their lifetimes. When people spoke of the growing gap between the "haves" and "have-nots," the focus was usually on the plight of the poor, those falling behind, not those pulling ahead.

Tom moved onto the other files. Each individual situation was different, but the abilities, achievements, and prospects were manifest in every case. The composite picture troubled Tom. It was almost a cliché that great men were commonly disappointed by their offspring. These fathers, however, must be enormously proud of their children. Where were the bums? The washouts? The addicts? The burnouts?

Tom checked his watch. It was time to go. He took a print of the original Art Basel photograph and examined it yet again. This assemblage, which had piqued his curiosity at the time, was now a profound mystery to him, one he was determined to unravel. He tucked the photo into his jacket pocket, knocked on the glass wall to let Amy know he was leaving, and left to meet its presumed architect, Claude Dumont.

11

Fifteen minutes later, Tom took the private elevator to the 95th floor of 432 Park Avenue. He had worked around and among wealthy people for his entire career, but he still wasn't accustomed to some of the material aspects of affluence that the rich seemed to take for granted.

When the doors opened, he stepped into an entry way. A female voice called out, "I'll be right there!"

The woman who appeared was stunning: tall with movie-star good looks, a fabulous figure, and gleaming auburn hair falling on tan shoulders. He recognized Nadine Dumont immediately from the file.

"You must be Tom," she said, extending her hand with a pleasant smile.

"Thank you for having me to your home, Mrs. Dumont."

"Claude has most of his meetings here when we're in New York. Come, I'll take you to him."

Amy's folder had included some

background on the Dumont's condo. Located on the second highest floor of the 1,400-foot-tall building, it had been on the market for a few years, then divided into two units, and finally recombined when Claude purchased both for $60 million. The cost of the subsequent renovation was not publicly available, but Tom could see that every aspect was of the finest quality and workmanship.

They crossed a vast, light-filled living room and entered a paneled study. The north and east-facing walls were vast windows with views of upper Manhattan and Long Island. The interior walls were dominated by two large oil paintings, one of Vaux-le-Vicomte, the Dumont chateau outside of Paris, and the other of a tasteful brick mansion set amidst rolling pastures. Tom would have liked to have studied them more closely, but his attention was immediately drawn to the man who rose to greet him.

"Mr. Dumont, it's a pleasure to finally meet you."

"And you must be the famous Thomas Wright." They shook hands. "And please, call me Claude. Everything does. Have a seat. Let's make ourselves comfortable."

"You know," Tom said, pointing to the chateau, "I visited in the 80's. It was spectacular, both inside and out."

"It is a marvel," Claude said, taking a

moment to gaze at the painting. "I assume you know the story."

"Bits and pieces, but not really."

"Nicolas Fouquet was a brilliant financier in Seventeenth Century France. In my humble opinion, he was singularly responsible for Louis XIV's early success as king. Unfortunately for Nicolas, he reached a point where he thought he deserved a greater reward for that service. Using state money, he hired the best architects and designers of his day to create his paradise. Louis came for a visit, was envious, and threw him in jail for the rest of his life."

"Doesn't seem fair."

Claude raised his index finger. "It's always unwise to outshine the Sun King. There's a lesson in that for all of us."

Tom wondered what that lesson had been for Dumont, or whether the anecdote was somehow meant as a warning for him. He pointed to the other painting. "This one I don't recognize."

"That is my heart," Claude said, smiling broadly. "It's *Les Champs*, our horse farm outside Lexington. When I was young, my mother and I stayed there with my aunt during the war. I returned almost every summer until she passed and left it to us. We spend at least half of the year there."

"*Les Champs*. Is that meant to be French for 'the fields' or English for champions?"

Claude chuckled politely. "I see that you're a man who appreciates a double entendre." Claude guided Tom to an overstuffed leather chair. "Can I get you something to drink?" Claude winked. "I know my office said coffee, but I presume you're not driving."

"I'll have whatever you're having."

"I have something you might like." Claude went to a side table and poured two cognacs. "This is distilled from one of my favorite vineyards." He handed Tom a snifter.

Tom smelled it and knew he was in for something special. He raised his glass to Claude and sipped. It was delicate, floral, and perfectly balanced. "This is exceptional. Where can I get this?"

"You can't, actually. There's a cognac maker, A. Harvey, that I've known for years. I bring them selected wines from time to time and they distill a few cases of this for me. It's an indulgence, I admit, but I'm glad you like it." Claude sat opposite Tom and crossed one leg over the other. "I understand that you're with *Future* magazine."

"That's right. I'm an investigative reporter there."

"Congratulations on your nomination. I reread your articles this morning."

"I'm flattered."

"It was excellent work. You know, Hank Summers is an old friend of mine. We've had many adventures together, I can tell you."

Tom and Summers were on relatively good terms at the moment, especially since the Pulitzer nomination, but Tom and the publisher had never joined on anything close to an *adventure*, and Tom doubted they never would.

"So," Claude continued, "I understand you're writing an article about Art Basel."

"Well, I'm actually interested in a photograph I took there a few days ago." Tom reached into his pocket and handed Claude the photo.

Claude sat back and examined it, a grin slowly forming. "Ah, yes, the Picassos. I thought that might be what you were really interested in. Do you want to see them?" Claude put his hands on the arms of his chair and started to rise.

"I saw them when I was there," Tom said. "What I'm more interested in, frankly, is the people in the photograph."

Claude settled back into his chair and looked at the photo again, nodding. "Many old friends. We like to reconnect at these sorts of occasions." He looked up.

"I've identified all of the men. It's an auspicious group."

"I've been fortunate in my friendships."

"What's most remarkable to me is that those young people are their children."

Claude shrugged as he took yet another look. "Yes, I suppose some of them...."

"All of them. I checked."

"How...curious." The temperature in the room seemed to fall as Claude handed the photo back to Tom. "Your assistant said you were working on a story. I don't understand where you're heading with this."

"I'm fascinated that men of that age could have children that young, and even more by how accomplished each of those children is."

Claude's smile faded. "There's no mystery there. These are fine people. Their example, their love, their close attention and devotion to their sons and daughters...combine all of that with the resources at their disposal, and it's no surprise to me that this next generation is exceptional."

"But their age..."

Claude laughed.

Nadine stuck her head into the room. "What's so funny in here?"

Claude waved her over to him. She sat on the arm of his chair, facing Tom. They were the very image of the perfect couple.

"Tom was in Miami last week and saw our little celebration over the paintings."

"It was a fun night," she told Tom, smiling brightly.

"Now he's interested in our friends' children."

She looked at her husband and then back at Tom. The smile was gone. "Why?"

"I find it fascinating that men of that age, highly successful men, could have such young and promising kids. I think our readers would too."

Nadine said, "There are many successful men – and women – with young, exceptional families. Do you have any children, Mr. Wright?"

"No," he said, wondering if she already knew the answer to her question, suspecting that she did. "My wife and son died in childbirth many years ago."

"I'm so sorry," she said, her gaze softening. "I can't imagine."

Claude frowned. "You know, Tom, I hope you'll find something else to write about. Our friends value their privacy. They don't want this kind of publicity, especially for their children. It attracts unwanted attention, from the media and worse. I'm sure you can understand."

"Nevertheless," Tom replied, probing, "I think there may be something important here, perhaps some medical advances that haven't been widely shared?"

Claude and Nadine exchanged looks, and Claude said, "That's very...imaginative." Claude put down his snifter and stood, stone-faced. "I have another engagement, but it was certainly a pleasure to meet you, Tom. I wish you success in whatever you chose as your next subject. You deserve that Pulitzer and I hope you get it."

Tom was disappointed that his interview

was ending so abruptly, but clearly he had struck a nerve, which was in itself informative. He finished the last of his cognac and, standing, said, "Thank you for seeing me on such short notice."

Claude raised his arm, smiling now, and gestured toward the open door. "Come, I'll show you to the elevator." As Claude crossed the room, he stopped to open a cupboard and removed a bottle.

Tom nodded to Nadine and followed Claude from the room, noting once again the incredible views of the city. He felt more like he was in an airplane than in a building. An awkward silence fell upon them, and Tom worried that he had been too aggressive in his initial questioning. He wanted to end their first meeting on a warmer note, hoping there would be others. "You have some exceptional homes," he said. "If you don't mind my asking, do you prefer living in this urban environment or in nature?"

"I love my vineyards and my horse farm, but nature is always all around us. When I look out over the city, do you know what I see?"

"Tell me."

"I see a reef built by millions of creatures over many decades, shelters bursting with beautiful, colorful life. That's what a city is to me. We humans, when all is said and done, are as natural as anything else." Claude grinned and handed the special bottle of cognac to Tom. "An early Pulitzer gift. Good luck!" Claude waved as the elevator door closed between them.

When Claude returned to his study, Nadine was still there, gazing out the window.

"I don't want him to write that story," she said. "It's an invasion of our privacy and the rights of our friends, and I don't like this 'old fathers' angle. It's ageist."

"I agree. I'll stop it." Claude sat at his desk and picked up the telephone. He hit a speed dial button and an assistant in Lexington answered immediately.

"Yes, Mr. Dumont?"

"Hi, Susanne. Hank Summers, please?" A moment later, "Hank! How are you?"

"Fine, fine, Claude. To what do I owe this pleasure?"

"It's been too long since I've seen you. Can you join me for dinner?"

"I'd love to. When are you free?"

"Well, I happen to be back in New York. Could you join me at Jean-George at, say, 8 p.m.?"

"Tonight?"

"Of course, if this is too short notice..." Claude winked at Nadine, who nodded.

"Oh, no, no. I'd love to. Will Nadine be joining?"

"Not this time. I have something I want to discuss with you. It'll just be the two of us," he

LEGACY

said warmly, "just like old times."
  "I'll be there."

12

Renard Bergeron had complained to Claude about his workload, but creating the Miller embryo would be neither taxing nor difficult. By now, his techniques were well developed, his equipment optimized, his storehouse of reagents, base-pair segments, and other supplies complete and at the ready. He only needed their DNA samples. Based on his experience, he was sure that Mr. and Mrs. Miller would decide to proceed. He used the hours before his flight to wrap up some loose ends in the lab.

Despite his generally sour disposition, Renard loved his life here. In medical school he'd come across the writings of Carl Jung and had been particularly impressed by the Swiss psychoanalyst's belief that "the privilege of a lifetime is to become who you truly are." This *individuation*, the process of personal fulfillment that embraces both one's conscious and unconscious self, had been a long journey for Renard, but under Claude's broad wing he had achieved it.

Renard was born in 1961 in New York City, by coincidence the same year that Carl Jung died. Renard's father was a wealthy investor and a close friend of Claude's from university days. Claude had known Renard since he was a baby. Renard's earliest memories were of sunny days at his parents' beach house in the Hamptons, where Claude often joined them. Nadine hadn't come along until much later.

Renard's father was French, a witty, urbane man who loved everything about money, whether making it or spending it. Claude had started with plenty, and Renard's father had been behind many of the famous investments that Claude had profited from over the decades. In Renard's opinion, Claude had never truly "worked." Rather, apart from rare flashes of staggering ruthlessness, Claude had glided from success to success, doing it with such joy, grace, and generosity that the span of his life took on the appearance of a continuous summer garden party.

Renard had never developed his parents' taste for society. His father could trace their lineage to French royalty through many paths in their family tree, but Renard thought it entirely irrelevant. He was an introvert, a serious person who had discovered science early and devoted his life to its pursuit. He and his father had frequently clashed. It was fortunate that Claude, perhaps at his father's request, had taken an interest in the quiet, intense boy. It was Claude who had given the young Renard a book entitled THE SELFISH GENE by biologist Richard Dawkins. Renard had devoured it over a weekend. That Sunday at dinner he surprised everyone at the table by announcing that he was going to be a geneticist. He was only fifteen, but his family and teachers noted a difference in him after that. He sailed through Harvard's undergraduate biochemistry program and entered a dual-track MD and PhD program. His initial laboratory work focused on the development of restriction enzymes that could cut DNA in specific, targeted places, a prerequisite for gene editing. He was a superb experimentalist and rapidly earned the faculty's respect for his accuracy and productivity.

But Renard was more ambitious than anyone imagined. He was intrigued by the potential of human stem cells, undifferentiated cells with the potential to develop into many kinds of cells – skin, nerves, bone, blood – in the body. Two Canadian scientists had first discovered the existence of stem cells in 1963, and by 1981 mouse stem cells could be removed from embryos. Without authorization, by 1987, Renard was secretly investigating techniques for deriving stem cells from human embryos. Enormously excited after a particularly successful experiment, he had shared his results with a trusted professor, a mistake that brought his world crashing down around him. His deliberate and flagrant departure from Food and Drug Administration and National Institutes of Health guidelines placed the entire university at risk. Renard was abruptly expelled from both the medical school and Harvard Graduate School of Arts and Sciences only weeks before he was to have graduated.

Claude, a trustee of Harvard, intervened behind the scenes and the decision was partly reversed. The PhD degree was awarded, but Renard was barred from practicing medicine, his research materials were confiscated, and his reputation was left in ruins. It was the lowest point in Renard's life.

A week later, however, Claude had presented Renard with the opportunity of a lifetime. They'd been having dinner together in Manhattan, just the two of them. Renard remembered Claude's pitch as if it had occurred yesterday. Claude had begun by sharing his frustration with the bureaucracy, red tape, and second-guessing that had descended upon the field of genetic research. A scientist with controversial ideas faced daunting opposition. Claude said he had always believed in Renard and still did. Despite the Harvard scandal, he offered to fund Renard through a private company that they would call Chromos. Renard's mandate would be to push ahead with basic as well as applied genetic research. From time to time, of course, Claude would have special projects for him, but he promised they wouldn't be burdensome.

It had been music to Renard's ears.

Claude had then launched into his vision for what genetic engineering could achieve in two areas of intense interest to him, the cultivation of grapes and the breeding of Thoroughbred racehorses. Claude was well-informed, and while Renard had questions, it certainly seemed possible to make progress on both, particularly with no resource constraints or oversight. It would mean a private life without wide recognition by peers, but Renard cared nothing about that. He had accepted Claude's proposal that very night. Within a few years, Chromos was far ahead of the field. Soon, Nobel Prizes were being awarded for discoveries that Chromos had made years earlier.

Their relationship had reached a new and deeper level when Claude married Nadine. Claude had been married twice before, but Nadine was special, his true love, and it showed in everything Claude said and did. She had desperately wanted to have children, something Claude had never achieved with previous wives. Claude knew why: he carried two defective genes of high penetration that had resulted in terminated pregnancies. One night Claude came to Renard's lab with a question. Could Renard manipulate the DNA in Claude's sperm to eliminate the defects? Both men understood that manipulating human germ cells, cells capable of developing into embryos, was strictly forbidden. But Renard was confident he could do it. Using zinc finger nucleases, at the time the leading technology for cutting DNA, he was able to create a healthy new genome and viable embryos. Nadine had twins, Chase and Aubrey, and they'd been their parents' pride and joy ever since.

Claude and Nadine had been deeply grateful and offered Renard any gift he could name. The reply was immediate: additional funding. Claude gave him a blank check. From that time on, everything Renard learned about genetic science was applied to human germ cells. It was only a matter of time before Claude had approached him to assist a desperate friend, and then another. Over the years, Renard had helped over twenty families, highly successfully with one notable exception, or, rather, a pair of them. The fees paid by the families were enormous, but no one else could provide what Renard offered. Claude had insisted that Renard keep all the proceeds. The payments for each procedure went straight into Renard's offshore account. He was now a very wealthy man.

In their partnership, Claude was the dreamer, strategist, and financier, Renard the researcher, technical expert, and master of detail. Renard constantly sought new knowledge, either in the form of data or, less commonly, from talented scientists who could be induced to work with them in secret. Many of their short-term recruits came from labs in China, in which case scientists received in a few months more than they could have expected to make in a lifetime. While Claude had an impressive grasp of genetic science and its possibilities, it fell to Renard to make countless pragmatic decisions along the way. There were simply too many highly technical issues that Claude didn't need to know about and might not have understood anyway. While that had created friction at times, Claude had long ago become reconciled to those choices.

One in particular had almost ended their relationship, yet bound them together forever.

13

Hank Summers was already seated when Claude Dumont entered Jean-George, one of New York City's finest French restaurants. Claude smiled and waved to acquaintances as the maître-de escorted him to their table. It could have accommodated six but was set for two.

Hank, a thin man of medium height with well-groomed grey hair and prominent black eyebrows, was struck, as always, by his friend's glowing vitality and warmth. They had known each other since the 1960s. Claude had been instrumental in helping Hank establish *Future* magazine, subsequently connecting Hank with many of the luminaries that formed the backbone of the publication's franchise.

Claude smiled warmly at Hank and shook his outstretched hand vigorously. As Claude was sitting down, Jean-George Vongerichten, the legendary founder of the restaurant, came rushing from the kitchen, his arms outstretched.

"Claude! I heard you were coming tonight!"

The two men embraced and then Jean-

George pulled out Claude's chair for him.

"It's been too long," Jean-George said.

Claude laughed, protesting, "I was here last week!"

"Still, too long. I've instructed the chef to make some special things for you tonight. I hope you enjoy."

When Jean-George was gone, Hank turned to Claude and said, "Eating out with you is like dining with no one else."

"Let's have some fun." Claude patted Hank's hand and raised a finger to get the sommelier's attention. The man appeared in an instant.

"Gaspard, we'd like to start with a bottle of the Screaming Eagle Cabernet. You pick the year."

"Right away, Mr. Dumont," the man said with a slight bow.

Claude turned to his dinner guest. "So, Hank, how have you been? How's Margie?"

"Oh, she's fine. Spends a lot of time with the grandkids, which is wonderful. She's with them in Philadelphia now. I was so glad when you called. I was dreading another quiet evening at home." Hank proceeded to update Claude on his family and the magazine. "I heard you bought some treasures down in Miami."

"Yes, they're wonderful. I was thrilled to get them both. You should stop by and see them."

"I'd like that very much."

Jean-George brought the bottle of wine himself as the sommelier watched discreetly from his side.

"Doing double-duty tonight?" Claude teased the famous restaurateur.

"Actually, Claude," Jean-George said in a hushed voice, "I have a favor to ask."

Claude turned to face him. "Name it."

"We are out of Chateau Dumont." He spoke rapidly, almost beseechingly. "I'm sorry to bother you with something like this, but I literally can't find it anywhere, and I have some regulars here who refuse to drink anything else."

"Call my office – you have my number? – and tell them from me to send you two cases from my private cellar," Claude said as the cork slid from the neck of the bottle.

"Thank you, so much. The usual terms?" Jean-George carefully decanted the bottle, the wine a deep, inviting purple.

"As always."

"And, of course, there will be no charge for this one," the owner said with a grin.

"You're too generous."

"A small commission for you, with my thanks." Jean-George poured wine into their glasses and left with a bow.

Hank chuckled quietly. "Doesn't this usually go for about $10,000 a bottle?"

Claude nodded, observing the wine's

color. "That's what scarcity will do for you. I've been experimenting a little with some of my own wines, trying to find the right price points." Claude lifted his glass in a toast, matched by Hank.

Claude closed his eyes, savoring the wine. It was peppery, energetic, and complex. The nose was marvelous and multilayered. "This is absolutely superb."

"I couldn't agree more," Hank said. "Now, you said you had something to discuss with me."

Claude looked serious for a moment as he gently swirled the wine in his glass. "As you know, because you asked about the paintings, I was at Art Basel in Miami. A writer that works for you took a picture of me and some friends while we were assembling for another photographer."

"How strange." Hank took a sip of the wine, nodding his appreciation. "Who was it?"

"His name is Tom Wright."

"I know Tom very well. What's this about? Is there a problem?"

"It's not the photograph that concerns me. He asked me for an interview, which I quickly accepted because of my relationship with you and the magazine. I thought it would be about the paintings, but it wasn't that at all. We met briefly this afternoon. He seems to be planning some sort of feature about my friends and their children."

"Their children?" Hank looked bewildered.

"Many of them were there, so naturally I wanted to include them in the photo."

"Why would he write something like that?"

Claude lowered his head, his expression animated. "That's just it. Why? There's nothing there, just some friends out for a good time. I don't want their privacy to be violated because I waved them into a picture. I'd be embarrassed."

"Of course, Claude. I'll kill the story first thing in the morning."

Claude visibly relaxed. "I'd appreciate that, Hank, I really would. I don't want to seem ungrateful for his interest. If there's something else I can help him with, I'll be happy to do it. I just think this is, well, it's inappropriate."

"Absolutely. I'm sorry you've had to deal with this. I had no idea. He's a good writer, tenacious, but a bit of a bull-in-the-china-shop. Don't give it a second thought."

They were immediately surrounded by waiters bearing culinary treasures from the famed kitchen.

Claude raised his glass to Hank. "To friendship."

"To our friendship, Claude. There's nothing I value more highly."

14

As Claude and Hank were finishing their meal, Tom Wright was in his 60th floor condo on West 57th Avenue, files spread before him on his dining room table, his cell phone on speaker. Slivers of Central Park were visible between the soaring skyscrapers that increasingly crowded its south side. He had a bottle open on the table, a finger of scotch remaining in his glass.

The phone on the other end picked up. "Hello?"

Tom leaned forward. "Is this Mr. Darwish? Khalil Darwish?"

"Yes, it is. How did you get this number?"

"I'm a reporter for *Future* magazine. We're running a feature on exceptional young leaders. Your son, Ahmet, was suggested as a strong candidate."

"He is exceptional," Darwish said, a note of pride in his voice. "I'll grant you that. I don't believe I caught your name?"

"Tom Wright."

"Tell me more about this article you're working on, Mr. Wright."

Tom ran his eyes down his notes. Darwish lived just outside the city in Westchester County, but his operations were based in Dubai. He owned some of the most important commercial buildings in the Gulf region. Eighty-two years old. Much younger wife. Their son was a math prodigy in his first year at Stanford, aged sixteen. International level gymnast. Student leader. Tom shook his head, not for the first time. "Ahmet is a most impressive young man."

"So you said. The article?"

Tom had carefully scripted his pitch to make the story as attractive to the parents as possible. "As you know, our magazine is oriented toward successful individuals and families. We hear so much about the haves and have-nots in our country. We think the exclusive focus on the have-nots is crowding out genuine appreciation for people of talent, people who are making something extraordinary out of their lives."

"I have to say I agree with that."

"At Art Basel this weekend our magazine obtained a photograph of a group of distinguished men and their children—"

"I never allow the press to photograph me or my family."

Tom felt a stab of irritation. Art Basel was a public event. What entitled a man like Khalil Darwish to say he couldn't be photographed by a member of the press? He pressed on, "You were in the photograph with Ahmet, a very handsome young man, I might add--"

"Wait a minute. Was this with Claude? The paintings?"

"Yes. That's exactly right."

After a long pause, Darwish spoke again, but his tone was icy, almost menacing. "Do not include us in your article. I forbid it."

"But why? This could increase your son's profile around the world--"

"His profile is just fine. Does Dumont know anything about this?"

"He does."

"And what did he say?"

"To be honest, he's not supportive of the project."

"Neither am I. Drop this, Mr. Wright. I promise you you'll be sorry if you don't." The line went dead.

Tom sat back on his couch. *What the hell was that?* He took a sip of his drink, felt the smoke against the back of his throat. Darwish was the third parent he'd been able to reach so far. Favorable exposure in *Future* should have been a great opportunity for Ahmet and the others. All three had reacted negatively as soon as the connection to Art Basel had been made, though only Darwish had threatened him so far. Tom's instincts told him these powerful families were hiding something.

Had this been the chance celebration of

an art purchase, or a reunion for an entirely different purpose? And why had the offspring been there in the first place? Somehow Tom was sure that the children were at the center of all of this. He reexamined the photograph. At the time of his own family tragedy, these elderly billionaires were having healthy babies. Were there technologies or medicines then that weren't being shared with the broad medical community? And if that were the case, what right did these families have to keep it for themselves? His frustration was slowly turning into anger. Whatever secret bound them together, he was going to get to the bottom of it whether the families cooperated or not.

He ran his finger down his list of parents. The next couple was Scott and Deborah Fiske. They had twins, Edward and Paul, but, unlike the other families, very little information about the boys was available. He found their number, dialed, and left a message.

15

The following morning Tom was researching the history of fertility treatments when Hank Summers stuck his head into Tom's office. "Have you got a minute?"

Tom looked up, surprised. Summers wasn't the kind of boss that wandered the halls. "Sure, Hank."

"Let's talk in my office."

Tom stood and followed. He'd worked for Summers for twenty years, but he couldn't remember the last time Summers had wanted to see him in his office. Maybe this about the Pulitzer, or maybe he was going to be scolded for not having a lead on his next big story. He debated whether it was too early to tell him about his Art Basel ideas. He decided he'd drop some heavy hints if pressed.

Tom's night had been frustrating. Of the parents he'd reached, none were interested in his story, and some were outright hostile. He'd finally called Britt to vent. She'd been sympathetic and then encouraging, reminding him of all the roadblocks he'd encountered in the past, only to achieve breakthroughs later. He was grateful for her support and friendship.

They walked by Summer's executive assistant, who smiled warmly at Tom. Summers' office was much larger than Tom's with big windows overlooking Broadway. The opposite wall was covered in framed photographs, most of them autographed. Summers sat behind his desk and gestured for Tom to shut the door.

"What's up?" Tom asked as he took a seat.

Summers looked at Tom for a moment and said, "I want to talk about your next story."

So that was it. Thanks for the Pulitzer buzz, but what have you done for me lately? Tom said, "I know my production has been a little down recently, but I think I may be onto something really important."

"Is that why you were down in Miami last weekend?"

"No, but that's where I got the idea."

"Well, you've upset a lot of people. Very important people."

Tom hadn't expected the families to call the magazine so soon. "I'm sorry to hear that."

With a pained expression, Summers said, "I'm killing the Art Basel piece. What else have you got?"

Tom felt like he'd been punched in the stomach. Summers had never tried to influence a major article before, at least not one of his. "What are you talking about?"

"You heard me. Shut it down. We're not invading the privacy of those families."

"Can we talk about this?" Tom fought his rising anger. He'd always had full discretion on his choice of topics. "Do you even know what I'm working on?"

"You took an unauthorized photo—"

"It was a public event!" Tom couldn't believe his ears. "There were cameras all over the place. I was hardly the only one doing it."

"Calm down, Tom. Let me finish. You took an unauthorized photo of some very powerful families, the kind that are the very backbone of our readership."

"You're making a big mistake. There's something going on with those kids. I think Dumont's been connecting his friends with illegal fertility procedures for years."

"Illegal?" Summers sputtered. "Claude Dumont? Do you know how ridiculous you sound?"

"Serious medical ethics issues are at stake here. Laws may have been broken."

"I've known Claude Dumont for thirty years—"

"Do you know the backgrounds of these children? They are not normal human beings."

"They come from outstanding families. They've had every resource and advantage. Tom, I know you have strong feelings about social inequality in this country. Your writing is excellent. I've never interfered with your work. You provide a thoughtful balance in the magazine. I'm proud of what you've produced here. But make no mistake about it: there is a growing and powerful aristocracy in this country and around the world. They are *our* future. We can't turn them against us."

"Dumont got to you," Tom seethed.

"Claude and I are old friends. Yes, he alerted me to this, but I also received calls from two of the families you interrupted last night, plus another from Claude this morning about Khalil Darwish. You don't want to mess around with people like that. *I* don't. This is a quality publication, not a tabloid. My God, Tom, you've been nominated for a Pulitzer. I assume you'd like to actually receive it. You know how the world works. I don't need to be telling you any of this."

Summers was giving him a clear order, but Tom was a professional investigative journalist. It wasn't just what he did, it was who he was. If his hypothesis was correct, there was medical knowledge twenty years ago that could have helped millions of families if it had been more widely available. He wasn't going to drop this story under any circumstances. "I've worked here for two decades because of the investigative freedom you've given me."

"You're a smart man. *Very* smart. You know our business. You have to understand my position."

"Hank, what are these people trying to hide?"

"They're just protecting their families."

"It's much more than that. I think there's some sort of secret fertility clinic that Claude and his friends have used—"

"And what if they did? Why is that anyone's business?"

"It's *everyone's* business! Twenty years ago, did we have advanced health care only available to the ultra-rich? That wasn't available for *my wife and child*? Should wealthy parents today have access to therapies that aren't legal for the rest of us? Does that sound right to you?" Tom suddenly felt tears well up and his throat constricted. "You attended the funeral."

"Oh, Tom." Summers stood and walked from behind his desk. "That was terrible for you. I haven't forgotten. But it was a long time ago and, well, I'm just not seeing the connection to this. We must deal in the present. This is about relationships, about business." He placed his hand on Tom's shoulder. "You've been pushing yourself hard. *I've* been pushing you. You're tired. Take some time off. Come back with a clear head and continue your great work for the magazine."

"I won't drop this."

Summers could no longer conceal his impatience. "Can you prove *anything*?"

"Not yet, but I'm sure some version of it is true. There's way too much smoke."

Summers shook his head. "It's pure speculation. Think of the risks you're taking. The litigation could cripple the magazine. And for what?" Summers let the silence hang as he returned to his desk. "My decision is final. We're not publishing this story. It's not what we're about."

Tom was suddenly on his feet, his cheeks burning. "Aren't we about the truth?"

"Enough, Tom. I don't want to hear another word about this. It's entirely inappropriate, it's bad for *Future*, and, well...I have so much respect for you, but...it's absurd."

"I'll tell you what it is," Tom yelled. "It's *corruption*." He turned on his heels and slammed the door behind him. Summers's executive assistant watched him pass with a look of shock.

Tom rushed to his office and shut the door. His head was pounding. He realized he was breathing rapidly, too rapidly. He sat heavily in his chair and leaned forward, his thumbs pressing his temples. He couldn't stop thinking about the rich families, their children, their privilege, their greed and arrogance. He looked up at his late wife's photograph, which only made him feel worse. Then he saw that he had a message on his desk phone. He wondered if Summers had changed his mind. He hit the play button. A woman's tentative voice said:

"This is…Deborah Fiske. I'm calling for Tom Wright. It's about your message last night. I can't talk over the phone, but I heard about the story you're writing and, well, I have important information for you. I'll meet you today at noon in front of the Bethesda Fountain. If you're not there, I'll…call again. Don't tell anyone about this. Please make sure you're not being followed. Okay. Bye."

A quiet knock on his door caused him to look up. It was Hank Summers, looking contrite.

"Look, Tom, that's not how I wanted that to go. I'm really sorry. If you want to talk about this, let's talk."

"I'm going to write this story. That's non-negotiable."

Summers sighed. "Please be reasonable."

"This may be the biggest story of my career. This matters to the world, and it matters to me personally."

"You're not publishing it here."

Tom was deeply disappointed that Hank could be so political, so *commercial*. Suddenly, he was seeing Summers and *Future* in an entirely new light. "I can't drop it, Hank. It's too important."

"My decision is final."

"Are you sure about that?"

"Absolutely sure."

"Then I quit. I'll clear out of my office today."

"Oh, come on, Tom," Summers pleaded. "I

don't want you to leave." Summers shook his head. "Don't be such a hothead. Take the rest of the day off. Think it over. Let's talk about it tomorrow."

"There's nothing to talk about." Tom slipped his laptop and a stack of folders into his briefcase, grabbed his jacket, and passed Summers on the way to the elevator.

"Hey!" Summers called after him. "You can't take that!"

"Try and stop me," Tom said flatly as the elevator doors closed.

16

The shock of his abrupt resignation lifted slowly as he walked north on Broadway, his briefcase heavy at his side. He knew he had a quick temper, a trait that had caused problems at various junctures in his life. Was this one of them? He had acted rashly, but he felt no regret. He owned his condo, had plenty of money stashed away, and had come into a moderate inheritance, which was safely invested. *Future* had been a comfortable and prestigious platform for his work, but he was known now. He could freelance, be his own boss. Most importantly, he might now have the just the lead he needed to break this story open.

He checked his watch as he reached Columbus Circle. It was 11:30 a.m. His meeting with Deborah Fiske was to take place mid-Park at around 72nd Street, so he had plenty of time. He turned right onto Central Park South and crossed to the north side. The day was beautiful, not a cloud in the sky. People were out walking, biking, roller-skating, and sunning on the grass. A horse-drawn carriage went by. He passed through a cluster of dark rock formations and wound his way around The Pond toward The Mall and the Bethesda Terrace.

A tall, stylishly dressed woman was standing directly in front of the fountain. She wore a long dress, a big floppy hat, and sunglasses, too much clothing for a warm day. Tom guessed by her disguise that she must be the woman he was meeting. He walked straight to her and introduced himself.

"Thank you for coming," she said, glancing behind him.

"You've certainly aroused my curiosity. What's this important information you mentioned?"

"I don't know where to start."

"Wherever you like. I suddenly have all the time in the world."

She dipped her glasses, revealing large green eyes. Now he recognized her from one of Amy's folders. "After I got your message I heard you were calling other families and I…well, I had to see you."

She was nervously scanning the terrace and Tom could see the tension in the rise of her shoulders. "Are you looking for someone?"

She turned to him. "Why do you ask?"

"You seem anxious."

After a short pause, she said, "I suppose I am."

"Then let's walk while we talk."

94

Tom led her to a footpath that followed the lake's shoreline. People rowed in small boats, seemingly without a care in the world.

"My husband, Scott, is a close friend of Claude Dumont," she said. "Do you who know who he is?"

"Dumont? Yes, I do." Tom also pictured Scott Fiske: the firm jawline, the thinning white hair, a tall, lean frame, the expensive suit. What was she afraid of? What risks was she taking by meeting with him now?

"Scott and I were married twenty-two years ago. He's older than me -- much older -- so we were in a hurry to have children. After years of trying, I'd all but given up. But Scott came home one day smelling of liquor, which I remember distinctly because he rarely drinks anything but wine. He said he had a new plan."

Tom recalled the fine brandy he'd shared with Dumont. He was beginning to get a sense of Dumont's modus operandi. He felt his pulse quickening. "I'm with you. Please go on."

"The next day we went to a doctor on Fifth Avenue. He examined both of us. He saw that I was ovulating and asked if he could harvest some eggs right away. I agreed, and Scott left some...sperm. I feel so uncomfortable talking about this—"

"This is very helpful. I need to hear all of it." Tom stopped and looked her in the eye. "This will stay strictly between the two of us until you tell me otherwise. You have my word."

She nodded and they resumed their walk. "A couple months later we flew down to Kentucky to visit Claude at his horse farm. I thought we were just going to look at horses and go riding. Claude had a facility there though, a lab, and a doctor took us aside and said that he could help us have a baby. He said that he'd used some proprietary technology to create embryos from the cells we'd provided in New York. We'd tried everything else, so I agreed. It was the biggest mistake I've ever made."

"What happened?"

"I got pregnant right away. At first, we were so happy. Ecstatic, really. We were even happier when we learned I was carrying twin boys, and happier still when they were born, six pounds each and apparently perfectly healthy."

Tom glanced at her, recalling that Amy had found nothing in the public record about the Fiske twins. "But they weren't?"

She slowed her pace. "My son, Paul, is a severe, violent schizophrenic. The symptoms first started when he was about ten years old, and we knew something was seriously wrong by the time he turned thirteen. Since then, it's gotten...well, it's...horrible."

"I'm so sorry. Where is he now?"

"It's hard to talk about this." She quickly looked away and wiped her cheek.

Tom desperately wanted her to continue,

but he saw how hard this was for her. Her pain and vulnerability touched him deeply. "We can meet another time."

"No, I need to tell you now. Time's running out." She took a deep breath. "As Paul's condition worsened, we built a...safe place for him in our home in Greenwich. We have round-the-clock nursing care. Even with that, he's a danger to himself and to others...even to me."

"What a nightmare," Tom said, digesting the implications of what she had told him. *So, there was a special clinic, advanced methods.* He thought he knew the answer but asked anyway: "Are you saying these health problems are connected to Dumont's clinic?"

"Of course, they are!"

Tom tried to remain calm. "I don't understand. What did he do?"

"When they created the embryos, they modified our genes."

"How do you know *that*?"

"They *told* us they did. We even gave our input," she added bitterly, "our 'wish list.' In the process, critical pieces of the boys' DNA were scrambled. They were doomed from the start. They never had a chance."

They started walking again, Tom's heart pounding. "What does your husband think about all of this?"

She waved away the mention of her husband. "Scott's a private banker. Claude is his biggest client by far. There's no way that Scott would ever take any action against him. He practically worships the man. They all do."

"I don't want to seem insensitive. I'm just trying to understand. How can you be so sure that Dumont tampered with your boys' genes? I understand they made claims, but couldn't it have been a random outcome? An accident of nature?"

"A few years ago, we had their DNA sequenced. We know for a fact that their mental illness is genetically based. Neither Scott nor I have those mutations."

"It seems Edward is less affected?"

"He's not as seriously ill, but he's definitely bi-polar. So far, it's been manageable. He's a brilliant musician, a pianist, but he can be miserable even when he's on medication. I often hear him cry himself to sleep. It's heartbreaking."

"I'd heard that a twin with schizophrenia will often have a brother or sister with bipolar disorder."

"They're identical twins. Their DNA's the same. Something in Paul's life pushed him in a terrible direction."

"Did you ever confront Dumont about this?"

"Scott did. He almost divorced me over it, but I told him I'd leave him if he didn't."

"What did Dumont say?"

"Oh, he was his typical empathetic, charming self. He denied any connection to the genetic damage. Then he reminded Scott in the nicest possible way that he's an older man, which put his offspring at higher risk. Claude said that out of friendship he'd create a trust to help care for both boys."

"Did he?"

She nodded, her lips pressed hard together. "He certainly did. Ten million dollars."

Tom whistled quietly.

"Like Scott needs the money," she whispered.

"And that settled things for your husband?"

"Between him and Claude? Absolutely. But Scott never forgave me for forcing the issue. He drifted away from us after that. Nowadays we hardly ever see him. Apparently, he prefers young French actresses. We have plans for my birthday in a few days. We'll see."

They walked in silence for a few moments.

"Now that you've told me these things, Deborah, what do you want me to do?"

She stopped and held his arm. "I want you to write this story. I want you to expose him. I want you do to it now. It's critically important."

"Why?"

"Because he's still *doing* it! My friend, Sue, is next."

"She told you this?"

"Yes! They've wanted a child for years. Her husband, Rick, just talked to Claude about it. They're going to go through with this."

Sue and Rick. "Are you talking about the Millers?"

Her grip tightened. "How did you know that?"

"Because I met them on the plane back from Art Basel this weekend. Have you told her about your suspicions?"

"Of course, I have. We've been close for years. She's seen what I've been through."

"But she doesn't believe you."

"She listens out of friendship, but no, she doesn't accept my explanation. She thinks it happened a long time ago, that Scott was too old to father children, and that the science must be better now. At this point she's not going to say no to Rick. Never has and never will. That's why we must expose Dumont. It's the only way to stop this."

"You've filled in so many gaps for me," Tom said carefully, "but if we're going to go public, I'm going to need a lot more information." Tom thought for a moment. "May I meet your boys? Talk to their doctors?"

"I can make arrangements to meet the doctors, but do you really think it's necessary to see my twins?"

"That's entirely up to you," Tom said, "but

yes, I'd like to meet your children. I want to truly understand what Dumont has done and what you've all been through."

Deborah took a deep breath as she gazed across the lake. "All right, then. I'll take you to them now."

17

Rick Miller's heart was in his throat as the Pilatus PC-12 aircraft passed within twenty feet of a scrubby ridgeline and then plunged its nose down. The forward cockpit window was suddenly filled with gray asphalt. Passengers gasped as Rick envisioned a fiery death. The pilot flared, pulling up to land the plane with a few minor bounces. Sunlight sparkled off the bright blue Atlantic at the end of the runway. As they taxied to the small terminal, Rick started breathing again. Welcome to St. Barts.

Rick had flown from a quarterly business meeting in Miami to St. Martin in a NetJets Gulfstream IV, a much larger and more luxurious aircraft than the one he was about to disembark. He didn't have to resort to fractional ownership, but he was a businessman to his core. He'd built his car empire on high-end markets, superb customer service, and a focus on cost control. He had strong general managers for each of his prospering dealerships, so his business travel usually amounted to only twenty hours of flight time per quarter, not nearly enough, in his view, to justify the expense of owning a jet outright. NetJets allowed him to get an airplane whenever he needed one. He rarely used them for personal purposes, but this meeting could not be missed.

Unfortunately, the landing strip at St. Barts' Gustaf III airport was only two thousand feet long, so only small propeller-driven aircraft could land there. Rick's heart rate had almost returned to normal by the time he passed through Customs and took a short taxi ride to Eden Rock, a small luxury hotel centered on a long, sandy beach called *Le Plage de Saint Jean*. He was an hour early, so he decided to wait at the bar, a large, tiered space with colorful couches and canvas awnings that opened to the beach and the ocean beyond. A good-looking young man with his hair pulled back in a ponytail led him to a corner table. After ordering his drink, Miller looked about him. The establishment was chic. Most of the customers were young and wearing bathing suits or cover-ups. He'd only been on the ground for a few minutes, but this already seemed like paradise. He did feel a little out of place in his dress shirt and blazer. As he nursed his drink, he wondered how the young people around him could afford to live like this. It was a Tuesday, after all. He thought of indulgent parents, and then back to the purpose of this trip.

He was on his second gin-and-tonic when a handsome man in his late 50's approached him.

"Mr. Miller?" the man said with a slight French accent.

"Yes." Miller stood and they shook hands. "Are you Dr. Bergeron?"

"I am." Bergeron sat across from him.

"Thanks for meeting me. I'm sorry to interrupt your vacation."

Bergeron smiled tightly and lit a cigarette. "I'm not sure what Claude told you, but he thought it was important for you to be able to ask me questions before you make any decisions."

Rick nodded. "Sue and I really appreciate your willingness to help us. We've been trying to have a child for a long time."

Bergeron shrugged, pursing his lips in a Gallic manner. He checked his watch and asked, "So, what do you want to know?"

"Well, for starters, how is it that you can do what no one else seems to be able to do?"

Bergeron gave a short laugh, rolling his eyes as he blew smoke into the breeze. "I can answer that easily, but first it's important that we have an understanding." He looked about to ensure no one was within hearing range. "I'm sure that Claude told you that what we do is entirely private and confidential. You must never speak of this with anyone. There could be enormous negative legal implications, possibly for us but most assuredly for you. Claude is extremely generous, but he is also a *very* powerful man. That entails inherent contradictions, *non*? I hope for your sake you never see that side of him. I have, and it's not what you want. Understood?"

"Claude made that very clear. I would never do anything to betray his trust, or yours."

"*Bon*." Bergeron nodded and took another drag on his cigarette. "We have the capabilities we do because we've fully embraced the science of genetics without restriction. Claude has funded my company, Chromos, for over twenty years. While the global research community has hobbled itself with regulation, religion, and bureaucracy, we've pushed ahead, unfettered and unconstrained. I believe that we are at least a decade ahead of what is currently regarded as cutting-edge science. You ask me: What is our edge? That's it."

"So, what exactly do you do?"

Bergeron gazed at Miller through the smoke curling up from his cigarette. "He didn't tell you much, did he?"

Miller smiled weakly. "Just that he would help us."

The Frenchman dropped his cigarette into an ashtray, speaking quickly. "At the end of the day, we are breeders. I'm sure you're aware of what Claude's stables have accomplished over the years. Champion after champion. We've had similar results with grapes. It's the secret to his best wines."

"All of that's due to your work on genes?"

105

LEGACY

Bergeron raised a brow. "You've no doubt heard debates about the influence of nature versus nurture?"

Miller nodded.

"Nurture is important to be sure, but it builds on nature. That nature is dictated by genes. Every cell in your body has a full copy of the blueprints that make you you." Bergeron tapped another cigarette out of a pack and placed it between his lips. "That manual is written in a substance called deoxyribonucleic acid. DNA? Are you following me?"

"I think so, yes."

"In a computer, all information is ultimately reduced to bits: one or zero. You're familiar with the concept?"

"Yes, of course."

"In biology, all that information is recorded in four letters: A, C, T, and G. They stand for adenine, cytosine, thymine, and guanine. Adenine always connects to cytosine, and thymine always links to guanine. Each of those combinations is called a base pair. You have about three billion of them, strung together in structures called chromosomes. When you put them all together, you have what's called your genome, your full instruction manual. Those three billion base pairs make up your 20,000 genes. It's more complicated than that, but...I don't want to confuse you."

"No, it's very interesting."

"This is what's important: if there are missing or misplaced letters in DNA, the process of life is disrupted, or may not start at all. How old are you, Mr. Miller?"

"I'm turning seventy."

"Then it's possible, even likely, that there are accumulated defects in your DNA that would directly impact the health of your child. How old is your wife?"

"She'll turn forty-eight next month."

Bergeron seemed to consider that for a moment. "Do you have a picture of her?"

Miller took his phone from his pocket and showed it to Bergeron. It was a flattering photo of the two of them on their wedding day. Rick had had a full head of dark brown hair in contrast to his current white wisps.

"I mean something current," Bergeron said, taking the phone and thumbing quickly through Miller's photos. He held up the phone. "Is this her?"

"Yes, that's Sue."

Bergeron frowned as he took another look. "She's a little heavy."

Miller was taken aback. "I wouldn't say that. I think she's a very attractive woman."

"I'm speaking purely from a scientific perspective. Is it your intention to have her carry the baby, or will you use a surrogate?"

"You mean, have the baby with another woman? How does that work?"

"We take your wife's egg and your sperm. We determine the structure of your respective DNA, fix any problems, and create healthy embryos. We can implant that embryo in your wife's uterus or someone else's. Nine months later: birth. It's still your baby. Your genes."

Rick had never even considered that possibility. "I'd have to ask her."

"I'm not trying to be an asshole," Bergeron said. "At her age and weight, the chances of a successful implantation are reduced. If she wants to carry the child to term, we can compensate for that risk by creating multiple embryos. It's your decision."

"What did you mean when you said you fix any problems?"

"We screen for hereditary diseases like Huntington's, cystic fibrosis, a number of cancers, that sort of thing. We know where to look for them. If we find problem areas, we cut out that segment of DNA and replace it with healthy base pairs." Bergeron took a deep pull on his cigarette and gazed at Miller through the exhaled smoke. "I imagine that Claude mentioned this, but we can also make enhancements."

Rick leaned forward. "He did touch on that, but what exactly can you do?"

"Just as we can correct errors, we can adjust base pairs to create more advantageous characteristics. For example, we can preprogram genes to create a better ability to build muscle mass, to prevent baldness, to enhance elements that affect intelligence, to influence temperament—"

"So, if I'm hearing you correctly, we can actually...design our child?"

"Yes, within limitations. Once I've examined your DNA, I'll be able to give you a set of options. Or, if you'd prefer, you can provide me with your wish list, and I'll let you know what's possible."

Miller felt overwhelmed. "This is a lot to take in. It's…" He sat back heavily, trying to process the enormity of what Bergeron was offering. He mopped his forehead with a handkerchief.

As the silence dragged on, Bergeron started to get up. "Perhaps we have wasted your time."

"No, no," Miller said, raising his hands. "I meant to say, it's *miraculous*. You're telling me that you can not only eliminate the chances of birth defects, but you can help us create someone exceptional."

"It will be your job as parents to create the exceptional. All I can do is give you the best possible natural abilities to build upon. So, tell me now. Are you interested?"

"You bet I am. Absolutely."

Bergeron waved discreetly to a young blonde who was sitting alone at a nearby table.

As she rose to leave, Bergeron took a card printed with a line of routing numbers from his shirt pocket and slid it across the table. Miller examined it. Bergeron leaned forward and lowered his voice. "The price for this procedure is $10 million cash. It is a one-time fee, but does not include surrogate compensation, routine prenatal care, or the delivery. That's up to your own OB-GYN. We guarantee a full-term pregnancy. If your wife loses a fetus, we will continue to implant the embryos at no additional charge. To the outside world, this will look like a straight-forward in vitro fertilization. Only you and I will know the origin of the embryos." Bergeron drew even closer. "Let me be very clear. This is completely illegal. It shouldn't be, but it is. That's why we are so strict about confidentiality."

"You can count on me."

Bergeron nodded. "Claude wouldn't have sent you here if he didn't trust you."

"Thank you, Doctor. When do we actually start?"

"Right now. I'll need a sperm sample."

"Now?"

Bergeron tilted his head toward a covered walkway that led to the street. "There are unisex bathrooms down that way. The second door is locked. Knock on it. The nurse I just waved to is waiting there for you."

Rick shook his head. This was all moving

so quickly.

Bergeron clasped Miller's shoulder as he stood. "Don't worry. If you need any assistance, she's very good."

18

Deborah Fiske made full use of the road-handling capabilities of her Aston Martin Rapide as they raced east on the Merritt Parkway. Passing traffic at high speed seemed to preoccupy her, limiting their conversation. Several times Tom was more than a little frightened. For the first time in his life, he prayed that they'd pass a state trooper on the side of the road, anything to be able to step out of the car. They crossed the Connecticut state line and turned south onto Round Hill Road. The Fiske estate was situated on twenty wooded acres, the large baronial mansion set amidst perfect lawns backed by a picturesque lake.

They pulled around a circular gravel driveway and stopped in front of an imposing stone entryway.

"Home sweet home," she said with a trace of bitterness.

A man in a blazer opened her door. She climbed out of the car, leaving the engine running, and thanked the attendant. Tom walked beside her to a massive oak door that opened as they approached. They stepped into a grand hall with a thirty-foot ceiling befitting a medieval castle. Tom had known they were rich, but this reflected serious money. Someone in another room was playing a Beethoven sonata. Tom was no expert, but the pianist was talented.

"Can I get you anything?" she asked as she laid her hat on the table and took off her sunglasses. Her face fully revealed, she was indeed a very attractive woman. Her dark hair was lustrous, her complexion without blemish, her green eyes flecked with gold. It was easy to imagine Scott Fiske falling instantly in love with her, and hard to fathom their subsequent estrangement.

"I'm fine," Tom said, "but thank you."

As they crossed the hall, the music grew louder. Tom caught a glimpse of the piano and its player in a sunlit conservatory as they passed.

"This is Edward," she said quietly. He was a handsome boy, perhaps sixteen or seventeen, with hair and a face like his mother's. He was totally focused on his music and didn't look up as they passed. Tom noted that Deborah didn't interrupt his playing.

"Paul is this way," she said. She opened another heavy wooden door and entered a tiled white hallway that seemed more suited to a hospital than to a home. They descended steps to a barred gate that could have been a prison door. She punched a five-digit code into a small box on the wall and the lock clicked open. She let Tom walk through and then ensured that the gate closed behind them. They followed another short hall and stopped in front of a small glass window set into a metal door.

"He's sedated," she said. She knocked on the door. A big man in a white hospital uniform opened it.

"Good afternoon, Mrs. Fiske," the nurse said.

"How is he?"

"Stable."

She stepped to the bed and gently stroked the boy's hair. "Tom, this is my other son."

Tom stood beside her. Paul looked much like his brother, though his face was thinner, his skin dull and blotchy. His right eye was heavily bandaged. Ugly, deep purple scratches marred his forehead. A bag of intravenous fluid was suspended from a stand beside the bed, a needle taped to the back of his hand. The boy would have looked like the victim of a serious automobile accident had it not been for the thick, padded nylon straps that held his wrists and ankles to the guardrails on each side of the bed.

"What happened?" Tom asked.

"He had a bad episode and...attacked himself," Deborah whispered, her voice catching.

Tom winced. "I can't imagine what this is like for you."

She nodded but didn't say anything. They stood there for what seemed like a long time.

"Being with you here, seeing your sons, I'm hesitant to ask any questions."

"Please do. That's why we're here."

Tom paused to order his thoughts. Deborah was being brave, but her pain was obvious. He wanted to help her and her friends and hoped he could. "First, if Paul's this violent, is it safe to keep him at home?"

"This didn't happen here. They were trying a new drug combination at the hospital and decided to keep him overnight for observation. If he'd been here with people that know him this never would have happened."

"I see." Tom tried to imagine the courage and fortitude it would take to live like this, to be a mother of two mentally ill children and the wife of a distant husband. Despite it all, he could tell by the way she touched her son that she loved him deeply. She turned to look at Tom.

"So, are you going to help us? Make sure this never happens to anyone again?"

It occurred to Tom that by agreeing to her request he would be taking on an additional heavy responsibility, as well as significantly accelerating his own timeline. His heart went out to Deborah and her sons, especially this restrained boy who appeared to have no chance of anything close to a normal life. If someone was responsible for this, he or she had to be held accountable. But while Deborah had his deepest sympathy, he needed facts. He said, "I clearly see the suffering you've all endured. I believe every word you told me about your interactions with Dumont and your husband. The missing piece for me is how Dumont's doctors damaged your sons' genes. Do you remember any names? I could reach out to them, check on their research and publications."

She shook her head. "I only remember one doctor from my visit to Lexington. He seemed to be French, but I don't think I ever knew his name. I would have remembered that. I have no idea whether he's still there, but they must have someone if they're making the same offer to Sue and Rick."

"I guess I'm also struggling with Dumont's motives. He's taken incredible risks."

"Oh, that's not hard," Deborah said quietly, "not if you know him."

"Can you explain?"

"It's quite simple, really. He thinks he's a modern-day king." She paused, then continued. "You have to remember that the Dumont family is French, a culture historically steeped in royalty, absolute power, and fabulous wealth. Everything Claude does can be understood in those terms."

Tom hadn't expected that level of insight from her. "Just how well do you know him?"

"I've probably had a dozen serious

conversations with him over the years: dinners with Scott, social events, a few visits to each other's homes. We bonded over art: literature, painting, music, statuary, and architecture. Claude is very well-educated, especially knowledgeable about seventeenth- and eighteenth-century Europe. He's obsessed with the concepts of monarchy and *noblesse oblige*. All of the priceless art, the horses, the estates, the homes, his generosity, the lifestyle – he's a reincarnated Louis XIV in his prime, above the law because he makes his own." She stroked her son's arm. "French kings decreed fabulous pensions, titles, and estates to bind people to them. Claude's done the same throughout his life. Ultimately, he was able to grant the most valuable treasure of all: children. It was risky and illegal, but he did it because he could, and the crime bound people to him more tightly than anything else could have. The problem is that he's never been as smart as he thinks he is. Mistakes were made. My boys continue to pay the price. No one else should ever have to suffer from Claude's arrogance."

Tom thought of the chateau at Vaux. The parallels with French kings resonated. "We'll need solid proof that there's a genetic basis to your sons' condition, and then of tampering. And I'll need to find that doctor."

She nodded. "I'll bring you to the medical experts. They can take you through the evidence and answer your more technical questions."

"When can I see them?"

She turned to him. "I was hoping we could do that now."

"Will they be available on such short notice?"

"Oh, they'll be available. Believe me, they owe us."

19

Nadine Dumont was having a very good day. She and three friends had just played tennis and were having lunch at Liz Hastings' home in Scarsdale, New York. Liz, a human rights lawyer, was married to Lord Hastings, one of Claude's oldest friends. The Hastings fortune had compounded over generations extending back to The Hundred Years War and a relative whose military prowess had earned the gratitude of an English king. Claire Darwish and Anika Mukerjee rounded out the group. Claire was a pediatrician, Anika a much sought-after interior designer with clients in Manhattan, Paris, and London. All four were highly rated tennis players. Nadine and Liz had defeated the others in straight sets. They were still in their tennis attire, drinking iced tea and mineral water.

"Your serve was really on today," Anika was telling Nadine. "How many aces was that? A dozen?"

"My pro's been having me face a wall and toss balls to the same exact point each time," Nadine said. "It seems to be working."

LEGACY

Members of Liz's kitchen staff appeared with a big bowl of salad, a platter of iced teas, and some sliced fruit.

As they were plating their meals, Claire asked, "Hey, by any chance did any of you get a call from a reporter asking about Art Basel?"

"Pratul did," Anika replied quickly, referring to her husband. "He started out saying he wanted to include our daughter in a story about young leaders. It turns out the guy's an investigative reporter for *Future* magazine. He was calling people he'd seen with Claude in Miami."

"What did Pratul tell him?" Nadine asked, putting down her fork.

"That we're not interested. We don't need that kind of attention, right? What's the upside?"

"The same guy, Tom Wright, came to see Claude yesterday," Nadine said. "Claude told him to mind his own business and contacted the publisher of the magazine."

"Do you think this is a coincidence?" Anika asked, looking to each of her friends. A silence fell upon them.

"It has to be," Liz said. "There's no way anyone could know."

"Unless someone's talking," Claire said.

"No one would be that stupid," Nadine said, although she had lingering doubts. Deborah Fiske made accusations years ago, but she'd been

120

warned, and Scott would never betray them.

"Okay," Anika said, "so, this reporter goes to Miami and takes a photo of Claude and our families and gets curious. If he keeps digging, the chances of him eventually finding something grows." She looked to each of them, her gaze settling on Nadine. "I don't want my daughter to ever have to deal with that."

"Claude's close to Hank Summers, isn't he?" Liz suggested to Nadine. "It seems like this should be easy to fix."

"One would think so," Nadine said. "Excuse me for a moment." She stood and walked to the couch where she'd placed her purse. She called Claude.

"Nadine! How was the tennis?" he asked cheerfully.

"I'm here with Liz, Claire, and Anika. Both the Mukerjees and the Darwishs were contacted by Tom Wright last night. What did Hank say at dinner?"

After a pause, Claude said, "He said he would kill the story."

"Do you think he did?"

"He'd be foolish not to. Leave this to me, my dear. I'll tend to it right away."

"This is the last thing any of us need."

"I couldn't agree more. Give the girls a hug from me."

20

The McAllister Hospital Psychiatric Treatment Center was housed in a brick building set in an affluent neighborhood of tree-lined streets. Tom and Deborah entered the front lobby. She told the receptionist who she was and they were immediately escorted to a conference room on the third floor. Two doctors were waiting for them. One was a white man in his sixties, a doctor Deborah had met many times, and the other was a petite black woman in her forties with short hair and large, expressive eyes.

"Mrs. Fiske," the older physician said, "let me begin by saying how sorry we are about Paul's attack. We've never seen this kind of reaction to this therapy." His name, Dr. Richard Bromley, was elegantly stitched in red above the breast pocket of his white jacket.

"Dr. Bromley, my husband and I are going to hold this hospital fully accountable for what happened to my son. We've obviously already been in contact with our attorneys."

Bromley took a deep breath, but his expression remained calm, even kind. "Be that as it may, how can we help you today?"

"As I said on the phone, I'm determined to increase public awareness of this disease. This is Thomas Wright. He's a journalist. As you've often explained to me, genetics and environment both play a role in the disease. Tom has some questions about the DNA sequencing you've done and how it relates to my sons' condition."

"I see," Bromley said. "I assume you're willing to waive any privacy concerns?"

"Yes," she said. "I'll sign forms to that effect."

"We'll have them ready for your signature before you leave," he said. "After you called, I asked Doctor Slater to join me. She has considerably more expertise on this area than I do."

"What's your background, Doctor?" Tom asked her.

"Shall we sit?" Bromley suggested.

As they took their seats, Doctor Slater said, "I went to medical school at Yale and had my residency at Massachusetts General Hospital. I did three years of post-doctoral work at the Innovative Genomics Institute at Cal Berkeley and the Karolinska University Hospital in Stockholm. I have an MD as well as a PhD in biochemistry."

Tom nodded. This woman was impressive.

"What would you like to know?" Slater asked.

"To start," Tom said, placing a notepad in front of him, "do the boys' diseases have a genetic basis?"

"Yes, they do," Slater said. "In some cases, it's difficult to point to a specific genetic cause, but they have clear markers."

She stopped, waiting as Tom took notes.

"Can you be more specific?" he asked, looking up.

"Do you have a scientific background, Mr. Wright?"

"Not formally," he confessed, "though I've written about science for decades."

Slater seemed to be choosing her words carefully. "I haven't been directly involved in Paul's treatment here, but I did review his records after Dr. Bromley invited me to this meeting. He has a severe case of hebephrenic schizophrenia. It usually develops between the ages of fifteen and twenty-five, so his case appeared early. The symptoms typically include disorganized behaviors and thoughts, delusions, hallucinations, and abnormal speech patterns. Violent and suicidal tendencies are not uncommon. The disease has no single specific biological cause. As Mrs. Fiske noted at the onset, both genes and external factors affect the course of the disease. Relevant to Paul, we know that people who have abnormalities in a neurochemical called dopamine are at higher risk. We also see more schizophrenia in patients with less neuronal matter in certain areas of the brain." She paused, looking between them. No one spoke, so she continued. "It's clear that deletions or duplications of genetic material in a number of chromosomes caused these two conditions to develop as Paul grew older. In particular, a small deletion in a region in chromosome 22 called 22q11 made him highly vulnerable."

"So, you've sequenced his entire genome?" Tom asked, looking to Deborah and then to Slater.

"Yes," Deborah replied, "about three years ago. All four of us were tested: Scott, me, and both boys."

"DNA is very complex," Slater said. "Just because something is coded in a gene doesn't necessarily mean it will express itself. The chemical building blocks that make DNA are constantly mutating and repairing themselves. With that in mind, the gene sequences for both Deborah and her husband are normal."

"Meaning," Tom said, "that if you'd looked at either set, you wouldn't have predicted that their child would develop this illness."

As they were talking, Dr. Bromley was typing a text message on his cell phone.

"Are we boring you, Doctor?" Deborah asked sharply.

"No," Bromley said, continuing for a moment before putting his phone down. "Not at all. But I don't want to delay you at the end of our meeting. The privacy waivers are being prepared as we speak."

"Thank you," she said, returning to Slater. "Please, continue."

"That's right," Slater said in reply to Tom's question. "Edward and Paul are monozygotic twins, meaning that they both came from a single egg that split into two. As identical twins, their genetic material should be identical, and for all practical purposes, they are. When we compared the four sequences, there were obviously many genes that came from the parents. I haven't yet studied the full sequences in detail, but there is no question that Scott and Deborah are the biological parents of these boys."

"Yet the boys do have genetic damage."

"Yes. The case is highly unusual for two reasons. The first is that there are a number of SNPs—"

Deborah held up her hand. "I don't know what those are."

"I'm sorry, there are single nucleotide polymorphisms and copy number variants, or CNVs, in both boys that are completely absent in either parent."

"So, there is damage," Tom said.

"Yes," said Slater.

"And what's the second reason you

126

mentioned?"

Slater let out a long, slow breath. "There appear to be segments of DNA in some chromosomes that could not have come from either the mother or the father. I can't explain that. Not yet."

Tom noticed Deborah bite her lower lip. Apparently, she hadn't shared her suspicions about Dumont's clinic. He simply asked, "How is that possible?"

"I don't know," Dr. Slater said. "I've never seen anything like this."

Choosing his words carefully, Tom said, "If I'm correct, the Fiskes used in vitro fertilization for the twins." Tom glanced at Deborah for confirmation and received a nod. "Is it possible that the boys' chromosomes were somehow manipulated before the embryos were placed in the uterus?"

"No," Dr. Slater said firmly, shaking her head. "The twins are seventeen years old. At the time of the implantation, doctors in my field didn't have the ability to edit the genes of human embryos. Not only was it not scientifically possible, but it also would have been completely unethical and illegal. No licensed medical doctor would have attempted it."

"You seem very sure about that," Deborah said, an edge in his voice.

"I'll look into this more deeply. There might have been some contamination at the clinic. All I can say is that something did go terribly wrong, and I'm so sorry for how it's affected you and your family."

21

It has long been said that clothes make the man, and a man in Hank Summers' position had to dress the part. It had been his custom since founding *Future* to buy two suits every quarter, a habit that ensured a crisp, contemporary appearance and a perfect fit over the years. He had just returned from his visit to Umberto, a tailor as skilled with his compliments as he was with a scissors and needle. Hank had recommended Umberto to countless friends and had grown into a major source of business for the enterprising clothier, deepening their relationship. Since his last visit, Umberto informed him, Hank had lost a full inch off his waistline and gained half an inch on his chest. Hank proudly recounted his recent squash victories at his club as he admired his improved physique in the tailor's mirror. It had made for a most pleasant afternoon, and, if events unfolded as expected, he would soon have need of the new suits.

He rode up the elevator to his office, hung up his coat, and collected phone messages from his executive assistant. One was potentially exciting. No less a personage than Lord Hastings was pulling strings to have Hank invited to the World Economic Forum. Held every January in Davos, Switzerland, it gathered thousands of leaders from government, business, society, and the arts to address issues of key concern to the world. More and more celebrities were attending the proceedings, and Hank felt strongly that it was important to the magazine that he should be there. Moreover, it would mark another step toward his rising importance on the world stage.

He closed the door to his office, picked up his phone, and dialed Hastings's private number.

"Hello?"

"John, it's Hank. I just got back to the office and received your message."

"Thanks for calling me back." Hastings, normally ebullient, sounded flat and hurried. "Look, Hank, this is about Davos. I'm afraid it's just not going to work out this year."

Summers couldn't conceal his disappointment. "But I thought it was all taken care of."

"I'm sorry. The committee has withdrawn you from consideration. Maybe next year? I know this was important to you."

"But why?"

"I'm limited in what I can say."

Summers felt the disappointment deep in the pit of his stomach. "Can you tell me anything

KEVIN BOREEN

at all?"

After a pause, Lord Hastings said, "Hank, we've been friends for many years, and I really do feel badly about this. Some concerns were raised."

"What could they possibly be? I'm precisely the sort of person that should be attending this event."

"In these circles, and Hank, you're the last person in the world that I need to explain this to, there is an expected degree of...engagement. Based on recent activity at *Future*, some people are wondering if you fully embrace that."

"But I—"

"I'm really sorry, but I have a call that I have to take. I'll see you soon, Hank, and I am sorry." Hastings disconnected.

Summers felt utterly deflated. He couldn't imagine how this had happened. Who could overrule Lord Hastings on something as trivial as an invitation that thousands of others would receive? He was trying to get his mind around that when his assistant cracked open the door. "Mr. Summers, your wife has been trying to reach you on your cell phone. She says it's important."

Summers fumbled for his cell, which he found in his jacket pocket. The screen showed several recent calls from his wife. He called her back and she picked up immediately.

"Oh, Hank! I don't know what's going on!"

"What's wrong? What's happened?"

"I don't know!" She sounded close to tears. "I got a call from Venessa Ferreira this morning. We were supposed to go to the Sundance Film Festival with them—"

Hank loved the film festival. "Are you saying we're not?"

"Well, they've had to cancel. Some conflict came up."

"And they won't give us their tickets?"

"There's more. Sue Covington called me less than an hour later apologizing that their box is going to be full at the Super Bowl."

"We've been disinvited from the Super Bowl?" Hank said faintly. They hadn't missed one for twenty-five years. His exclusion from Davos was now taking on an entirely new and ominous significance.

"Something's wrong, Hank. People aren't returning my calls." She lowered her voice and asked, "Did something happen between you and Claude Dumont? That's what people are saying."

Hank was stunned. "No, nothing happened. We had a perfectly delightful dinner together the other night. This doesn't make any sense."

"Well, maybe you'd better look into it while I still have a friend left." She hung up.

Summers took a deep breath. He glanced at his calendar and noted that it was December 7th, the anniversary of the attack on Pearl Harbor.

He certainly felt he was under attack, but by whom? He was sure he remained on good terms with Claude. They'd been friends for years, not just social acquaintances, but close confidants. He dialed Claude's private line. Claude picked up on the second ring.

"Hank, how are you?"

"I've been better. All of our plans for the next two months seem to have fallen through in a single morning."

"Hmmm.... I was afraid something like this might happen."

"So, you know about this?"

"Hank, when we were at dinner the other night, I suggested something to you as a friend. Do you recall what I said?"

"Of course, I do. You asked me to kill the Art Basel story."

"And?"

"I killed it the very next morning. Things turned ugly. I had to fire Tom Wright," Summers lied, wanting to appear strong. "He's no longer at the magazine."

After a long silence, Claude's voice took on a hard edge that Summers had never heard from his friend. "I didn't ask you to *fire* him. I told you that the story needed be stopped, that a lot of people would be upset if he continued."

"But—"

"I wanted you to *control* him. How can you control him if he no longer works for you?"

"How do you know he's continuing his investigation?"

"Can you think of another reason for him to be visiting the psychiatric hospital that's been treating Paul Fiske?"

For the third time in mere minutes, Hank's line died.

22

The Eurocopter Mercedes-Benz EC 145 approached Bergeron's hilltop villa from the east, settling lightly on a square of lawn beside his illuminated swimming pool. He boarded and settled into a white leather seat trimmed in black. It only took ten minutes to fly from St. Barts to Princess Juliana International Airport in St Martin. Claude's jet, a Falcon Dassault 2000, awaited him there. The flight to Lexington, Kentucky, took three hours. Blue Grass Airport was quiet when he arrived. He put his brief case and overnight bag in the trunk of his car, turned onto Man O War Boulevard, then onto US Route 68, heading south away from the city. From there, it took just twenty minutes to get to the farm.

It was past midnight when he arrived. He drove fast up the winding entrance road, past the stables and guest relations building, past the driveway to the Dumonts' sprawling home, through fence-lined pastures, and into the restricted area.

Claude had been right: he'd needed to get

away. Although it had been just a few days, he felt refreshed and motivated. It was late, but he liked to work at night when no one else was around. He had two tasks tonight. If all went well, he would finish them both before dawn.

Bypassing the parking garage, he pulled in front of the main entrance, took his brief case from the trunk, and stared into the retinal scanner beside the door. The lock opened with a quiet snap.

He crossed a foyer, his heels clicking against the marble floor. The main reception desk was dark. He entered the broad hall and walked past the office suite. He didn't know who would be on duty tonight, but he wasn't in the mood for chit-chat. He descended the stairs to the basement.

"I didn't expect to see you back tonight, Dr. Bergeron," the security guard said from behind his desk. "How was the island?"

"Very nice. I'll be a few hours."

"Yes, sir."

Bergeron looked into another retinal scanner and entered the central laboratory. He crossed to the other side where he unlocked the door to his own private lab. Overhead fluorescent lights turned on automatically as the door closed behind him.

Bergeron felt like he'd spent half of his life in this room. The walls were lined with workbenches, shelves, and cabinets. The center of the room was dominated by a large island with sinks, microscopes, ventilation hoods, and glassware. His desk was on the far side of the island. He felt a familiar sense of pride as he took it all in: the electronic and analytical weighing stations, pH meters and pH adjustment apparatus, freezers, gel staining and visualization equipment, several microscopes, heat blocks and microwaves, autoclaves and drying ovens, micro pipette stands, centrifuges, and, of course, the gene sequencing machines. Whatever he'd ever needed had been provided by Claude with no questions asked. It had cost a fortune, but Bergeron knew his boss was more than satisfied with the returns on his investment.

He opened his brief case and took out the sample that Rick Miller had provided. He allowed himself a grin: the nurse had assured him that little assistance had been required, a good sign. He unpacked the vial and turned on the machines he would need. The lab had been an excellent customer for makers of gene sequencers over the years. He owned several cutting-edge devices from the likes of Applied Biosystems, Illumina, and Thermo-Fisher Scientific. Tonight he would use his Ion Torrent Genexus System, a tool that would give him a complete, high-resolution, base-by-base view of Miller's entire genome within twenty-four hours.

LEGACY

He took a reagent kit from a cabinet, donned rubber gloves, a mask, and eye goggles, and prepared the sample. Decades of laboratory experience showed in the speed and fluidity of his movements. The system used a process called capillary electrophoresis. Electrodes placed on either end of gel containing the DNA sample would cause molecules to move through the gel, allowing the sequencing machine to read the order of the DNA bases.

By this time tomorrow, he thought, he would have his latest patient's full genome in hand. After rechecking the settings, Bergeron initiated the sequencer. "Let's see what you're made of, Mr. Miller."

He prepared the remaining portion of Miller's sample for freezing, following the same procedure he had used for the racehorse before his trip to St. Barts. He would use this material later as Rick Miller's input for the genetically modified embryos. That accomplished, he turned to his second task of the night, setting about the painstaking, intricate process of creating a new kind of Thoroughbred.

23

Tom handed the taxi driver a twenty-dollar bill and stepped onto the corner of 116th Street and Broadway. After Tuesday's discouraging meeting with Dr. Slater, he had spent two days calling attorneys that might know something about the legal aspects of tampering with human genes. None of them seemed particularly knowledgeable about that field of law, but one had recommended contacting HUGO, the Human Genome Organization. Tom learned online that HUGO included a Committee on Ethics, Law, and Society. It consisted of nine members spread around the world, and by good fortune its chairman, Dr. Bradley Fisher, was a professor of bioethics at Columbia University. Tom called him immediately. Fisher said he was leaving on a trip the next day but could meet for half an hour that afternoon.

Fisher's office was in Lewisohn Hall, a stately brick building on Broadway in northern Manhattan. Tom climbed some steps and followed the walkway to the front of the building, which faced a peaceful courtyard.

Some students were reading on a bench beneath a leafless tree.

Dr. Fisher was a thin, athletic looking man with spare, sandy hair and alert eyes. Tom guessed he was in his early forties. They sat in comfortable chairs around a small round table in the corner of his office, traffic and pedestrians passing soundlessly on the street below.

"Thank you squeezing me in," Tom began.

"Not at all," Fisher said. "This kind of public outreach is exactly why our committee exists. How can I help you?"

"As I said on the phone, I'm working on a potential story. I'm still gathering background, so this might not amount to anything."

"You've managed my expectations."

Tom took a notepad from his jacket pocket. "To start off, is it legal to edit human genes?"

"Well, I'm going to have to answer partly yes and partly no."

"Please explain that."

"You should think about gene editing in two categories. One pertains to germline cells and the other to somatic cells. By germline I mean genes that can get passed on to children and their children. This includes sperm, eggs, and embryos. Somatic cells are basically everything else: skin, bone, muscle, organs. Generally, gene research and modification are allowed for somatic cells, subject to regulatory approvals. Gene research that affects the germline is broadly forbidden. Is that helpful?"

"Very. So, if I understand you correctly, it would be flat-out illegal to manipulate the genes of a sperm, egg, or embryo."

"I wish it were that clear cut, but it isn't. There is no universally recognized set of rules or laws that explicitly prohibits human germline gene editing. There are, however, a number of barriers in place."

"Go on."

"I don't know if you followed the story a few years back, but in 2018 a Chinese scientist named He Jianku announced that he had used gene-editing technology called CRISPR to introduce mutations in the CCR5 gene of human embryos. When that gene is non-functional, the HIV virus can't bind to white blood cells. People with that mutation are immune from AIDS."

"That would be a good thing, wouldn't it?"

"It might have been if he'd followed procedures and gotten the proper approvals. Unfortunately for him, he did neither. He was convicted for malpractice, fraud, and violating medical ethics and sentenced to three years in prison and a heavy fine."

"That seems like a stiff punishment for a well-intended experiment."

"You have to step back a little and consider the big picture. When you use a gene therapy to, say, fight melanoma, you're treating

LEGACY

somatic cells that exist in that one patient. There's no risk that the modified genes will be passed on to future generations. But when you modify germline cells, you are altering the future for generations, potentially of our entire species."

Tom nodded. Clearly, he had found the right person to answer his questions. "So, in the case of the modified Chinese babies, the added AIDS resistance would pass to their children."

"In theory, yes. What made that intervention so monstrous was that Jianku took unknowable risks with the lives of those children and their descendants. He couldn't possibly have known what might have gone wrong. The therapy might have accidentally delivered genetic changes to unintended places in the genome. A mishap could have created mutant children with thwarted, abnormal, or painful development. An altered gene might eventually create toxic proteins. The global medical community universally condemned what Jianku and his team did. It was a major blow to Chinese biotech's prestige and reputation. They're still struggling to recover."

"You mentioned something called CRISPR. What's that?"

Fisher smiled. "It stands for clustered regularly interspaced short palindromic repeats."

"I'm sorry I asked."

"It's a relatively new technology for cutting and splicing DNA at particular points. It's a real breakthrough that recently won Doudna and Charpentier a Nobel Prize in Chemistry. What used to take weeks or months can now be done in a matter of days or even hours."

"If you don't my asking, how does it work?"

Fisher checked his watch. "Maybe we can continue this after I get back from my trip, but very briefly, your genetic code consists of bases that we call A, C, T, and G. In one area of your genome, the sequence might be A-A-C-G-G-T-T-T and so forth. CRISPR is able to locate that exact pattern and then use an enzyme called Cas9 to cut it at a particular point."

Tom scribbled quickly, then looked up at the professor. "I know you're getting ready to travel so I want to be respectful of your time. Could I ask just two more questions?"

"Sure."

"The example you gave was from China. What about the United States? What are the laws here?"

"There aren't any specific US laws that address this directly, but there are restrictions on funding and marketing. The 1995 Dickey-Wicker Amendment states that the National Institutes for Health can't fund any research involving the editing of human embryos. Then in 2015, Congress passed a law that says the FDA must approve any human clinical trials that involve gene editing. And, of course, if you want to sell a DNA treatment in the United States, the FDA has to approve it."

"So, theoretically, there's nothing to stop a private laboratory from using technology like CRISPR to conduct research on human gene therapies."

"I suppose, but what would be the purpose? You wouldn't be able to use it or sell it. If you're an academic at a university, the funding and reputational risks would be enormous."

Tom nodded. "Here's my last question, Doctor. I've been contacted by the parent of a seventeen-year-old boy who's convinced that botched gene editing resulted in her child's severe schizophrenia. Is that possible?"

"No," the doctor said quickly.

"And why is that?"

"Because the technology to edit genes in human embryos didn't exist seventeen years ago."

24

Deborah had been raised in a loving middle-class family. Her father had joined his family's carpentry business after high school and shortly thereafter had married her mother, who went on to earn her nursing degree at night school while raising three children. Her parents still lived in the simple ranch-style home where she'd grown up. As children they had had all the necessities and very few luxuries, but each birthday had been celebrated as if it were Christmas. Those days were among her fondest memories. Her husband Scott, who had not come from a close family, had been moved early on by her stories and had picked up on the tradition.

Today was her birthday. Scott had promised to fly back from Europe and she expected him to be home by 4 p.m. Then they were going to a party in her honor at the home of Catalina and Lucas Montez, old friends who shared a love of horses and riding. They had a two-hundred-acre estate in Putnam County, not far from Carmel. Scott had helped Lucas expand his holdings in South America, and Deborah and Catalina had ridden together frequently before Paul's medical problems had consumed her life. Deborah had bought a new dress and shoes for the occasion. They were neatly arranged in her dressing room, along with the carefully chosen accessories she was planning to wear. For the first time in a long time, she was looking forward to an evening with friends.

She was about to apply her make-up when her phone rang. It was Scott.

"I'm sorry, Deb, but I'm not going to be able to make it."

"What do you mean? Where are you now?"

"I'm in London. Some things came up."

Deborah opened her mouth soundlessly as she pressed her hand to her chest. "London? You've been away for months. Paul is under sedation after...after nearly killing himself." She knew her anger would make him defensive, but she couldn't help herself. "Today is my birthday. You should be here. You should be at home with your family!"

After a long silence, Scott said wearily, "Deb, I need to ask you a question."

"What?"

"Have you been discussing Paul with people you shouldn't be talking to?"

"I can talk about my son with whomever I want."

146

"No, you cannot." She heard him sigh on the other end of the line. Then, he said, "I got a call from the doctors at McAllister. They said you brought a *reporter* with you. Are you still pushing your conspiracy theory that someone altered the boys' genes?"

"It's not a theory. It's a fact. It's science."

"No, it is not science. We've been assured of that by experts. But I'll tell you what is a fact: you're attacking on my closest friend, the man who is singularly responsible for the home you live in, paying the medical expenses of our children, and my livelihood. You can't keep blaming others for the tragedy of the twins. This has to stop. You're ruining everyone's life, mine included."

"*I'm* ruining? You're the one that abandoned us. You're the one who left me to deal with all of this on my own. You don't need to be in Europe to do your job—"

"Oh, now you're going to tell me how to run my business?"

"You started going to Europe when Paul got sick. You're still in the same profession, right? What changed, Scott?"

"Happy birthday, Deborah." Scott hung up the phone.

She tried to call him back but her calls just went to his voicemail. She threw her phone blindly and collapsed onto her bed, sobbing.

Time passed. She was just so disappointed, so furious. She struggled to calm herself. Fine. Scott could stay where he was. She'd go by herself. Catalina was her friend, after all. She'd have a better time without him.

She showered and sat at her vanity to put on her makeup. She heard a faint ringing from her phone. Thinking it might be Scott calling to apologize, she got up and walked back to her bedroom. The phone was muffled, but she found it under some pillows. The screen said CATALINA.

"Hello?" she said, trying to steady her voice.

Her friend sounded sad. "Hi, Deb. I just wanted to call to wish you a happy birthday."

"Thanks, but you can tell me in person. Scott's still in Europe, so it will just be me."

"Well, actually, we're going to have to cancel. I'm really sorry. Lucas isn't feeling well, and both the Hastings's and the Darwish's had a last-minute change of plans."

"Oh..." was all that Deborah could manage. She felt fresh tears forming.

"I'm really sorry. We'll get together soon, okay?"

"Sure."

"Okay. Bye."

She pressed the end button on her phone and let it fall to the bed. This was no coincidence.

She was putting on a bathrobe when she heard a knock on her door.

"Not now," she said.

The door cracked open. It was one of the house servants. "Mrs. Fiske, there's someone asking for you at the front door."

"Who is it?"

"He wouldn't say, but he said it's important that he talk to you."

Her first thought was that it might be Tom. Maybe he had learned something new that could help them. She put on some slippers, hurried down the stairs, and crossed the great hall. She opened the door but didn't recognize the middle-aged man standing there.

"Are you Deborah Fiske?" he asked.

"Yes, I am."

He handed her an envelope. "You've been served."

Dumbfounded, she slowly walked back into the great hall. She slumped onto a couch and opened the envelope. She read the contents. Scott had filed for divorce. The papers were dated that morning. She realized he'd never had any intention of coming back today. She wondered if Catalina and the others had already known. Of course, Scott would have thought all of this through, planned everything to the last detail.

This was obviously all because she'd approached Tom. No one wanted to be on the wrong side of the great Claude Dumont.

She reread the filing. So, it had come to this.

She had made so many mistakes: marrying Scott, having his children, letting him get away with not being a good husband and father.

And, as of tonight, having signed their prenup.

25

Rick and Sue Miller sat side by side on the terrace of their Fifth Avenue penthouse, enjoying a glass of wine. Central Park spread below them as if it were their own front yard. Beyond the park, the dark silhouettes of buildings on the Upper West Side rose against a deep amber sky. A bottle of Chassagne Montrachet beaded with water rested in a crystal ice bucket.

"It's good to have you home," Sue said. "How was Miami?"

"Business is going well." He sipped his wine. "I stopped in St. Barts on the way back."

"Oh? You didn't tell me you were going there."

"I should have. Claude's doctor had time to see me. I'm sworn to secrecy, but it doesn't feel right to keep any of this from you."

"So don't." She leaned forward. "What do you think?"

"Claude says he's a brilliant man, and I don't doubt it. He's also an arrogant son-of-a-bitch." Rick took another sip of wine and held it in his mouth, savoring it. He'd been a beer-drinker before he met Sue, but now he maintained a cellar with two thousand bottles.

"And?"

"I think we should do it."

"You know I want that more than anything else in the world, but I keep going back and forth. You're almost seventy, Rick. We can't ignore the risks that come with that."

"That's why my talk with Dr. Bergeron was so encouraging. First, they guarantee a full-term pregnancy. Second, they check for any potential genetic defects and fix them at the outset."

"Really? Is that possible?"

Rick nodded. "Claude's been referring couples like us to Bergeron for years. Apparently, he has an excellent track record."

"It's not one hundred percent, though."

"You're talking about the Fiske boys?"

"Deborah's certain they mishandled the embryos. She's been talking about it for years."

"Well, I don't know her well, but I do know Scott. I respect his judgment. He looked into it, and the guy knows how to do due diligence. The Fiske kids were just an unfortunate tragedy. Besides, that was almost twenty years ago. The science must have advanced a lot since then." He stopped to refill their glasses, giving her a meaningful look. "Which raises another very exciting opportunity."

"And what's that?"

"We can't say a word about this to anyone. It's a big deal."

"It hasn't stopped Deborah." She bit her lip. "I feel so sorry for her, Rick. I really do. You can't imagine what she's been through."

"Well, you see what's happening to her now. That could be us if we're not careful. We're never going to break this promise. Agreed?"

"Okay..." she said tentatively, watching the sunset.

"I'm not going to ask you to break off your friendship with Deborah, but she can't know about this."

"You're right," she admitted, knowing she had already broached the subject with her. "I'll keep the secret from now on. But stop being so mysterious, Rick. Tell me what he said."

He took her hand. "This isn't just about having a full-term pregnancy. It isn't just having a defect-free baby." He paused. "We can actually direct Bergeron to include some augmentations, some improvements."

"What, like blue eyes and blonde hair?"

"Yes, like that. Or maybe a more athletic body or higher intelligence."

"My God, Rick. Do you think the others took advantage of this?"

"Of course, they did. You know those kids. Haven't you ever wondered?"

"I never thought about it. It never

occurred to me that it was even possible, but yes, I can see now."

"We'll give our child every advantage and opportunity. But wouldn't it be wonderful if the aptitudes were there from the outset?" Rick leaned forward and took her hand. "This is the future of humanity. Claude's offering us an incredible opportunity."

"You've worked hard all your life," she said, patting his hand. "We deserve this."

The temperature dropped quickly as night fell, so they moved inside. Talking quickly and eagerly, they sat side-by-side on the couch in front of a warm fire, feeling the wine as they designed their baby.

26

"Are you ready to go?" Natalie Dumont asked her husband. Their luggage was neatly lined up by the elevator to be taken down to their limousine. Their jet was fueled and waiting at Teterboro Airport, across the Hudson River in New Jersey.

"Something's come up," Claude said, kissing her forehead. "I'll need fifteen minutes."

"What is it?"

"That reporter's coming by. Says it's imperative that I see him."

"That horrible man. I wish we could just ignore him."

"That's just it. We can't."

"Hank couldn't stop this?"

"He agreed to kill it, but Wright left the magazine. I figure the best thing I can do at this stage is to humor him and perhaps offer some inducements."

The phone rang. Natalie picked up the receiver and listened for a moment.

She turned to Claude. "He's downstairs."

"Send him up."

155

Claude walked down the hall and stopped before a window in his study. It was dark over Manhattan, countless windows glowing, car lights on the avenues in long strings of red and white. He turned his back to the view. What mattered most to him was represented in this room: photographs of Natalie, Chase, and Audrey, depictions of the chateau and the horse farm, his wines, the piano, his desk, and a few favorite trophies. This was the life he had made for himself. He had been born with advantages and worked hard to cultivate them. He felt the same way about his friends and the people he admired. He deeply resented Tom Wright's unwanted trespass into his world, voyeurism justified as journalism. The children were simply none of the man's business.

Claude also knew, of course, that his views were unlikely to have any impact on the reporter. He tried to put himself in Tom Wright's shoes. He was a journalist, a bit of a vigilante. He was driven by his ego, pride, curiosity, and desire to climb in the world and to be recognized. He was hungry for success and cautious about appearing a fool. Now that he was on his own, he might also have more concern about his finances. These were the facts and points of reference that mattered in the coming contest. Claude considered how he would use them.

Nadine entered the room, followed by Tom.

"Thank you, Nadine," Claude said. "We'll be just a few minutes."

Tom said, "I saw your luggage. I hope I'm not delaying your departure."

"We do have a plane waiting for us, so I'm sure you'll understand that I'd like to get straight to the point." Claude led him to a couch as Nadine left, closing the door behind her. Claude did not offer a drink.

Both men sat. "Mr. Dumont—"

"Claude, please."

"Yes. Claude, do you know Deborah Fiske?"

"Of course. She's a wonderful woman, married to my close friend, Scott. He's been one of my bankers for, oh, it must be forty years now."

"So, you also know that her son is schizophrenic and his twin brother is bipolar."

Claude frowned and nodded. "Yes, yes, of course. It's a tragedy. Scott and Deborah deserve so much better. They've both done their absolute best for those boys. I admire them for it."

"Were you involved with the process that led to that pregnancy?" Wright asked.

"Excuse me?"

"Did you recommend the medical experts that helped Mrs. Fiske become pregnant?"

"That was so many years ago." Claude paused, his eyebrows knit in thought. "It's possible, I suppose. I know they'd tried to have children for years. Scott may have come to me. I may well have recommended some doctors. Nadine and I had had a difficult time ourselves. I'd researched the field extensively and had many contacts."

"There are some who believe that the boys' mental illnesses were caused by genetic defects."

"Well, that's entirely possible. Everyone knows that genes play a role." Claude checked his watch. "Tom, what are you getting at? Why are we having this conversation?"

"I'm hoping that you can put me in touch with the doctors that helped Deborah become pregnant. She has unanswered questions, and it's important for the story I'm working on."

"Why didn't Deborah come to me directly?"

"She tells me she has."

"I haven't spoken to her in years."

"Perhaps this is why."

"I'm afraid I can't help you."

"Can't, or won't?"

Claude raised his outstretched hands. "This is absurd. Scott Fiske is my age. He was almost seventy when Deborah got pregnant. That alone is a high risk factor for schizophrenia. If you do your research, you'll also find that nutrition during pregnancy comes into play, and I know from Scott that his wife had some, well, let's call them eating issues at that time. That's all that I'm prepared to say about it." Claude stood. "Stop this nonsense, Tom. You're wasting your time and enormous talents. I know you're a fine journalist. Find a worthy topic. I'll help you on your next story in any way I can."

Tom stood. "If you would just give me the doctors' names…"

"All you're going to do is to invade people's privacy and potentially embarrass them. The Fiskes are going through a difficult time right now and this is the last thing they need in their lives. There *is* no story here. Please drop it. Nothing good will come from this. You've lost your job. Do you now want to lose your reputation?"

"I didn't lose my job. I resigned in protest. This could be the most important story of our age."

"Do you hear yourself? What you're saying? It's delusional."

Tom shook his head. "Just give me the names of the doctors. I'll be out of your hair."

"I have no names to give you." Claude walked behind his desk and opened a drawer. "Tom, I've never done anything like this, but I will pay you to stop this line of inquiry." He pulled out a leather checkbook, opened it, and poised a pen above it. "Name your price."

"Not on your life."

"I'm serious. I'm prepared to offer you a considerable sum."

"I'm not remotely interested in your offer."

"Then our business here is done." Claude tossed his checkbook onto his desk. "You should go now."

The elevator door was open and waiting as Tom reached the vestibule. He stepped inside and felt his cell phone buzz. As the door hushed closed, he read a text message from Deborah:

> SUE AND RICK ARE FLYING TO KENTUCKY AT NOON TOMORROW TO LOOK AT HORSES. THEY DON'T RIDE. HURRY.

27

Renard Bergeron took notes as, on the other end of the call, Rick Miller read the list of characteristics that he and Sue had chosen for their baby. Except for the cone of his desk lamp, it was dark in his office. Smoke rose from the cigarette in his ash tray and swirled in the light. Renard had just finished sequencing Sue Miller's DNA, which he had extracted from frozen eggs her doctor had forwarded from Manhattan.

"We want a boy. He'll be tall, perhaps six-foot-four, and muscular. We'd like him to be smart as hell and a hard worker. Blond with blue eyes, if that's possible. Obviously, no defects or diseases. Athletic ability. Strength. Handsome. Good teeth. Good health. You know, good cholesterol, that sort of thing. We want him to have an aggressive personality, but not too aggressive. We want a winner. Oh, and a sweet disposition. I don't know if that's genetically based, but Sue asked me to mention it."

"Musical ability?" Bergeron asked, an amused expression on his face.

"Nah. My boy's going to be a football

player and then a successful businessman. I don't need a fiddler."

"Anything else?"

"That's what we came up with. What do you think?"

Bergeron studied the list for a moment. "The birth defects and propensities for diseases are things we routinely do, so that's not a problem. If I remember correctly, you have brown eyes."

"Yes, that's right."

"And your wife has hazel eyes."

"Uh...how do you know that?"

"You showed me her photograph."

"You have a good memory."

"Yes, I do. But tell me this: how are you going to explain blue eyes to people when they meet your son?"

"What do you mean?"

"The color of the iris is an allele of a gene for the eye. Blue eyes are a recessive trait, so if either parent has brown eyes that's likely to dominate. That doesn't mean that you or your wife must have blue eyes to have a blue-eyed baby. Sometimes a recessive trait can skip a generation, but you'll avoid awkward questions in the future if you just let the eye color occur naturally. You may have a blue-eyed baby at first anyway. The melanin that makes brown eyes develops as the child grows."

"Come to think of it, I don't know of any

blue eyes on either side of the family."

"Then I think you have your answer."

"Okay, scratch that off the list."

"Muscle mass I can help with, but obviously nutrition and conditioning as the child grows will be critically important."

"So, how does that work? I want my boy to be strong."

"We can adjust a gene that humans have in common with horses, which I've done a great deal of work on for Mr. Dumont. Don't worry. Your child will be muscular."

"Is there a risk of creating a freak? I'm not asking for the Incredible Hulk."

"The alteration is routine for us, and it's safe." Bergeron sensed Miller needed a little more reassurance. "The mutation is written IVS1+5G>A. The gene is located at 2q32.2, which is the large arm of chromosome 2 at position 32.2. As I said, we've done a lot of work on this."

"Sounds like you have. How about height?"

"You're, what, about six-foot-two? And your wife's about five-ten?"

"Close enough. Again, how'd you know—"

"You showed me your wedding photo."

"Man, you're something else."

"Your child is likely to be on the tall side if we do nothing at all, but there's a single letter DNA substitution that I can make on a gene called HMGA2. If I do it for both of you, on average it would add a centimeter to your child's adult height. I can't guarantee six-four, but we can get you close."

"That's fine. Hey, Doctor, you said something about doing it for both of you. What does that mean, exactly?"

"Your child's genome is a combination of genes it inherits from you and its mother." Bergeron drew smoke into his lungs and exhaled. "I've sequenced your respective DNA. You're both pretty healthy genetically, so there are just a few adjustments I'll make along those lines. I'll then add the augmentations. In some cases, I'll just be knocking out a particular base pair. In other cases, I'll be adding larger segments or turning some off. Once I'm satisfied that the genetic material from you and your wife is optimal, I'll directly inject your combined chromosomes into your wife's egg. The process will proceed naturally from there until the embryo is mature enough to be implanted. Have you decided whether to use a surrogate?"

"Sue wants to carry the baby. She doesn't trust anyone else to do that."

"That's fine. I'll make a few extra embryos, just in case. Anything else?"

"Just one more question: how will you make him smart?"

"Intelligence is highly polygenic, spread across five hundred genes. There are seven regions of chromosome 7 that are particularly important." Bergeron smiled to himself over a secret that only he and Claude shared. "We've had excellent success in this area. You'll be pleased with the result."

"I'm sure we will be. You'll do all of this before we come down?"

"Yes, we have very advanced systems here. If any problems come up, and I don't expect any, I'll let you know."

"I just have to say, this is the most impressive interaction I've ever had in the health care field, and I've had colon cancer. Where did you say you went to medical school?"

"I went to Harvard," Bergeron replied, "but I'm a PhD, not an MD."

"Oh. Does that matter?"

"Not for what we're doing. Believe me, Mr. Miller, you found the right person."

28

Maxim Fedorov, Dumont's head of security, was still in New York City, having supervised the delivery of the two Picassos. Claude called him from the limousine and asked him to meet them at Teterboro.

"What are you going to do?" Nadine asked as they headed south on Third Avenue, the meeting with Tom Wright very much on her mind.

"Increase the pressure," Claude said. "I don't want this getting out any more than you do."

"If Wright finds out about Renard and that he's not a medical doctor…"

"He won't. Even if Deborah had remembered his name from eighteen years ago, and I don't remember if they actually met, there's no public record of his existence. We took care of that years ago. None of the others will ever talk. Wright will never find him."

"What are you going to have Max do?"

"Gather information. Conduct surveillance." Claude took her hand and smiled.

166

"Don't worry. I'm not turning into Don Claude."

Nadine laughed. "No, that's definitely not your style."

The ride from the condo to the airport took sixteen minutes. Their limousine hushed to a stop beside their waiting jet as a police helicopter landed two hundred feet away. A very large man stepped out of it, ducking as he stepped out of the rotor wash. Even from this distance, his bearing indicated that he was every inch a soldier.

Claude strode to him, patted his shoulder, and gestured for him to follow Nadine onto the jet. Maxim greeted her and, at Claude's direction, took the rear-facing seat in front of his boss. Their cabin attendant closed the door as their luggage was loaded into an aft compartment. Moments later they were airborne, climbing to 39,000 feet on a southwest heading.

"Thank you for joining us," Claude told Maxim. He smiled and added, "It's fortunate that you happened to be near a helicopter."

"I was with some friends in the NYPD when you called. They kindly gave me a lift. I'm glad I didn't hold you up."

"We would have happily waited."

The cabin attendant brought three glasses and a bottle of red wine. Maxim declined, but the Dumonts each accepted one.

"Max, I have some work for you. It's sensitive."

LEGACY

"Name it."

Claude reflected that so many of the blessings in his life had come through friendships. In his case, that friend was a man named Mircea Snegur. A graduate of the University of Moldova, Snegur had received his PhD in Agricultural Sciences from the Department of Animal Husbandry. He had collaborated with Dumont in the 1970s on many projects, and their shared passion for animal breeding led to a close and lasting friendship. Meanwhile, Snegur rose rapidly in the communist party of the former USSR. In 1991, after the collapse of the Soviet Union, Moldova became an independent republic. Claude had been delighted when Snegur was elected its first president.

Maxim Fedorov had been twenty-four years old at time, serving in a special forces unit. Hailing from the small town of Falesti, he had remained in Moldova and was handpicked for Snegur's team of bodyguards, eventually advancing to lead it. When Snegur left office in 1997, he'd recommended Maxim to Claude. Maxim had quickly become one of his most important and trusted employees.

"An investigative reporter named Thomas Wright is becoming a nuisance. Until recently he worked for *Future* magazine. He saw a group of us at Art Basel last week and has been harassing our friends with inappropriate questions about their children. I've promised to take care of this."

Maxim nodded.

"I've repeatedly asked Wright to stop his project, but he's continuing. We have to convince him it's not in his best interests."

"What do you have in mind?"

"Place him under close surveillance. Hire whomever you want. I want to know who he sees and where he goes. It might be helpful if he figures out that he's being followed, but I'll leave that to you. My lawyers are arranging a subpoena, so we'll soon have his phone records. I want to know who he's been calling, how often, and when. We're building a dossier. There may be useful things in his past. I know he's been married twice. His second wife passed about twenty years ago and he's been a bachelor since. There might be something in that. He was traveling with Britt Nielsen in Miami."

"Perhaps we can create some inconveniences for him," Maxim said.

Claude moved his head noncommittally. "Let's be careful about how we do that, but yes, I want him to realize it's foolish to continue."

"Anything else?" Maxim asked.

"Focus on Wright for now, but there's a woman involved, Deborah Fiske, who seems to think I'm responsible for the mental state of her two sons."

Maxim raised an eyebrow but said nothing.

"She's contained for now. I mention her because she's pulled Wright into this. No one else seems to be listening to her, so if we handle the reporter, we should be in the clear. Max, act fast. I want to put this behind us quickly."

"I'll get to work." Maxim stood, pulling out his cell phone as he moved to the back of the cabin.

Nadine slipped into the seat he'd just occupied. "Thank you," she said to her husband.

Claude smiled serenely as he patted her hand. "We'll handle this."

"You always do."

29

Tom Wright was from a small farm in upstate New York. His family had raised berries and apples and maintained a herd of about sixty dairy cows. As a side business, his father also bred Bloodhounds. Aside from his parents, who had passed a few years ago, his most vivid memories were of those dogs. Tom had always been fascinated by them, remarkable creatures with a sense of smell a thousand times more sensitive than humans. For them, an odor conveyed far more information than a photograph for a human. Once introduced to a scent, a trained Bloodhound won't stop until it's found the source.

Tom now had a scent, and he was just as tenacious. He'd meant what he said to Dumont. If it were true that Dumont possessed technologies that could edit genes twenty years ago, this would be the most important story of the decade. God only knew what therapies Dumont might have developed since, and what he was doing with them now.

Tom had finally called Amy to tell her

about his resignation, profusely apologizing for not having done so earlier. It had been three days, so she had obviously already heard the news. She was furious with the magazine and offered to resign herself, but Tom urged her to finish the internship, knowing the imprimatur of *Future* would strengthen her resume. Summers had ordered her not to do any further work on the Art Basel story, but she offered to help Tom in any way she could. Tom was grateful but didn't want to put her at risk. Accordingly, he kept his immediate plans to himself, such as they were. They agreed to keep in close touch.

It had taken several phone calls to upscale hotels in the Lexington area, but Tom had learned that the Miller's had a reservation at The Kentucky Castle in Versailles, a town just outside of Lexington. All sixteen of the Castle's rooms were taken, however, so he'd arranged to stay at the Griffin Gate. He booked a flight that night through Charlotte, realizing too late that the charges had gone to his corporate credit card. Apparently, his departure from *Future* hadn't been processed yet. If Summers was having second thoughts, Tom definitely was not.

Beyond that, his plans were vague. He had no idea what kind of facilities Dumont had at the farm. The Dumont Stables website was filled with photographs of pastures and magnificent Thoroughbreds but was light on information. There appeared to be a well-appointed visitor center. He'd start there, try to meet some staff members, and learn the names of any medical or scientific personnel that worked on the farm. That might generate leads to who had treated Deborah years ago. Somehow, he had to establish contact with the Millers. Perhaps they would inadvertently share some useful information. Failing that, if he could establish a relationship with them, he might be in a better position to follow the course of the pregnancy and their child's development. Working with a long time horizon had served him well in the past. Many of his best stories had involved years of patient, diligent research. That time frame might be too long for Deborah's purposes, but there was nothing he could do without facts. If Deborah hadn't been able to convince Sue of her claims, Tom was in no position to do any better.

He checked his watch. It was time to head to the airport. He grabbed the overnight bag he'd packed, a backpack containing his laptop, and a jacket. He took the elevator down to the ground floor and hailed a taxi.

"LaGuardia, please," Tom said. "American Airlines."

"How do you want to go?" the driver asked.

"Take the Midtown Tunnel."

"You got it."

LEGACY

As they were pulling away from the curb, Tom's phone rang.

"Hello?"

"It this Thomas Wright?" said a man's slightly accented voice.

He didn't recognize it. "Yes, it is."

"Drop your story or you'll regret it."

Tom angrily looked at his screen. The caller ID was UNKNOWN. "Who is this?"

"You've been warned." The call ended.

Tom felt his cheeks flush. This wasn't something that Hank Summers would do. Could it be one of the families? Dumont himself? Tom wondered how far they would go to try to stop him.

Whatever the taxi driver might have heard, he wasn't showing any reaction. Traffic was heavy for this time at night. Tom kept checking his watch. They turned south on Third Avenue and then east to pass through the Midtown Tunnel to Long Island. Tom had made this trip to the airport countless times. Everything was so familiar to him. They passed through the toll booth and followed the Queens Midtown Expressway to the Brooklyn Queens Expressway. Soon Tom could see the lights of planes taking off over headlights on Interstate 278, the Grand Central Parkway.

His driver seemed to be looking more and more into his rear-view mirror. "Some jerk is right on my ass," he said.

Tom looked to his right. The car in the adjacent lane wasn't exactly tailgating them, but its bumper was just inches away from their right rear wheel. When the taxi driver accelerated, the other car kept up with them.

Tom looked ahead. They were approaching a fork in the expressway. The left lane led to the interstate and the airport.

Two hundred feet before the fork in the road, the car veered into them.

"Watch out!" Tom warned.

The cars collided, the taxi rocking on its suspension. It wasn't a crash so much as it was a firm push.

"Son of a bitch!" the taxi driver yelled.

Tom felt the rear of the taxi slide to the left, their front moving to the right. The taxi started to lift onto its left wheels. Tom feared it would roll, but the taxi fell back heavily onto its four tires, continuing to spin to the right, sliding onto the painted median between the diverging roads and skidding to a stop a few feet in front of a concrete barrier. By then their assailant was far past them and out of sight.

"Are you okay?" the driver asked, eyes wide.

"Yeah."

"What the hell was that guy thinking?"

"No idea," Tom said, knowing better.

"I'm calling the police." The driver reached for his phone.

"I'll tell you what," Tom said, quickly checking his watch again, seeing how little time he had to spare. "I've got to make this flight. Can you make your report after you drop me off? Here, I'll give you my business card. I'll back you up one hundred percent: your boss, the police, the insurance company...whatever you need." Tom took a card from his wallet and added a one-hundred-dollar bill.

The driver tucked the money into his shirt pocket and examined the card. "*Future* magazine, huh? You're a reporter?"

"That's right. It'll be easy to find me."

"Okay, boss." The driver slipped the card into his pocket, put the car into gear, and pulled onto the expressway.

Five minutes later Tom entered the terminal at LaGuardia. Thankfully, the security lines were short. Once through, he sprinted the length of the nearly empty terminal, winded by the time he reached the two gate attendants. The aircraft door closed right behind him as he boarded.

30

Tom used the following morning to make inquiries before the Millers arrived. A talkative waitress at breakfast had told him about the Kentucky Horsepark Campground located just a few miles north of the hotel. It seemed as good place as any to ask about the Dumonts and their employees. The compound included the International Museum of the Horse, the American Saddlebred Museum, and the headquarters for both the United States Equestrian Federation and the Kentucky Thoroughbred Association. He stopped at each, casually inquiring about public tours. Any questions related to the Dumonts or *Les Champs* unleashed torrents of praise bordering on reverence. He collected pamphlets and phone numbers wherever he went, all potential leads.

At his last stop, a young man mentioned the Hagyard Equine Medical Institute, the largest private veterinary practice for horses in the world. Hoping there might be links between Hagyard and Dumont's breeding efforts, he headed to Iron Works Pike. The institute was a sprawling compound of low buildings, stables, and fenced pastures. He parked and entered the lobby.

"Can I help you?" a receptionist asked.

"I hope so. I have some technical questions. Is there anyone I can talk to?"

"There should be somebody at McGee."

"Is that here?"

"Yes, sir, it's our fertility clinic." She gave him directions and offered to call ahead for him.

He found it easily, a small cluster of barns and sheds.

A tall, lanky man wearing jeans, boots, and a checkered shirt greeted him at the entrance. He had bright blue eyes set in a deeply weathered face. Tom followed his host down a short hall and into a cramped office.

The man sat behind his desk and gestured to a small oak stool. The walls were covered with certificates and diplomas in the name of Terry Stanley. One was from the American College of Theriogenologists.

"How can I help you this morning?" Stanley asked.

"Well, to start, what is a theriogenologist?" Tom said with a grin.

Stanley looked over his shoulder and then back at Tom. "You're not the first to ask. *Therio* means beast or animal, *gen* means genesis or creation, and *ology*—"

"The study of. So, you're an expert in

horse reproduction."

"I'd like to think so. I've worked here for about thirty-five years."

"I'm writing a piece about breeding. Do you, by chance, do any work with *Les Champs*?"

"Some," Stanley said. "Why do you ask?"

"I know they're nearby, and they have an uncanny way of raising champions."

"You're right about that."

Tom handed him a business card. "Tom Wright. I used to work at *Fortune*."

"Used to?"

"I recently decided to freelance."

Stanley examined the card. "I don't run across reporters very often."

"Nor I across theriogenologists." That earned a slow smile. "Right now, I'm just looking for background. I grew up on a farm, but we didn't have horses. What sorts of things to you do for *Les Champs*?"

"Same as anybody. Everything we do here at McGee is centered around producing healthy foals."

"Can you be more specific?"

"Don't think I should be." Stanley looked back at him for a moment. "That's a first-rate operation they have going there. There's big money in these racehorses."

"I'm not looking for any trade secrets."

"I don't know that I'm privy to any secrets, but I wouldn't want to accidentally divulge something I shouldn't. It's probably a better question for them, Mr. Wright."

Tom nodded, trying to conceal his disappointment. "Fair enough. I'd think the same in your shoes, I suppose. I'll reach out to them directly. I appreciate your time."

Stanley started to get up, saying, "I'm not sure if I helped you any."

Tom stood with him. "Maybe there is one more thing."

"What's that?"

"Could you give me a point of contact? I wouldn't want to trouble Mr. Dumont with something like this, but I don't know anyone else over there."

Stanley took a black Moleskine calendar book from his drawer, flipped to the back, squinted, and wrote down a name and number.

"This guy may be able to help you. He's not the most friendly person you'll ever meet, but he's smart as hell."

Tom took the piece of paper. It had a phone number and a name: Renard Bergeron.

31

The Millers' plane touched down at Blue Grass Airport at noon. Sue was delighted that Rick had chartered a plane for the trip. Instead of taxiing to the public passenger terminal, they stopped on the tarmac in front of TAC Air, a fixed base operator that catered to private jets. They passed through a small VIP lounge where they were met by a representative of The Castle.

"Your limo is waiting just outside," the well-dressed young woman said. She listened to her earpiece for a moment, then extended her arm. "Your luggage is already in the trunk. Welcome to Lexington and enjoy this beautiful weather."

The Millers followed her to the waiting vehicle. It was immaculate. Rick was in the business of selling expensive automobiles to demanding people, and his success had hinged largely on exceptional service. He appreciated it whenever he saw it, and he was experiencing it now. He wondered if this was The Castle's standard or Dumont's. Perhaps both.

It had been an unusually mild December

LEGACY

in New York, and it was even warmer here. They passed through rolling green hills beneath a clear blue sky. Sue excitedly pointed to horses when they came into view. This was the heart of Thoroughbred country, and the beautiful, perfectly formed animals were wonderful to see. Rick couldn't help but think of the baby they were about to create and how deeply satisfying it would be to watch him grow. It had been a lifelong dream. Now it was finally coming true.

Rick couldn't remember a time when he'd been this happy. He was healthy for his age. Other than blood pressure pills and statins for cholesterol, he took no other medications. A survivor of colon cancer, his past medical issues, he'd been assured, were behind him. He'd lost fifty pounds, improved his diet, and given up his penchant for smoked meats. His doctor had recently told him that it would not be unreasonable for him to expect to live another twenty years, perhaps longer. He would live to see his son cross the threshold of manhood. He took Sue's hand. They both smiled.

They arrived at their hotel, and it really did look like a castle. The receptionist informed them that check-in had been prearranged by *Les Champs*. While their bags were brought to their room, they were led to a grassy court and offered glasses of champagne. They picked two Adirondack chairs and toasted one another.

"Are you excited?" he asked his wife.

"Yes, very." She smiled from behind her glass, then added, "I guess I won't be having any more of this for a while."

"Will you miss it?"

"A little, but it's nothing compared to the baby." She put her glass on a side table.

"I'd almost given up on ever being a father. Thank you for doing this. It means so much to me."

"Don't thank me. I want this as much as you do." She looked to the horizon for a long moment.

"Where did you go?" he asked, smiling.

"The important thing is having the baby. Our baby. That's going to be enough for me. Yes, I want him to be perfect, but what matters is that he's ours and that we're going to love him unconditionally."

"Do you think I feel any differently?"

"We can't push him too hard, Rick. We can't expect too much. His upbringing must be positive and joyful. It has to be normal."

"Of course," he said, sipping his champagne as he wondered why she was telling him this. It hadn't occurred to him until now that they might have different approaches to parenting. He inwardly shrugged it off. It was a bridge they would cross later.

A tall young man approached them. "Mr. and Mrs. Miller?"

"Yes?" Rick said, turning.

LEGACY

"There is absolutely no rush, but your ride to *Les Champs* is ready when you are."

32

The winding driveway leading onto the farm was a scene from horse heaven. White split-rail fences extended as far as the eye could see. As they crested the hill, a long stone building with a steeply sloped slate roof spread before them. Something about the building struck Rick as unusual. Then he realized it was the windows. They were smaller and higher than a home would have. He realized that this magnificent chateau was in fact a stable.

A sweeping circular drive brought them to a grand entrance graced with Doric columns. Claude Dumont was waiting between them, dressed in a white linen suit, and smiling broadly.

"Rick!" He clasped Miller on the shoulder and then took Sue's hand gently in his and gave her a warm hug. "Welcome to the farm. I'm so happy you could come."

Nadine rushed out the door, looking as lovely as ever in a knee-length cotton dress. "I'm so sorry I'm late. I was on the phone when I heard you'd arrived."

"We just got here," Sue said, hugging her. Rick gave Nadine a peck on the cheek.

"Do you need some time to freshen up?" Nadine asked, slipping her arm around Sue's. "Did you just fly in?"

"We dropped off our bags at The Castle," Rick said. "Gorgeous place."

Nadine looked to Claude and then back to Sue. "But you should stay with us here! We have plenty of room."

"Thanks, Nadine," Sue said, "but we're fine there." Quietly, she added, "I really appreciate the offer, but I'm not sure how I'm going to feel after all of this. It might be good to have, you know..."

"Of course," Nadine said. "I completely understand. But next time you're down here, you'll stay with us. Okay?"

"I promise."

"Good. And don't worry. We're going to take great care of you."

They entered a great hall. The interior was of post and beam construction, heavy dark timbers contrasting with white walls and a high ceiling of pale oak.

"The stalls are down this way," Claude said, extending his arm, "and our offices are here to the right." They strode across wide floorboards and then through glass doors into a well-appointed conference room. The wall facing the central hall was entirely of glass, the stalls visible beyond. The opposite wall was covered with photographs and paintings of horses. The walls at either end of the long conference table supported shelves filled with trophies of every size and description, some bright and shiny, some tarnished with age.

"Does this all happen here?" Sue asked, looking a little confused. "I guess I expected a hospital, or something like that."

"Not here, but nearby," Claude said, smiling reassuringly. "We have the most advanced genetics laboratory in the world. You might say it's our secret workshop. We've created championship horses, the finest wines, and now we're able to help our close friends have the families they want and deserve."

"What do genes have to do with wine?" Sue asked.

Claude smiled. "Have you ever heard of a wine called Chateau Petrus?"

"Vaguely," Sue said.

"I had it once," Rick said. "Superb."

"I quite agree. It's a Bordeaux made entirely of merlot grapes. It's a right-bank Pomerol appellation, not the most prestigious location, but the soil! The twenty-eight-acre estate is on a rise of forty-million-year-old blue clay with greatly reduced iron content. It yields a grape that makes a sublime wine. The soil is so special that that one small parcel of land has been valued at one billion euros. Can you imagine? I tried to buy it, but they wouldn't sell. So, what did I do? I hired a brilliant young scientist and set him up in his own business. It took years of research, but he was able to use a technology called TALEN to edit merlot grape genes to duplicate the wines from that button of land."

"TALEN?" Sue asked, looking to Rick.

"I'm sorry," Claude said. "I get carried away. It was an early technology for gene editing. Now we use a technique called CRISPR/Cas9. That's what our clinic used to create your new baby."

"Everything's ready?" Rick asked.

"Yes. You'll have to ask him about any details – I've respected your privacy and haven't asked him any questions – but he said he was able to meet all of your criteria."

"That's terrific news," Rick said, grinning at Sue as he grasped her hand.

"The procedure to implant the embryo is very straightforward," Nadine said to Sue. "The transfer takes about thirty minutes. It's not painful and you don't need any anesthesia. After you've rested for a few hours, you'll be free to resume normal activities."

"When do we start?" Sue asked.

Claude said, "The doctor's set aside 9 a.m. tomorrow, but we can accommodate whatever you wish."

Rick looked to Sue, who said, "That's fine."

"Excellent," Claude said. "I'll let him know." He started to get up. "Why don't we show you around and then bring you up to the house to relax?"

As they all stood, Sue wiped a tear from her cheek.

"Is everything all right?" Claude asked.

"Oh, yes," she said quickly. "It's just that you've been so kind to us."

Claude hugged her. "What are friends for?"

33

Tom checked his watch as he drove to *Les Champs*. Deborah had texted that the Millers were flying down at noon, but he didn't know if that was their departure or arrival time. He hoped he'd have time to see the Visitor Center before they arrived, but he pulled into the stables parking lot just in time to see a long black limo drop them off. He considered joining them inside, but immediately dismissed the idea when he saw Claude emerge from between two thick columns. He decided to wait. He'd follow them back to their hotel and, he hoped, meet them on more neutral ground.

He retrieved the piece of paper that Stanley had given him. *Renard Bergeron*. He decided to search the name before calling. Nothing came up. Nothing at all. That struck Tom as odd. He rechecked the spelling. He'd entered it correctly. No Facebook account. No Instagram posts. Nothing on Twitter. Zero on LinkedIn. No publications or blogs. Who didn't have at least some modest presence on the web? Was Bergeron just a farm hand, perhaps even an illegal alien? He doubted it. Stanley had described Bergeron as "smart as hell," and Dumont could certainly afford anyone he wanted. Tom's instincts told him that this was significant.

Keeping a close eye on the stables entrance, he dialed Britt Nielsen.

"I was wondering when you were going to get back to me," she said after the first ring.

"Sorry. I've been totally preoccupied with this Dumont story."

"Is it true that you left *Future*?"

"Why am I not surprised that you already know?"

"I can't wait to hear all about it. Apparently, you're still working on the story. Making any progress?"

"All of a sudden, it seems I am. There's no way you're going to know this guy, but I'm hoping you can talk to some of your horseracing friends. Maybe they've heard of him."

"I can call around. What's up?"

"I don't want to go into too much detail over the phone, but I'm trying to learn more about the scientists or doctors that work in Dumont's breeding operation."

"What's the name?"

"Renard Bergeron." Tom spelled it for her. "He's got no presence on the web at all. Really weird."

"How'd you hear about him?"

LEGACY

"A horse veterinarian at a clinic here in Lexington gave it to me."

"Did he give you Bergeron's number?"

"He did. I haven't tried it yet. It's weird that he seems to be completely off the grid. If he's erased himself, he might not be pleased to hear from me. I'd like to know what I'm getting myself into before I call him out of the blue."

"It all sounds very cloak and dagger. Do you want me to fly up? I could be your wing-woman. It was fun last time."

"I appreciate the offer, but I don't expect to be here much longer."

"I miss you. We always have such fun."

"Why don't you come up to New York instead?"

"Hmmm. That sounds nice. This weekend?"

"Make it a long one?"

She laughed. "You're on. I'll book a flight."

"That'll be great. Call me if you come across anything in the meantime, okay?"

"I will. See you soon."

The hours passed slowly. Tom was tempted to visit the stables but was afraid he'd miss the Millers when they returned or, worse, bump into Claude. A few cars came and went. The incident outside LaGuardia the night before was still very much on his mind, but he convinced himself that Dumont and his friends wouldn't risk acting against him while he was in Lexington. When The Castle limousine didn't return, Tom wondered whether the Millers would spend the night with the Dumonts, but they had a reservation and hadn't brought any luggage, so he concluded they would go back to the hotel at some point. As the parking lot started to empty at the end of the workday, he felt increasingly conspicuous. He decided to wait for them in Versailles.

Traffic was light on the way to The Castle. The hotel grounds were magnificent, and the main entrance opened to a large, two-story hall with a high, vaulted ceiling. His hotel was nice, but he wished he'd been able to get a room here. He checked at reception and learned that there had been a cancellation for Monday night, so he booked a room. That felt like progress. He pulled a book from a shelf, ordered a scotch, and found an overstuffed chair where he had a good view of the entrance. He was nursing his third drink when the Millers appeared. Rick seemed a little tipsy. Sue steadied him as they climbed the stairs to their room. They both seemed happy and excited, but Tom had missed his last chance for the day.

Tom had little to show for his day in Lexington aside from a name that might not mean anything. Still, he was encouraged. He'd seen the Millers with Dumont. The secret clinic was almost surely on the grounds of *Les Champs*. In the morning he'd visit the stables. Perhaps he'd find a staff directory. He would inquire about Bergeron, and with any luck Britt would learn something by morning. He paid his tab, put the book back on its shelf, and walked to his car.

He knew that Deborah wanted him to stop the Millers from going through with the implantation, but that was currently beyond his control. They were going to do whatever it was that they had come here to do. His instincts told him was onto something enormous. All those gifted children at Art Basel were not a coincidence. Nor was the connection of the elderly billionaire parents to Claude Dumont, the world's most successful breeder, an accident. Sue and Rick Miller were trying, with Claude's help, to have a child, and whether the parents knew it or not, it would be a child with altered genes that might affect the evolution of the human race.

When he arrived at his own hotel, the lobby was empty. The bar behind the elevators was quiet with only a few couples. Suddenly he felt tired. He didn't want to talk to anyone. He went to his room and straight to bed.

Hours later, his alarm startled him. It was completely dark outside his window. He checked his cell phone. There had been no text or call from Britt. He sighed but knew that had been

KEVIN BOREEN

a long shot anyway. He ordered a room service breakfast, showered, shaved, and got dressed. Someone knocked on his door. He accepted a tray of scrambled eggs, ham, toast, and coffee. He logged onto his laptop and checked his e-mail and the news, seeing nothing of note. He decided to leave his computer in his room for the day. He picked up his binoculars and a leather notepad and left at 5:45 a.m.

The hotel lobby was as empty now as it had been the night before. He walked past a wide circular fountain and found his car.

"Oh, shit." During the night someone had backed into his rental. The rear bumper was an ugly remnant of shredded plastic. He pulled away a big piece that was jammed against the right rear tire. As he crouched by the side of the car, a pick-up truck stopped close behind him, its headlights bright.

The truck's window slid down. "Do you need some help?" a man asked. It sounded like he had a Slavic accent.

"Looks like someone backed into me."

The motor still running, the man stepped out of the truck and crouched beside Tom to inspect the damage. Tom couldn't see his face inside the hood of his sweatshirt.

"There are people," the man said quietly, "who don't want you here."

"Did you do this?" Tom stood abruptly, pointing to the damage. "I'm going to call the

195

police."

"To be honest, I don't think the local police want you here either."

The man rose slowly. He was a full head taller than Tom and had huge shoulders and a distinctly military air about him. Now Tom could make out his high cheekbones and square jaw. He quickly concluded that an altercation was a very bad idea.

"Leave the families alone. You don't know what you're dealing with here."

"Why don't you enlighten me?"

"My advice is to get your things, go home, and find something else to write about." The man turned, got back into this truck, and drove away.

Tom realized he was shaking. Why was someone – almost certainly Dumont – trying to intimidate him? He turned quickly, realizing too late he should have taken the license plate of the truck. It was already exiting the parking lot.

He started the car and took a deep breath. He had been threatened throughout his career but had never been one to back down. He took his profession seriously. He was a journalist, and these desperate acts only confirmed that he was onto an important story. If the world's most respected businessman was violating medical norms by editing genes for wealthy parents, the world should know. Mankind had a right to that technology, as well as an obligation to ensure that it was used responsibly. He put the car into reverse, backed up carefully, and drove out of the hotel lot. Minutes later he was on the interstate heading toward Versailles, the remnants of his bumper vibrating in the airflow.

He arrived at The Castle just in time to see Rick and Sue Miller get into their limousine. His report to the police would have to wait. He drove slowly to the Pisgah Pike, heading south in the slow lane, his eyes on his rearview mirror. He had just turned into Route 60 headed toward Lexington when their limo passed him. He fell in behind it and tightened his grip on the steering wheel. Dumont knew he was here now, so it was pointless to hide. One way or another, today he was going to speak with the Millers.

34

Five miles before the turnoff to the farm, Tom accelerated and passed the limousine, intending to arrive a few minutes before them. He'd greet Rick like an old friend and hope that shaking the tree would yield some fruit. Then Tom would look for a staff directory.

He followed the circular driveway and parked in a gravel lot to the left of the stables. He hadn't noticed anyone following him and no one seemed to be paying attention to him now. He locked his car and walked through the main entrance. A woman looked up from behind a desk, smiled at him, and resumed whatever she'd been doing. There was an empty, glass-walled conference room on the right with exhibits on both ends. He walked to those, playing the visitor while keeping an eye on the front entrance.

Moments later, Rick and Sue Miller entered. Rick was wearing khaki trousers, a blue blazer, and a white shirt with no tie. She wore a comfortable track suit. Tom stepped away from a display case and made eye contact with Rick.

Rick recognized him, smiled, and approached him with his hand extended, every bit the car salesman.

"It's Tom, right?" Miller said.

"Yes, Rick. What a coincidence."

They shook hands. Sue joined them.

"What brings you here?" Tom asked.

Rick and Sue looked at each other. The pause was momentary, but it told Tom everything he needed to know. Today was the day.

Rick recovered and said, "We've known Claude Dumont for ages but had never been here. We decided to take him up on his invitation."

"So, just a social visit?"

"That's right," Rick said. "And you?"

"I'm working on a story."

"What's it about?" Rick asked.

Just then, Claude entered the hall. His smile faded when he saw Tom with the Millers.

"I didn't realize you knew each other," Dumont said, striding toward them.

"We sat next to each other on a flight last week," Rick said. "Small world."

"Yes, indeed," Claude replied.

A handsome man in a white lab coat walked through the front entrance. "Mr. and Mrs. Miller," he said with a noticeable French accent, nodding in greeting. "You're right on time."

Claude said, "Tom, would you come with me for a minute? I have something I need to discuss with you."

Tom's gaze lingered on the man in the lab coat. Could this be Bergeron? He appeared to be in his fifties, so the timeline fit. Tom extended his hand and said, "And you would be?"

But the Frenchman had already turned and was leading the Millers to the door.

"Tom?" Claude said from behind him in a firmer tone.

Tom followed Dumont past the conference room through an oversized wooden door that led to an elegant corner office. Walls of windows overlooked verdant pastures. Two older horses stood close together by a fence.

Claude closed the door and faced him. "What are you doing here?"

"I told you. I'm writing this story."

"I thought we'd gone through all of that. I thought I'd been clear."

"It's clear that you don't want me writing about your little human breeding operation."

Claude shook his head slowly.

"I'm going to get to the bottom of this. I'm going to expose you."

"There's nothing to expose. You're making a fool of yourself."

"Why do you care? If there's nothing to tell, nothing to hide, why don't you just back off and let me do my job?"

"Because you're intruding on the privacy of some of my dearest friends. They don't want

KEVIN BOREEN

this kind of sensationalism and publicity. I'm asking you again: please stop this."

"I advise you to call off your goons. Crimes have been committed. I'm going to report all of it."

Claude winced. "I have no idea what you're talking about."

"Don't act like you don't know about my taxi ride to the airport or my car this morning."

"I don't. I have nothing to do with anything that may have happened to you, although you do strike me as the kind of person who would have lots of enemies. Don't make one out of me."

"Was that man Renard Bergeron?"

After the briefest of pauses, Claude said, "That's none of your business."

"Why did the Millers come here?"

"They are dear friends who are here for a pleasant visit. What concern is that of yours?"

"Will it be a mere coincidence if nine months from now we learn that Mrs. Miller has had a baby?"

Claude stared back at him.

"You can't hide something like that. I assure you I'll be paying very close attention."

Claude said, "This is private property, my property, and I want you to leave immediately. As of this moment, you're trespassing, and I have very good relationships with the local authorities."

201

"So I've heard, but that won't be necessary. I'll go, but you'll be hearing more from me."

Tom grinned at Dumont's reddening face and calmly walked past him and out of the office. As Tom crossed the large hall, he glimpsed the Millers getting into what appeared to be a six-seat golf cart with the man in the white lab coat. Rick waved at Tom, who waved back as the cart drove away. Tom decided he'd come back later to ask about a directory. He went directly to his car, relieved to find that it was still drivable. As he was pulling out of the lot, he saw the golf cart turn right, heading deeper into the property. The highway lay to the left. Acting on impulse, Tom turned right, following the cart at a distance.

The road was paved but had no lines painted on it. It passed between five-board white fences with pastures on both sides. Large leafy trees became more and more prevalent. He saw a NO TRESPASSING sign but kept going. The golf cart was far ahead and barely in view. He looked through his binoculars and saw it stop at a gate with a small guardhouse. Thick foliage extended on both sides, obscuring his view of what lay beyond. A tall iron gate slid open, and the cart pulled forward. The gate closed behind them.

Tom pulled over onto a stretch of bare dirt where it looked like tractors had recently accessed the pasture. He opened a gate and drove through, parking under an ancient maple. Scanning through the binoculars, he didn't see

KEVIN BOREEN

any sign that the guards had noticed him. He got out of the car and continued on foot toward the gate, using the fence as cover. The pasture ended in a sharp corner when it reached the guardhouse. Beyond the fence, a tall green hedge rose, blocking his view. Crouching, he hurried about a hundred yards away from the gate and climbed over the fence. No one was in sight.

He probed the foliage and found it dense with long, sharp thorns, thicker in some places than others. Eventually he found a thinner area of vegetation. Pushing branches aside, he slowly eased himself part-way through, getting scratched as thorns tore at his clothes. On the other side, he saw a tall electric fence. A yellow warning sign read: DANGER. 10,000 VOLTS, the maximum, Tom remembered, allowed by international regulations. Whatever lay behind that fence, Dumont didn't want anyone to see it, and that's where the Millers had been taken. He shifted his position to improve his view and saw that another fence, chain link topped by barbed wire, ran beyond the electric one. The fences extended as far as his field of vision. The enclosure must be enormous.

That's when he heard dogs barking in the distance, barks that quickly grew louder. Enormous German Shepherds appeared beyond the fences, growling and baring their teeth. Tom had grown up around dogs but had never encountered canines like these. They were not only enormous in stature, but their musculature was developed beyond anything he had ever seen.

"Sir," someone said from behind him in a soft Kentucky drawl. "Would you please join us out here?"

Tom looked back and saw two security guards in black uniforms. Both wore pistols, which he was glad to see were still in their holsters. One of them carried a tactical twelve-gauge shot gun. Both had nylon zip-ties hanging from their belts. Tom slowly climbed back through the hedge, taking care not to tear his clothing on the stiff branches.

"Did you notice the posted trespassing signs?" one of them asked.

"Yes, I did. I'm sorry."

"What do you think you're doing?" the other asked.

"I'm working on a story."

"You're a journalist?"

"That's right."

"Well, you've got some explaining to do. Come with us." As they led him back to the guardhouse, one of the guards spoke quietly into his headset. By the time they arrived there, Tom noticed someone approaching in a golf cart from the direction of the visitor center. It was Claude Dumont. A big man rode with him. Tom guessed he was the same man he had met in the parking lot that morning.

Claude stopped in front of the gate and turned to Tom. He grinned thinly and said, "It looks like you took a wrong turn from the stables."

"I told you I'm going to get to the bottom of this."

Claude nodded. "I can see that now. I believe you've met Maxim?"

"Briefly."

Claude looked to the horizon and then back at Tom. "You know, my friend, I've had a change of heart. Hop in. Let me satisfy your curiosity."

Tom wondered what kind of a game Dumont was playing. Did he seriously think he could talk Tom out of this story? But the opportunity to see the compound was too good to pass up. Maxim moved to a back seat and Tom sat beside Claude. The heavy iron gates swung open, and they entered the restricted area.

35

Claude drove in silence as they passed beneath the high branches of trees that lined the private road. They passed pastures, woods, paddocks, and kennels. In the distance Tom saw impossibly large cattle and horses of all sizes and descriptions. The German Shepherds ran along the fence line, shadowing their progress. Tom noticed that Claude drove with great precision and skill, controlling the golf cart as if it were a jet aircraft or a race car. The man gave every appearance of being perfect, yet Tom increasingly believed a monster resided within.

"Where are we going?" Tom finally asked.

"I'm going to show you our laboratory." Claude glanced at him. "I can see how determined you are. I respect that. But when you know everything, I think you'll agree to drop this. It's the only rational decision. I'm sure of it."

"No promises."

They pulled in front of a one-story brick building fronted with six large windows and a glass lobby. The roof line was steep, reminding

Tom of the stables. A cart identical to theirs was parked at the entrance. Claude stopped behind it. Tom assumed that the Millers had arrived in the other vehicle and wondered whether he'd see them inside. He'd taken a big risk peeking through the fence, but he was now glad he had. Maxim's silent presence was worrisome, but if they'd wanted to hurt him, he could have easily done so in the lot that morning.

They walked into the reception area. A young, athletic looking man sitting behind a broad desk rose to his feet.

"Good afternoon, Mr. Dumont."

"Phil," Dumont said, nodding to the younger man as they passed.

A short hallway led to what appeared to be a museum of sorts. The ceiling rose to the roofline, the sun shining through several skylights. Claude led him past the displays and into an office suite. Maxim stayed behind. An attractive young woman greeted Claude and smiled pleasantly at Tom. Claude opened the door to his office and gestured for Tom to precede him. The door closed with a solid click.

The oak-paneled office was spacious. A leather topped desk faced a stone fireplace. A desktop computer and a striking bronze of a horse topped an adjoining credenza. Windows looked out over pastures to the south and west. Two leather couches faced one another.

"Would you like anything to drink?"

Claude asked.

"Not just yet," Tom said.

"I think I might." Dumont gestured toward the couch and Tom sat. Dumont opened a cabinet and took out a bottle and two glasses. He poured himself a finger of amber liquid and put the bottle and the other glass down in front of Tom. "In case you change your mind." He sat directly across from Tom on the facing couch.

"So," Tom said, "we're here."

Claude looked about him. "Yes. This is my inner sanctum."

Tom suspected that Dumont was aggravated if not outraged, but there wasn't a trace of malice in his expression or behavior. He asked, "So, where's the lab?"

"Beneath us. On this floor we have our library, the lounge, guest offices for visiting scientists and clients, a conference room, that sort of thing. The lab itself is considerably bigger than the surface building. It has about ten thousand feet of working space and just about every piece of life sciences equipment you can imagine. It's beyond state-of-the-art."

"How many people work here?"

"Inside the compound, I'd say we have about thirty support people: security, admin, cleaning staff, and animal handlers. The scientific complement varies considerably depending on what we're working on. Early on when so many processes were manual, we might

KEVIN BOREEN

have had a few dozen. Nowadays, we tend to run much leaner."

Tom was about to ask again about Bergeron when his attention was drawn to a painting hanging above Claude's desk. He did a double take. "Is that what I think it is?"

Claude turned toward it. "Yes, it certainly is."

"The *Salvatore Mundi*. I guess I'd always assumed it was in the dacha or mega-yacht of some Russian oligarch, but I guess this makes sense."

"An extraordinary work by an extraordinary man." Claude drank from his glass as he shook his finger at the masterpiece. "What I would love to find now is the horse he made for Lodovico Sforza. Now *that* would be something."

"I'm not familiar with that item."

"Not many people are. It was never completed. It was supposed to be a bronze statue to commemorate Lodovico's father, Francesco. Da Vinci first made a plaster model. The horse and rider were twenty-six feet high. It was put on display and became an immediate sensation. Sonnets were written about it. But he needed fifty tons of bronze to cast it, and Lodovico was short of funds. When the French captured Milan in 1499 their bowmen broke pieces off it, and according to lore, the remains were carted back to France as trophies. The trail vanishes after that, but if they ever turn up, I'll hear of it."

LEGACY

Tom decided to have a drink after all. As he poured, he said, "You remind me a little of Leonardo."

"Oh, and how is that?"

"He was a man of extraordinary gifts who lived an unusually charmed life."

"I'll agree that applies to him, but his talents were so far beyond mine that any comparison is absurd," Dumont said. "But he did have a fatal defect."

"Which was?"

"His failure to complete so many of the things he started. He was such a wide-ranging genius that once he had solved a technical problem in his mind," Claude tapped the side of his head, "the actual implementation bored him. He'd simply move on to the next thing that caught his interest. In that way, the great artist and I are not at all alike. And that brings us to why you and I are sitting here now."

"I'm listening."

"I believe with every fiber of my being that we are at the threshold of a new age, an age driven by a new and deeper understanding of biology. I have committed my energy and my wealth to advancing that science. I'm immensely proud of the extraordinary progress we've made in the face of enormous impediments."

"By impediments, are you referring to the law? Medical ethics? Deeply held religious beliefs? The future evolution of our species?"

Dumont slowly shook his head. "Do you study history, Tom?"

"I read widely."

"As I look back over the ages, I'm constantly struck by the persistent and powerful forces that stand in the way of progress."

"I'm more optimistic. Mankind's made incredible advances. I'll send you a copy of Pinker's *Enlightenment Now*. You might find it encouraging."

"I've read it twice, but I have a different perspective, perhaps born of my own experience and observations. I'll give you an example." Claude took a sip of cognac. "The ancient Greeks had profound scientific understandings and insights that didn't reemerge in the West for well over a thousand years. Do you know why?"

"The Dark Ages?"

"That was a symptom, not a cause. The curious, logical Greeks were conquered by the Romans, who were much more interested in wealth and power than in the pursuit of science. When Rome in turn submitted to the invasions of barbarians, the power void was filled by the Christian church, which was much more concerned about the eternal afterlife than man's condition here on Earth. Any thought that strayed from orthodox dogma was punished as heresy and schism. Scientific progress didn't just stop. It was actively suppressed for a millennium. History shows that the search for truth is more like a rising and falling tide than a flowing river."

"How is this relevant?"

"It's entirely relevant. For centuries scientists were silenced and persecuted for seeking the truth. We don't burn people at the stake anymore, but the deadening inertia of dogma, ignorance, and narrow self-interest continues to interfere with critical research that doesn't happen to conform to society's prevailing prejudices."

"But you've continued...in secret."

"That's right. I found my modern-day Leonardo—"

"Renard Bergeron."

"--provided him with every resource, and personally ensured that we relentlessly advanced. As a result, we are at least ten years ahead of the field. In time society will embrace the enormous opportunity to improve human biology. When that happens, we'll have that technology, and we'll eagerly share it."

"You're already sharing it. That's why the Millers are here, right?"

Claude leaned forward and looked directly at Tom with his clear blue eyes. "How cruel would it be to have the power to grant the greatest and most noble wish a man and woman could have, the desire to bear and raise a child, and refuse to do so?"

"What about the Fiskes?"

"What about them?"

"I've seen Paul. Did you know that he just recently gouged out his own eye?"

Claude nodded gravely. "Such a tragedy."

"Do you accept your responsibility for their suffering?"

Claude sighed deeply. "I've done everything I can for those boys and their parents."

"Deborah doesn't seem to think so."

"Well, I've tried, believe me. And in all the years that I've been helping couples, I'd never experienced anyone more enthusiastic and grateful than she was...until the problems started."

"They're enormous problems. Now she's concerned about Sue Miller."

"The Fiske boys were conceived eighteen years ago. We are so much farther along now. Our knowledge then was almost primitive in comparison. Sue and her child will be completely safe." Claude extended upturned hands toward Tom. "Do you see now why it's so important that you drop this? Do you comprehend the extent of the damage you could do? The people you'll hurt? The science you'll set back?"

"Much bigger issues are at stake. There's no way you can know how these alterations will play out over time. I can't stand by while you take the future of our species into your own hands. What gives you the right to play God? Deborah Fiske showed me what a mistake looks like, your mistake—"

"There's no conclusive proof that those boys were doomed by our edits. Our mistake wasn't in commission. We might have missed something, but we didn't cause anything."

"Without your so-called help they might not have been conceived in the first place," Tom said. "As to whether Paul's schizophrenia is a result of your meddling, the science is advancing rapidly. The doctors I spoke with already know there's genetic content in the boys' genomes that didn't come from either parent. Someday soon we'll know the truth."

Tom sensed that his words had found their mark, because Claude stared back at him for what seemed a long time. "Tom, what do I have to do to get you to drop this? What's your heart's desire? What can I give you?"

Tom shook his head.

"I'll pay you to drop it," Claude said. "Name your price."

"I don't want your money."

"I'll give you ten million dollars, Tom. I'll write you a check right here and now."

"I said no."

Claude stood and walked to the window, suddenly seeming much older. He put his hands on his hips, looked down at the floor, and then turned to face Tom. "Think through the implications if you write this story. Think of what it would mean for these families, these people who placed their trust in me. I couldn't bear to see the world pointing to these precious children and labeling them as freaks. I would truly rather die."

"I understand your feelings, but what you've told me today only strengthens my resolve to tell this story. What you and your scientists have done is monstrous. It has to be stopped, exposed, and regulated."

Claude rubbed his face and walked slowly to his desk. He opened a drawer and withdrew a pistol.

Tom jumped to his feet, speechless.

"You have to understand," Claude said, his voice catching. "These children are a part of me. I created them." He raised the pistol and pressed the barrel against his temple. "If this story comes out it will ruin everything I value in the world: my family, my friendships, my reputation, the science I've worked so hard to advance, and most of all these children."

Tom took a step forward, his mouth dry, his heart pounding. "Please put down the gun. You don't have to do this."

"I'll ask once more: how much money do you want to drop this story?"

"Claude, for God's sake, put down the gun."

Claude pulled back the hammer. "You've literally left me no choice."

Tom took another step forward. "It's not worth killing yourself!"

"Oh," Claude said, "that was never my intention." He trained the gun on Tom with a steady hand and fired a low velocity 9-millimeter bullet straight into Tom's forehead.

36

Claude walked around his desk and gazed down at the body. Tom's eyes were wide open. Blood was welling in a dark red circle one inch above the bridge of his nose. There was no question that the man was dead.

Claude opened his heavy office door a crack. Renee, one of his executive assistants, was at her desk. She looked up immediately and took out her earbuds.

"Yes, Mr. Dumont?"

"Could you please ask Renard and Maxim to come to my office immediately?"

"Of course."

"Thank you, Renee." Claude closed the door. He walked to a closet and took out a shallow rectangular pan that he normally used to hold his riding boots when they were wet. He knelt by Wright's body and slipped the pan under his head, noticing that there was no exit wound in the back of it. Blood had drained down the front of Wright's face and stained a small circle in the oriental carpet. No matter. It could be easily replaced.

He walked to his desk, sat, and thought about what to do next.

There was a quiet knock on the door and both Maxim and Renard stepped into the room.

Renard froze in place when he saw the body. "What the hell happened?"

"I tried everything," Claude said, shaking his head, "but he wouldn't listen. I offered him ten million."

Both men looked up at Claude.

"*Merde*, Claude!" Renard rushed to the corpse. "You shot him?"

"It was the only way. He knew your name."

"How?"

"I don't know. How is Sue Miller?"

"Fine," Renard said distractedly. "It's done."

"What do you want us to do?" Maxim asked.

Claude pressed his hands flat against his desk and said, "Take Wright to the lab. There's a bullet in the skull that needs to come out. Destroy it. Incinerate his clothes. Feed the body to the dogs." Claude paused, then continued. "Drive his rental car back to the Griffin Gate, collect his things, especially his laptop, and park the car in the long-term lot at Blue Grass. Renard, I'll need you to pose as Wright and get on a charter plane to Miami. Use his credit cards. My jet will meet you there and bring you back. We'll also need to burn this carpet. Bleach the floor beneath. Delete the security footage." Claude looked up at them. "I'll leave other details to you. Any thoughts?"

"We shouldn't use the dogs," Maxim said. "They can't digest teeth. If anyone thought to look, that would be evidence."

"I hadn't thought of that," Claude said, sitting back. "What do you suggest?"

"When I drop off his car at the airport, I'll bring back some jet fuel. I'll put the body in a 50-gallon drum and burn it. In two hours, there will be nothing left but ashes."

"Is that so? All right. Do it."

Renard crouched beside the body.

"Are you okay, Renard?" Claude asked.

Renard met his gaze. "I can't believe you did this. This is…insane."

"It was perfectly sane. Once you get over the shock of it, you'll see."

"People will know he was here. What will we say?"

"I offered him millions to kill an unpleasant story. He accepted. I wired it to his offshore account." Claude lifted his hands at his side. "He left."

"Works for me," Maxim said. "I'll send Renee on an errand. We'll roll the body in the carpet and take the elevator to the lab."

"Thank you, gentlemen."

Claude went into his private bathroom

and washed his hands carefully. He was sincerely sorry that he'd had to shoot the reporter, but Wright had left him no other option. Claude reflected on the choices people make. The reporter could have been jetting off to an exotic island with ten million dollars in his pocket. Ten million? Claude shook his head. He would have paid any price.

Renee was busy with something in the display area as Claude made his way to the exit. He smiled at her and wished her a good day. Then, stopping, he said, "Renee, when you get back to your desk, could you please call my friend, Hank Summers, and invite him to dinner in Manhattan the day after tomorrow? Say, eight o'clock?"

"Yes, Mr. Dumont. I'll be happy to do that."

"Tell him I'm sorry about our last conversation. I want to make it up to him."

"I'll do that, sir."

Claude strode to the golf cart he'd parked at the entrance. He took a deep breath and looked up at the sky. His conscience was clear. He had tried everything, and in the end, he'd done what needed to be done. There was no point in dwelling upon it. He trusted Renard and Maxim to take care of the rest. They always had.

It was a beautiful day. The leather seat of the Rolls Royce Phantom was soft and warm and as comfortable as a lounge chair. He'd bought the two of them from Rick Miller years ago. He accelerated quietly, admiring the pastures and trees as he drove through the compound gate and then onto the farm.

Nadine greeted him at the entrance to their mansion.

"How is she feeling?" Claude asked, kissing his wife on the lips.

"She's in high spirits," Nadine said brightly. "Why wouldn't she be? She's going to be a mother."

Arm-in-arm they went inside to congratulate their expectant friends.

37

"Can you believe this?" Renard asked as they rolled the corpse in the stained oriental rug. The shock of the murder had temporarily overwhelmed Renard's distaste for Maxim.

"He had it coming."

"I've never seen Claude do anything like this. This is crazy. Who knows what this guy might have said to people? How many people know he was here?"

"We'll clean it all up. There's no point worrying about it."

"We're accessories to a murder," Renard muttered.

"Not my first," Maxim said flatly. "Besides, it was self-defense. Wright was going to ruin many lives. He was warned. He was a fool to defy a man like Claude."

"There is no man like Claude."

They both lifted. Between the two of them, the weight was easily manageable. Bergeron unlocked the office elevator with a retinal scanner and pushed a button to descend to the laboratory, bypassing the basement

KEVIN BOREEN

security guard. The descent was long and slow, reminding Renard why he rarely came this way. They passed through the central work area, activated a second scanner, and placed the rug on the floor of Bergeron's private lab. They unrolled it and lifted Wright's corpse onto a broad stainless-steel counter.

"How long will you need?" Maxim asked.

"Thirty minutes."

"I'll go to his hotel and take care of the car." Maxim reached inside Wright's pockets and removed his wallet, phone, and keys. He handed Renard two credit cards. "For your trip. Make sure you use them." Wright's hotel room key was in a small paper envelope in the bill section of the wallet. Maxim held it up for Renard to see: the room number was written in pen on the envelope.

"I'll have him ready when you get back," Renard said.

Maxim nodded and left.

Renard turned to the remains of Tom Wright. He was used to working with cells and nuclei, not complete adult corpses. He hadn't dissected a body since medical school. He found a steel pan and placed it under the head. Wright's face had no expression: eyes open, mouth ajar, skin pale, the ugly round hole dead center in the forehead. Claude's aim had been perfect, of course. Renard went to a cabinet and retrieved surgical gloves and a box of heavy gauze. He

223

cleaned around the wound and turned the head to the side, feeling the back of the skull through the man's thick grey hair. The bullet had not passed through the parietal bones at the back. Renard wondered what kind of ammunition Claude had used, but quickly concluded that if you were going to shoot someone in a confined office, you'd want to use low-velocity rounds. Claude would have thought of that. Had he planned this all along?

He turned the body onto its stomach, adjusting the steel pan to catch any fluids that might leak from the wound. The brain is as soft as pudding and wouldn't slow a bullet, so he assumed that the projectile had stopped at the left or right parietal bone. He didn't know if Claude had been sitting or standing when he fired, but he assumed the bullet had entered at the center of the skull's frontal bone and then proceeded on a slightly upward path to the back of the brain. He went to another cabinet and returned with a flat plastic case. He opened it and removed a number 10 scalpel and a diamond-coated flexible wire connected to two handles, a Gigli saw, both wrapped in a sterile pouch. He removed them, laying them out on the counter. The scalpel blade was curved and mounted to a green plastic holder. It felt good in his hand, bringing back memories from medical school. He cut through the scalp in a clean straight line, cut two vertical lines, and pulled down a bloody flap of hair and skin, exposing the back of the skull. The suture line between the two parietal bones looked like an aerial view of a winding river. He took the handles of the Gigli saw in each hand, made the thread wire taut, and sawed through the back of the head. The bullet was right there, a shiny slug slightly dented on its round end, the only evidence that could connect this death to Claude's gun.

Renard took the slug to the sink and rinsed it off. His first thought was to place it in an autoclave. He did so, setting the temperature at 340 degrees Fahrenheit and the timer for thirty minutes. Then his eyes settled onto one of his Bunsen burners. That seemed like a better option. He recalled that bullets were made mostly of lead mixed with a little antimony for hardness. He went to his computer and looked up the melting points. Lead melted at 622 degrees, antimony at 1,167 degrees, and copper at 1,984 degrees. The Bunsen burner reached 2700, more than enough. He found some forceps and removed the bullet from the autoclave. He lit the burner. It took only a minute to melt the bullet into a small steel pan.

Satisfied that the slug had been utterly destroyed, he folded the stained carpet and forced it into a large plastic contractor bag. He then put the circle of bone back in place and folded the flap of scalp over it, tying it in place with a few stitches. He wrapped the head in a plastic bag, taped it around the neck to prevent leakage, and then wrapped the entire corpse in more plastic bags, taping the seams.

That was as much as he could do for now. Renard checked his watch. Maxim would be back soon. He called a local air charter company and booked a flight to Miami under the dead journalist's name using Wright's corporate card.

38

Maxim had one of the security guards drive him to Wright's rental car, which they found parked under a maple tree in one of the pastures. He pulled on nitrile gloves, opened the door, and turned on the ignition. The gas tank was three quarters full. The last thing he needed now was to run out of fuel. He made a three-point turn and headed in the direction of the stables, continuing past them, following the winding drive to the highway, and turning left toward the center of Lexington.

The twenty-minute drive to the Griffin Gate passed quickly. He parked in the center of the crowded parking lot. He removed his gloves and slipped them into his jacket pocket. It was close to 3 p.m. and the hotel lobby was crowded with new arrivals. Maxim walked straight through.

He took the elevator to the third floor and found room 319. Checking to ensure the hall was clear, he put his gloves back on. The door unlocked with a quiet click. The bed had been made and fresh towels left in the

LEGACY

bathroom. A small black backpack was tucked under one of the nightstands. He zipped it open and found a passport, some cash, a return ticket to New York, and a printed e-mail reservation for the Kentucky Castle for the following night. He returned everything to the pack but the reservation. He found an overnight bag in the closet, opened every drawer, and placed whatever clothing he found in the bag. A toiletries case rested on the bathroom counter. He found a laptop inside the desk drawer, as well as a notebook. He packed those with the clothes. Checking the room once more, he placed the backpack and the overnight bag by the door. Then he dialed the front desk.

"Yes, Mr. Wright?" said the receptionist.

"My plans have changed. I'll be checking out this afternoon. Could you please put everything on my card?"

"We had you leaving us tomorrow morning, Mr. Wright."

"Yes, that's right. I'll understand if you need to charge me for tonight."

"I'm afraid we will. Check-out time is usually 11:00 a.m."

"I understand." Maxim hung up the phone.

He then dialed the number on the reservation.

"Kentucky Castle, how may I help you?" said a bright young voice.

228

"My name is Thomas Wright. I have a reservation for tomorrow night."

"Yes, Mr. Wright, I have it right here."

"My plans have changed and I won't be needing it. Is it too late to cancel?"

"No, sir. That's fine. I'll take care of that for you right now."

Maxim grabbed the two bags and cracked open the door. Some people were walking down the hall. He closed the door and waited until they were gone. He pulled the door shut behind him and removed his gloves, returning them to a pocket. He took the stairs down and, rather than crossing the lobby, followed a long hall that led to a side exit. Once outside, he doubled back to where he'd parked. He put the bags in the back seat and drove to Blue Grass airport, where he parked in the short-term lot, noting the space number. He took the rental agreement from the glove compartment and slipped it into his breast pocket. He removed Wright's bags and caught a taxi to the private hangar where Dumont kept his plane.

He found one of the Dumont aircraft mechanics and explained what he needed. Ten minutes later, a black Suburban pulled in front of the hangar. A man in coveralls got out, the engine still running.

"It's in the back, Mr. Fedorov. Twenty-five gallons of Jet A."

"Thanks," Maxim said. He got behind the

steering wheel and drove back to the farm. He passed through the gates and parked behind the lab on a concrete lot with large industrial dumpsters on the far side. Beyond those, three fifty-gallon steel burn barrels were set apart. He took five five-gallon containers of kerosene from the back of the Suburban and filled one of the barrels about half-way, saving a few gallons. He called Renard to let him know that he was coming, and then drove the Suburban to the back to the lab, parking beside a set of storm cellar doors that led down to the basement. Renard opened the doors and Maxim followed him inside the laboratory. They brought Wright's wrapped body to the Suburban, and then the folded carpet in a contractor bag. They drove to the barrels and lowered the corpse headfirst into the kerosene. Renard turned away as Maxim twisted limbs to fit the body completely inside the drum. Then Maxim took out a Zippo lighter.

"Is that safe?" Renard asked with a raised eyebrow, stepping back.

"It's jet fuel, not volatile like gasoline." Between the fuel and the body, the drum was nearly full. Maxim lit the lighter and tossed it into the barrel, which caught fire immediately. Maxim then put the carpet in another barrel, added the remaining fuel, and lit it with a piece of cardboard that he ignited from the first barrel.

"I'll keep watch here until it's done," Maxim said. "Here's the car rental agreement. I wrote the parking spot number on it. Call them on Wright's phone and tell them where it is once you're airborne. The keys are above the visor. The doors are unlocked."

"They'll be pissed."

"Wait until they see what I did to the rear bumper." Maxim moved away from the billowing smoke. "Anyway, they can take that up with Mr. Wright. I checked him out of the Griffin Gate and cancelled his reservation at The Castle."

"Looks like he got away with ten million dollars."

"Some guys have all the luck."

39

The following afternoon, Claude was waiting on the tarmac as his jet taxied to the hangar and Renard descended the airstairs.

"It sounds like everything went smoothly," Claude said.

"It did," Renard said, looking a little rumpled. "Where are you off to now?"

"Back to Manhattan. I've got some loose ends to tie up." Claude drew close to him. "Are you okay?"

"What do you mean?"

"You seemed upset with me yesterday."

"I was. It was shocking. I wish there had been another way."

"Me too, but there wasn't. Just think of what could have happened. He had to be stopped at all costs."

"Well, it's done. We move on, right?"

"Right." Claude patted Renard's shoulder. "I've been meaning to ask, how are you coming along on our First Love project?"

"Quite well. We should be ready to implant the fetus by the end of this week."

"Excellent. I can't wait to see that foal." Claude climbed into his Dassault Falcon and waved at Renard from the open door. The stairs retracted, the door swung shut, and the jet taxied for takeoff.

Claude accepted a glass of scotch from the cabin attendant and took a folded handwritten list from his breast pocket. The first name on the list was Scott Fiske. It had three tick marks under it and the words WINE, DEB, and ART. He scrolled through the contacts list on his phone and pressed the call button.

"Scott! It's Claude Dumont."

"Afternoon, Claude. What can I do for you?"

"Well, as it happens, I have an important undertaking for you. I don't know if I've ever mentioned it, but I own vineyards in southern Australia, 300 acres in the Eden Valley and another 500 in the Barossa."

"No, I wasn't aware. I thought all of your wine operations were in France."

"They will be. I want you to sell all 800 acres."

"Do you have a price in mind?"

"The vines are exceptional. I imagine they'll sell for a nice premium. I'll leave that in your capable hands. We'll use our customary terms. This one should be quite profitable for you."

"I appreciate that. Thank you, Claude."

After a short pause, Claude said, "I heard from friends that you and Deborah may be getting a divorce. Is that true?"

"Yes, I'm afraid so."

"I'm very sorry to hear that." Claude waited a moment and then continued, "Believe me, I don't want to intrude on your personal affairs, but I couldn't help but notice that the timing of this coincides with this unpleasantness about *Future* magazine and that aggressive reporter."

Claude heard a heavy sigh over the phone.

"I'm so sorry about that, Claude. I don't know what got into her. I don't know why she—"

"What I'm trying to say, and I'm saying it poorly, is that I understand. Deb's been under so much pressure. The boys, your work in Europe, the recent tragedy at the hospital…. It's more than anyone could bear."

"I owe you so much. We both do."

"What you don't owe me is a divorce, my friend. I've taken steps to stop the story. That's behind us now. Again, your life is yours to lead, but I'll be very sorry if this ends up causing a permanent rift between you and your family."

"I appreciate that. I do. I've…well, I've been having some second thoughts about it all."

"Listen to your heart, Scott. You know, I haven't seen Deborah much in recent years. Maybe it would be good to catch up. I could have

KEVIN BOREEN

Nadine reach out to her. What do you think?"

"I think that would be very generous of you both, under the circumstances."

"Not at all. We'll do that. And Scott, good luck with those Adelaide properties. You might want to go out there and look for yourself, maybe take Deb with you? It's beautiful there this time of year."

"I'll look into it."

"There is one other thing you could help me with."

"Name it."

"I'm buying a painting in Belgium, an Albrecht Durer."

"I didn't know one was for sale."

"It's in a private collection. No one outside the family has seen it for generations. They've agreed to sell it to me for $10 million."

"Congratulations. I'm surprised the Germans are letting you get away with that."

"They wouldn't if they knew about it. That's why I need your help. The Alte Pinakothek's been using every pressure tactic to take the painting back to Munich. The greedy bastards already have his *Four Apostles*, for Christ's sake. Happily, they annoyed the sellers enough that they've reached out to me. Obviously, they want it to be kept quiet. That's where you come in."

"You need to make a discreet payment."

"Exactly, my friend. The account's

already set up in Grand Cayman. I'll have the details sent to your office."

"Easy enough. Just send the numbers though. No names."

"Perfect," Claud said, grinning to himself. "The funds will be available to you within the hour."

"Consider it done."

Claude ended the call, pleased with how it had gone. Scott would be in a much better position to keep Deborah under control if they remained married, and Scott had to realize that he needed her to take care of those boys. The Cayman account was in Wright's name, creating a plausible explanation for his disappearance. As for the land in Australia, Dumont had his hands full in France, and he thought it was prudent to sell in a strong market before buyers realized that climate change would eventually turn the state of Victoria into a desert.

The next name on his list was Lord Sterling.

"John! It's Claude Dumont."

"Good to hear from you. Where are you now?"

"I'm flying from the farm to Manhattan. I'm sure you're busy so I'm going to jump to the point. I'd like you to do a favor for me."

"Of course."

"Can you get Hank Summers back on the Davos invitation list?"

KEVIN BOREEN

"That's not a problem, but I thought—"

"The situation has changed. The reporter and I reached an accommodation. We need to bring Hank back into the fold. I might have overreacted."

"I don't think stopping that story was an overreaction."

"Hank tried his best. I got impatient with him. We should move on."

"I'll take care of it right away. What did it cost?"

Claude chuckled. "Do you really want to know?"

"I am curious."

"Ten million."

"Worth every penny, if you ask me."

If only you knew. "Thanks, John."

"No, thank you, on behalf of all of us."

Claude ended the call. Everything was coming together nicely. He asked for another scotch and continued working down his list until his jet touched down at Teterboro.

40

Hank Summers sat at his desk, shoulders slumped and lost in thought as he played absently with a number two pencil. Despite all the trouble Wright had caused, Summers regretted his resignation and wished he'd handled it differently. Tom was a unique talent who had added considerably to the reputation of magazine. Word of his quitting would bring negative publicity, particularly when the Pulitzers came out. Summers wanted to avoid that at all costs. Unfortunately, Tom wasn't returning his messages. He hoped his star reporter hadn't gone on a binge and done something crazy. It had happened before.

He walked down the hall and stopped at Tom's office. His desk was empty, but Amy was typing in the conference room. She took off her ear pods when she noticed him.

"Any word from Tom?" Summers asked from the doorway.

"No."

Summers stepped into the conference room and took a seat. "Do you have any idea

KEVIN BOREEN

where he might have gone?"

"It would only be a guess." After a pause, she reminded him, "You told me to stop working on the story."

"Yes, I know, and I regret that now. He's a good man. If possible, I'd like to get him back. I'd like to fix this."

"So, you've changed your mind about Art Basel?"

"I didn't say that." Sensing the young woman's hostility, he scanned the busy whiteboard, covered with photographs, index cards, and post-it notes. "What have you got here?"

"This is where we were when Tom left."

"Can you take me quickly through it?"

"Sure. Tom became curious after he saw some elderly men with young children at Art Basel—"

"Yes, he told me that."

"At first, we had no idea what we were looking for, but then Tom got a call from a woman named Deborah Fiske. Her husband was in the photos. She claimed that she'd had fertility treatments at a clinic affiliated with Claude Dumont, and that the genes of her twins had been damaged, leading to severe mental illnesses."

"That's crazy," Summers muttered.

"Mrs. Fiske introduced Tom to her doctors, and they confirmed that the illnesses were caused by defective genes."

"That doesn't mean that it was Dumont's fault," Summers protested.

"He's a horse breeder, Mr. Summers," Amy countered. "Why is he treating women in the first place? *Human* women? Deborah also told Tom that a friend of hers, Sue Miller, was about to go down to the Dumont farm to get a similar treatment. You asked me where he might have gone. I'll bet that Tom followed them down there."

"Did he tell you that?" Hank asked.

"No," Amy replied, "Deborah did. She called the office asking for Tom. I called her back, hoping she might know something."

"What did he hope to accomplish there?"

"She told me he was hoping to get the names of some of the technical people at *Les Champs*. They might help us figure out who has been performing these procedures."

"And did he?"

"We don't know. But there's more. We got a call from the police this morning. They're looking for Tom in connection with an accident two nights ago."

"What kind of an accident?" Summers had feared as much.

"Just outside LaGuardia. It appears someone tried to run his taxi off the road. They want to take his statement."

"So, he wasn't driving," Summers said,

relieved.

"Do you think that was a coincidence?"

"What connects that to his disappearance?"

Amy stared back at him.

"Okay," he said. "I'll admit it raises questions."

"Someone was clearly trying to dissuade him from going down there."

Summers pursed his lips. "I suppose it could be one of the families." If anything, this only confirmed his decision to kill the story. He thought back to the argument he'd had with Tom him before he resigned. Tom's subsequent persistence had been remarkable but not at all surprising. Hank knew that Tom's wife and child had died due to complications during childbirth, something about anesthesiology during an emergency C-section. Tom had never gotten over it. This had clearly become personal for him.

"Well, thanks for the update." Summers stood. "How much longer will you be here at the magazine?"

"Three more weeks."

"What are you working on?"

"This and that."

Summers considered whether keeping her on board was a risk worth taking. "Let's meet tomorrow in my office to see where we go from here." He stopped at the door and added, "If you hear anything about Tom's whereabouts, please let me know immediately."

"I will," Amy said.

Summers left her. As he approached his office, he saw a very attractive blonde sitting across from his assistant. She looked familiar but he couldn't quite place her.

"Do we have an appointment?" he asked, looking between them.

The woman stood. In heels, she towered over him.

"I'm Britt Nielsen, a friend of Tom's."

"Britt! Of course. I knew I recognized you. I have a meeting in a few minutes, but please, come into my office."

He held the door for her and closed it behind them.

"Have you heard anything from Tom? We've been trying to track him down." Summers gestured to a chair as he took his seat.

"No. That's why I'm here. He invited me up for the weekend. I can't reach him by phone and he's not at his condo."

"When's the last time you spoke with him?"

"He called me from Dumont's farm. I'm worried that something happened to him. He'd never abandon me like this."

There was a knock on the door.

"Come in."

It was Amy. "I'm sorry to interrupt, Mr.

Summers. The police just called again, looking for Tom. What do you want me to tell them?"

"Just tell them the truth, Amy. We don't know who where he is."

Britt asked, "Are you the Amy that works with Tom?"

"Yes."

The desk phone rang and, after answering it, Summers said, "Britt, it was very nice to meet you, but my appointment's here. I'll call you as soon as I hear anything. I hope you'll do the same."

"Of course," she said. Rising to follow Amy, she stopped at the door to add, "Maybe Claude Dumont can help us track him down."

That was the last call that Summers wanted to make, but he said, "Absolutely. I'm sure he'll be eager to help."

No sooner had the door closed than his office phone rang again. He picked up the handset.

"Hank, it's John Hastings. How are you doing this morning?"

"I'm fine, John," Summers replied, unconsciously straightening his tie. He checked the time. His appointment would have to wait. "To what do I owe this pleasure?"

"I have some good news for you. If you're still interested, you're back on the list for Davos."

Hank sat up straight in his chair. "That's terrific news. Thank you, John."

243

"You'll be getting the invitation shortly, but I thought you'd want to know right away."

"I can't tell you how much I appreciate this. What changed?"

"Just between you and me, Claude made some calls. He thought you should be there, so you will be."

Summers felt a warm wave of relief. "We're having dinner tonight. I'll be sure to thank him."

"We're all looking forward to seeing you there. Be sure to let me know where you're staying. There are some panels that may interest you."

"Of course."

The line went dead. Hank's heart beat a little faster as a broad grin spread across his face. He thought of the new suits he'd bought with Davos in mind. He couldn't wait to tell his wife.

After a hurried, hushed conversation in the hallway, Amy brought Britt to Tom's conference room and closed the door.

"Tom had a lead down there," Britt said, "a man named Renard Bergeron."

"Do we know anything about him?"

"Nothing at all. I asked around. No one's ever heard of him. Nothing online, either."

"What's the connection?"

"Tom met some kind of veterinarian

down there who said that Bergeron was his point of contact at *Les Champs*."

"And later that day, Tom disappeared." Amy tensed her jaw. "We need to report this to the police. I know he'd just quit the magazine and that people tend to resurface…"

"He never would have asked me up here and not shown up himself. Something's happened to him. He may need our help. He may even be…"

"Don't say it," Amy said. "I can't even bear the thought of it."

"Neither can I."

41

Summers arrived at Jean-George ten minutes early and was shown directly to the same table where they had eaten days earlier. Claude was already there, speaking with the sommelier. As soon as Claude saw Hank, he rose to his feet and approached him with an outstretched hand.

"Hank! Thank you for joining me."

Hank took his hand. Claude exuded friendship and good will. It was inconceivable that he could be behind any violence against Tom. "The pleasure's all mine."

The two men walked back to the table and sat.

"I received some good news from Lord Hastings," Hank said.

"Oh?" Claude's expression was neutral. "What was it?"

"I'll be going to Davos in February. I'm thrilled."

"That's wonderful news! I haven't missed it in thirty years. You'll love it."

"I understand you had something to do

KEVIN BOREEN

with my invitation."

"Did I?" Claude winked. "I suppose I might have said a word."

"I can't thank you enough."

"Don't give it another thought. You'll have to let me know what your plans are. There are some parties you won't want to miss."

The sommelier appeared beside their table with two bottles of Chateau Petrus. He said, "As you requested, we have both the 1989 and 1990 vintages."

Claude grinned at Hank. "I thought it would be fun to have a taste test. Gaspard, open both."

"I'll bring two more glasses," the man said, slipping away.

"I absolutely adore Petrus," Claude said. "Only twenty-five hundred cases produced a year and no second wine. All of the rejected grapes are sold to make generic Pomerol."

"I didn't realize that."

"Their commitment to quality is absolute. I remember, in 1987, they had too much rain late in the season and," Claude chuckled, "they brought in a *helicopter* to hover over the vines to dry them. Can you imagine? I never would have thought of that."

The sommelier returned with two assistants, poured the wines, and waited. Claude tasted the 1989 and closed his eyes. "Perfection." He opened his eyes and added, "I'm sure the other is as well. That's all for now, Gaspard. Thank you."

The three men bowed and stepped away.

"This is a lavish treat," Hank said, tasting the 1990.

Claude lowered his voice and drew closer. "My friend, I want to apologize for our last phone conversation. You caught me at a bad time, which is no excuse. I was worried and said more than I should have, and certainly more than I meant."

"We were all frustrated," Hank said, putting down his glass.

"Wright came to see me in Lexington," Claude said. "Did you know that?"

"I heard about it after the fact. It's very strange. No one seems to know where he is now."

Claude grinned thinly as he met his gaze. "I'm sure he'll turn up."

"What did he want?"

"He was still looking for a story." Claude drank some wine. "I eventually talked him out of it."

"And how did you do that?" Hank doubted that even Claude Dumont had such powers of persuasion.

"I made him an offer he couldn't refuse."

"You paid him?"

Claude nodded, quietly adding, "Ten million dollars, but that's just between you and me."

Hank's head inclined forward as he silently mouthed *ten million.* "You're not serious."

"Completely serious. I wired it to his numbered account in Grand Cayman."

"I didn't know he kept off-shore accounts."

Claude shrugged. "Maybe this was his plan all along. He chartered a jet and flew off that same afternoon. Like I said, I'm sure he'll be in touch when he's finished celebrating his new fortune. Money's a lot of fun at first, but the novelty wears off."

Hank shook his head. "I've known Tom for years, professionally more than personally, but I must say, I'm surprised." As the menus arrived, Hank wondered to himself why someone would pay ten million dollars to stop a story about nothing, but when he considered the families and their privacy concerns, he understood. It was so like Claude Dumont to take that burden onto himself.

Claude refilled Hank's glass of the 1989, and the conversation turned to Claude's guest list at the Royal Ascot, a coveted invitation. Hank and his wife, of course, would be among the guests, if they were free.

"She'll be thrilled," Hank said, offering a toast.

42

The next morning, Summers was waiting for his meeting with Amy when his cell phone rang. His wife's name appeared on the screen.

"Yes, honey?"

"I have great news!"

"What is it?"

"I just got a call from Nadine Dumont. They've invited us to the Super Bowl!"

"I hope you accepted."

"Of course, silly! We're going. We *have* to go."

"Well, that's wonderful. I'm delighted. Oh, wait a minute. Does that conflict with Davos?"

"No. In fact, Nadine suggested that we fly back from Switzerland on their plane."

Even better. "Wow. That's kind of them."

"They are such wonderful people. Nadine spoke so highly of you. I couldn't be more excited! We'll talk tonight."

Hank ended the call. It occurred to him that the Dumonts had been exceedingly generous since Tom's disappearance, but that was understandable. Hank had tried his best to control Tom, Claude now realized that, and the subsequent apology was warranted.

This was so much better than the invitation that had been withdrawn. The magazine had reported that the rental alone for the Dumont's luxury suite at the previous Super Bowl had been over a million dollars. Hank wondered who the other guests would be and looked forward to finding out. Now that he was back on Claude's good side, of course, the risks of keeping Amy onboard were even greater. He'd struggled with his decision, but now he knew what he had to do.

He remained seated as Amy walked into his office, manila files and a laptop under her arm. He saw no need to disillusion Amy about her mentor. If Tom had accepted ten million dollars to drop a story that Summers had already killed, that was his business, not theirs. The ethics around accepting a payoff troubled Summers, of course, but Tom no longer worked for the magazine, and he clearly wasn't coming back.

Summers had contacted Human Resources in preparation for their meeting. He learned that Tom had filed a glowing performance evaluation and letter of recommendation for Amy a week ago. The man was nothing if not thorough.

"After our talk yesterday," Summers

LEGACY

began, "I thought about your next three weeks. I want you to know that I'm grateful for all of your hard work, but without knowing where Tom is or when he'll come back, this might be a logical endpoint for your internship."

"I was counting on completing it," she said, slightly reddening.

"That won't be necessary." Summers looked down at this desk, nodding gravely. "Tom wrote a strong review for you, as well as a letter of recommendation. Coming from a person as demanding as he is, that means a lot. Until he resurfaces, please feel free to list me as your manager in your future job searches or applications. I'll be more than happy to put in a good word for you. And, of course, you'll be fully paid for the rest of your contract with us. Think of it as a well-deserved, paid vacation."

"This was an unpaid internship."

"Oh," Hank said, feeling foolish. "Well, then..."

After a pause, Amy asked, "May I ask a question?"

"Of course."

"Do you know if anyone has reported Tom's disappearance to the police?"

"I don't know. I haven't."

"Should we?" Amy asked.

Summers let out a long, slow breath, wondering how much he should say. "You know, Amy, I have good reason to believe that Tom is

KEVIN BOREEN

fine."

"Have you heard from him?" she asked, leaning forward.

"Not directly. I'm afraid that's all I can say at this point, but I wouldn't worry about him if I were you. He's fine."

"So, where is he?" she pressed. "How do you know he's okay?"

"I just told you I'm not at liberty to say."

An uncomfortable silence fell upon the room. Summers was about to end the meeting when Amy asked, "What do you want me to do with our research materials?"

Summers linked his fingers on his desk. "We're never going to use it, and the information is personal and sensitive. Just get rid of it. That's your final assignment."

After another awkward silence, Amy said, "So that's it?"

Summers smiled and rose from his chair. "Yes, I suppose it is. Be sure to stop by Human Resources before you leave. Thank you for all of your work here at *Future* magazine, and good luck."

As Amy returned to the conference room, she was filled with conflicting emotions: concern about Tom, anger at Summers, and frustration with what appeared to be a cover-up by both Dumont and the magazine. She couldn't think of any reason that Tom would let Summers

LEGACY

know where he was and then not also reach out to her, Britt, or Deborah. It made no sense unless he was in trouble.

She looked around the room where she had worked the last few months. She had come to *Future* with such excitement and hope. Tom had exceeded her expectations in every way. Not only was he smart and professional, but he was also kind. He'd taken a personal interest in her. She felt that he really wanted her to succeed. He had taken her under his wing more than any professor or editor she'd ever had. Now instead of being her mentor, he was missing.

So, today was to be her last day at *Future*. She grabbed a legal pad and wrote down three bullets: *Research*, *Deborah/Britt*, and *Missing Persons*.

Summers had instructed her to get rid of all the Art Basel documentation. She suspected he wanted to protect the magazine from any future legal action from the families pictured in Tom's photograph. But he hadn't explicitly told her to *destroy* them. When Tom returned, *if* he returned, he'd want to have all of this. She gathered the photos and files and packed them into a carboard banker's box. She thought about taking the hard drive from the conference room desktop computer, but that would be theft of company property and would look suspicious. She had copies of all their files on her own laptop, so she simply deleted everything on the

254

office hard drive. She didn't have access to Tom's desktop. She assumed that Summers would have the IT department wipe that clean, so she hoped that she already had most of Tom's own research.

Amy knew that she would need allies. Deborah and Britt each had strong reasons to care about Tom and his safety, and they'd all be more effective if they worked together. She added Deborah's number to her contacts list and made a mental note to call her later.

Then Amy went online, found the website for the New York Police Department, and dialed the Detective Bureau's Missing Persons Squad.

43

The phone rang seven times before someone answered. "NYPD. How can I help you?"

"Hi. My name is Amy Klar. I want to report a missing person."

She heard a sigh on the other end of the line. "Why do you think the person is missing?"

"I'm not sure that he is. It's just that no one has heard from him in a few days."

"Does he have a history of drug abuse or mental illness?"

"Not that I know of."

"How old is this person?"

"I'm not sure. I guess in his late fifties, early sixties."

"When was he last seen?"

"Three days ago in Lexington, Kentucky, but he's a resident of New York City."

"Is there anything suspicious surrounding this?"

"He's a journalist. He flew down to Kentucky for a story he was working on. On the way to the airport, he was a passenger in a taxi

KEVIN BOREEN

that was nearly run off the road."

"Was that reported?"

"Yes. The police have left messages at his office to get his statement."

"Anything else?"

"When he was in Kentucky, he invited a friend to come visit him here this weekend. He wasn't at his condo when she arrived. He hadn't called her to cancel. Now all her calls are going to his voicemail."

"Maybe he stood her up."

"I don't think so. Neither does she."

The detective said, "I can take his name and details and make some preliminary checks, but that's not a lot to go on. You have to understand that at any given time in this country there are a hundred thousand people reported as missing."

"I thought that people were supposed to contact the police as soon as they think someone has disappeared."

"Not always. Usually we're most concerned about children. In this case you have a grown man with no history of illness or addiction. Maybe he flew off to Vegas or Atlantic City. Is he married? Does he have family?"

"No. His wife passed away years ago."

"Well, I suggest you reach out to his friends and associates and wait for a few days."

"Is there anything else we can do in the meantime?"

LEGACY

"A next step could be to obtain a DNA sample that we could check against unidentified remains held in coroner's offices and medical examiners. We've got about forty thousand bodies across the country. But I don't think we're there yet. I suggest you wait for now."

Amy gave the detective Tom's details and left her cell number. She hung up the phone, discouraged. Then she called Deborah Fiske.

44

Deborah was feeling completely overwhelmed. She had interviewed several divorce attorneys, and there were many to choose from in Greenwich. All agreed that the history of cruelty, infidelity, and abandonment would work in her favor. She retained the one with the best record of navigating through prenuptial agreements, potentially the weakest part of her case.

The doctors had been in nearly constant contact. They'd once again modified her son's mix of medications. She hadn't seen any improvement thus far, but she sat by Paul's side for hours every day, hoping for a miracle.

She hadn't heard from Tom since he left for Lexington. She worried about Sue Miller and whether she'd gone through with the procedure, though she feared that she had. Dr. Slater had called that morning to say that she had important new information regarding the twins. They had arranged to meet that evening at the hospital.

She was walking back to her son's room

when her cell phone rang. She didn't recognize the number.

"Hello?"

"Hi," said a young woman's voice. "Is this Mrs. Deborah Fiske?"

"Speaking."

"It's Amy Klar from Tom's office."

Hoping for good news, Deborah asked, "Have you heard anything from him?"

"No."

Deborah leaned wearily against a wall. "I'm worried about him."

"So am I." After a pause, Amy said, "I have Tom's notes and files. The publisher told us this morning to get rid of them. They're of no use to us, but I thought you might want them."

"Yes, absolutely."

"If and when Tom comes back, I'll let him know where they are."

"I'll keep them safe. Wait a minute: did you just say *if*?"

"Mrs. Fiske, we're learning of disturbing circumstances around Tom's visit to Lexington."

"Like what?"

"According to the police, someone may have tried to push his taxi off the road on the way to LaGuardia, and he was supposed to be back in New York this weekend to meet a close friend, a woman named Britt. She went to his condo and he wasn't there. He's not returning anyone's calls. I think something's happened to him."

260

"Do you think he's been hurt?"

"I don't know. I hope not. I'm just telling you this because...you should be careful."

A second call started to ring on Deborah's phone. It was from her husband.

"I'm sorry, Amy. I have to take another call. When do you want to give me the files?"

"Could I bring them to you tomorrow?"

"That would be amazing. Thank you. I'm sorry to have to cut this so short. I'll text my address."

"I have it. See you soon."

Deborah hung up and picked up Scott's call.

"How are you?" her husband asked, his voice quiet, even gentle.

"I've been better."

"I've...been thinking."

"And?"

"Our last call. Your birthday. The divorce papers. I was angry and preoccupied with work. I was anxious about Claude, worried about my firm. I took some time off to think. You're right. I haven't been there for you and the boys, not for a long time. What I'm trying to say is, this is my fault. I'm sorry about the filing. I'm sorry about so many things."

This was not at all what she expected from Scott. She walked to a nearby couch and sat. "Are you saying you don't want the divorce?"

"That is what I'm saying. That was a

mistake committed in anger. Can we talk about all of this?"

"Where are you now?"

"I'm at Heathrow. I'm flying back tonight."

"Are you coming home?"

"If you'll have me."

She took a slow, deep breath. She had been so busy between the boys and the lawyers that she hadn't stopped to assess how she really felt. The truth hit her immediately: she didn't want Scott back. He had hurt her too badly, and too many times. She had loved him once, but that was long ago. She was about to say so when she thought of how this decision would affect her boys, how much their lives would change after a divorce. Given the terms of the prenup, their situation would almost certainly be better if she remained married. Whatever she ultimately decided, it was worth having a conversation.

"Deb?"

"Come home," she said. "We'll talk."

"Thank you."

She ended the call and checked her watch. It was a little after 4 p.m., time to leave for the hospital. She heard Edward playing in the conservatory, a Chopin polonaise. She went to him. He was so focused that he didn't look up, even when she put her hand on his shoulder. He was trapped in a world that was entirely his own. He concluded with three massive chords and looked up at her, a look of wild intensity in his eyes.

"I'm going out for a little bit," she said.

He nodded.

"I'll make you dinner when I get back."

"I'm not hungry."

"When's the last time you had something to eat?"

He started playing again, his fingers flying across the keys so fast she couldn't track them through the tears welling in her eyes.

45

Deborah parked behind McAllister Hospital and paused in the car to gather herself. In the rearview mirror she saw how tired she looked. She applied some lipstick and gave her hair a few strokes with a brush she kept in the glove compartment. Two minutes before her appointment, she got out and walked to the entrance.

Dr. Slater was waiting in the lobby. The first time they'd met, Deborah had been angry and upset, more focused on the psychiatrist and Tom's reactions than on this new physician. Seeing Slater now, Deborah noticed how petite and pretty she was. The young black woman exuded a quiet self-confidence, her posture erect, her gaze direct. Slater held a thin laptop computer and a manila folder in the crook of her arm.

"How are you holding up?" Dr. Slater said, walking briskly to her, her expression grave.

"I'm okay. What have you learned?"

"Let's find a conference room. I have a lot to tell you."

They walked past the receptionist and

264

entered a small room with a round table and three colorful plastic chairs. Dr. Slater shut the door behind them and placed her laptop and folder on the side of the table.

"When we last met, I told you I thought it was impossible that your boys' genes had been manipulated," Dr. Slater began. "I was wrong."

Deborah caught her breath. Could this be the proof she'd been seeking for so long?

Slater took a stack of complex, colorful charts from the folder and started to lay them side by side on the table. They were densely covered in bars and lines with countless numbers and short alphanumeric symbols.

"Dr. Slater," Deborah said, placing her outstretched hands gently on the reports, "nothing in the world is more important to me than understanding what happened to my boys, but I don't know enough to grasp the technical detail on these charts. Can you explain this to me in terms I can understand?"

Slater looked up at her. "Mrs. Fiske--"

"Please call me Deborah." She forced a grin. "I don't really know who Mrs. Fiske is these days."

Slater nodded. "Okay. This is complicated. You want to know what happened to Paul and Edward. I don't have all the answers yet. There are many things about this that I still don't understand."

"These charts represent their DNA

sequences, right?"

"Yes, and you're correct, they're more than we need right now." Slater gathered the displays and put them back in the folder. "When I analyzed them last night and this morning, I found a number of mutations in the boys' DNA that very likely contributed to their mental condition. I can't positively prove that those particular mutations were the result of any outside interference..."

Deborah felt her spirits sink.

"...but I did find something that I can't explain. In fact, it's shocking."

"What is it?"

"Nearly every cell in your body has an identical set of forty-six chromatids, or twenty-three chromosome pairs. The exceptions are the genetic material in eggs and sperm, which each contain half that number. When an egg is fertilized by sperm, these chromatids find their partner and join at a point called a centromere. One side is from the father, one is from the mother."

Deborah nodded.

"When your sons' sequences were analyzed in the past, doctors looked at specific areas associated with schizophrenia. Looking at their notes now, I see that a lot was missed. When I examined Paul and Edward's entire genomes, I found something unusual in chromosome 7. Instead of having one chromatid

KEVIN BOREEN

from each parent, they have a condition called uniparental disomy, or UPD."

"What's that?"

"It means that the two chromatids that make up that chromosome are from the same parent."

"Does that cause schizophrenia?"

"No. UPD can lead to a number of diseases, depending on which chromosomes are involved and the underlying health of the DNA. In this instance, your boys' mutations occur in a region of chromosome 7 associated with Williams-Beuren Syndrome."

"And what does that cause?"

"Let me be clear. Your twins don't have WBS. In fact, they have the opposite, something I've never seen before."

Deborah shifted uncomfortably in her seat. "I'm sorry. You're losing me."

"WBS has a number of manifestations, such as difficulty with language, mild mental retardation, and heart problems. It's caused when a series of repeating genes are deleted at a place on the chromosome 7 called band q11.23. This region is prone to deletion because it's bounded by blocks of DNA that are very similar to one another. But for your sons, rather than a deletion there are many additional *repeats*. Instead of retarding their development, it's possible, and I'm reaching a bit here, that this might have led to *heightened* abilities."

"Edward's a gifted musician," Deborah said. "Paul was brilliant before his troubles started. He spoke four languages before he was ten. But what's the significance of this?"

"Your boys have a uniparental disomy at chromosome 7 with what appears to be a highly unusual augmentation," she said, placing her hand on Deborah's, "but neither chromatid came from you or your husband. They are completely foreign."

"So, you're saying…."

"Your sons have a chromosome that came from someone else."

46

Deborah stared back at Dr. Slater. "What do you mean, someone else? That's impossible."

"The seventh chromosome in your boys is not from you or their father. I don't know how, but somehow new DNA was substituted before the embryos were implanted in your uterus."

"Then where did it come from?"

"From another person, Deborah. No one can build a complete human chromosome."

"How can you be so sure? Maybe it--I don't know the right words--mutated?"

"Impossible. That chromosome has 159 million base pairs and 862 individual genes. It wasn't constructed. It didn't appear by accident. I'm so sorry to have to tell you this."

"So, you're saying that my boys have a third parent? Another father?"

"Or mother. We don't know the sex of the donor, but the entire chromosome came from one person. Its two chromatids are nearly identical."

Deborah struggled with her emotions. She'd wanted evidence to punish the person or people who had doomed her children. Now she'd just learned that her boys weren't entirely hers and Scott's, at least biologically. It was the most painful, intimate violation imaginable.

"Deborah, tell me everything you can remember from when the boys were conceived."

Deborah took a moment to compose herself. "There's not much to tell," she said with difficulty. "Scott came home one day and said that Claude knew a fertility specialist that could help us. Our doctor collected eggs and sperm from us. Scott gave them to Claude's contacts. We were sworn to secrecy. They implanted the fertilized embryos about three weeks later."

"That's a long time," Slater said. "I wonder why it took so long?"

"Scott told me they'd been sent to a special lab in Lexington, Kentucky. That's where the work was done."

"What did they tell you they were going to do? What could they offer that a fertility clinic couldn't?"

"Scott went on and on about this scientist that Claude had set up with his own lab. They supposedly had special capabilities to produce healthy, viable embryos. It was outside the health care system, of course, totally secret. Claude was doing us this big favor. It cost a fortune, but we decided it was worth it."

"Maybe they saw something abnormal in the DNA you sent them. Maybe they thought

KEVIN BOREEN

the pregnancy would be more successful if they swapped in another chromosome."

"Without telling us?" Deborah said. "Who were they to make that kind of a decision? It's outrageous!"

"It is. It really is." Dr. Slater was quiet for a moment. "If they were making these kinds of radical changes, it might well have caused unintended damage in other chromosomes. I can't prove that, but it's entirely possible."

"They shouldn't have been gambling with my children's lives in the first place. I'm going to hold them accountable if it's the last thing I do."

"I'm wondering, Deborah. Were there other mothers? If we could look at the genomes of other affected children—"

"There were." Deborah looked closely at Slater. "And you just said *we*. Are you offering to work with me on this? It could get very difficult. The reporter you met, Tom, has disappeared. I've been warned. We don't know what these people might do to stop us."

"I don't think I really have a choice at this point. It's my duty to help you. The potential consequences of this for our *species* is almost beyond imagination, especially if they've kept advancing. We need to find out what's happened here, for your boys and for any others that might be affected."

Deborah thought about her call with

271

Amy. Tom had been investigating Claude's friends and their children. She knew at least some of them had used the same service. Amy's files would contain others. "I think I can get you at least a partial list."

"If we could check those children and see if there were other manipulations…"

"We'll have to be careful. We have to protect these families. We can't upend their lives."

"Let's take this one step at a time. Get the list. Then we'll come up with a plan."

"Yes, we will. And Doctor…thank you."

Deborah walked out of the hospital in a daze. She had so much to process. She dreaded having to deal with her husband later that night, but he'd have jet lag. She'd be able to put off any serious discussions until tomorrow.

What mattered now was to find out what had happened to her sons.

47

The following morning, Amy took a train to Greenwich Station and then an Uber to the Fiske estate. The car pulled into the circular driveway and stopped in front of an impressive entrance. The gravel extended all the way to the stone front of the mansion, much like English manor houses she'd seen on television dramas. Though the lawns, trees, and shrubs were beautifully maintained, Amy thought there was something austere, even sad, about the place.

A man stepped forward and opened the car door. "Miss Klar?"

"Yes," she said, climbing out. "Please, I'm Amy. I'm here to see Mrs. Fiske."

"Of course. She's waiting for you in the conservatory. I'll show you the way."

Amy took her box out of the back seat and followed the man inside. They passed through a marble foyer into a great hall with a massive stone fireplace. It opened to the left, where they entered a bright room with expansive windows looking out over a colorful garden. A black concert grand piano dominated the center of the room.

Deborah rose upon seeing her. Amy had seen photos of her, but none had done her justice. She was a striking woman, tall and well-proportioned with luxuriant dark hair and bright green eyes. Only the dark circles beneath them betrayed the pressures she was under.

"Thank you for coming all this way," Deborah said. "I've been so busy. This is an enormous help. Please, let's sit by the window."

She guided her to two white couches arranged perpendicularly in a corner.

Amy placed the box on the floor and sat, tucking one leg under her. "Have you heard anything from Tom?"

"No. I take it that you haven't either."

Amy shook her head. "I called the police. At this point they said there's nothing they can do. They say he'll probably just turn up, or that he may not want to be found."

Deborah took a deep breath and looked directly at her. "I think something happened to him in Lexington."

"Britt and I feel the same way, but we don't have a shred of proof."

"Is Britt another intern?"

"No," Amy said with a quick laugh.

"What's so funny?"

"When you meet her, you'll understand. She's a close friend of Tom's. She flew up to see him this weekend, but…"

"So, she must be as worried as we are."

"She is, and she wants to help."

"Then please bring her along the next time we meet. We can use all the help we can get." Deborah's eyes fell to the box. "I take it these are Tom's research notes?"

"Yes. We researched the fathers in a photo that Tom had taken at an art show in Miami, and then their children. It proved to be quite an exceptional collection of people. You might say it was all too good to be true, but we didn't know where to go with it until you called."

"Tom had left me a message, and then I heard that he was also contacting other friends. I knew someone who was about to go through this herself and felt I had to do something. But why isn't the magazine pursuing this? It's such an important story."

"I know. It's so frustrating." Amy shook her head. "I understand there's a tension between the ideals of journalism and running a business. *Future* is a small, private company. A man like Claude Dumont is extremely influential among its readership, and its advertisers. The owner thinks the risks to himself and the magazine outweigh the benefits."

"Well, I think he's a coward." Deborah folded her hands in her lap and shook her head. "Anyway, Amy, thank you for dropping them off. They're very timely, because we need to…"

A tall, elderly man wearing a silk

bathrobe and slippers walked into the room. He nodded to Deborah and smiled thinly at Amy. "I didn't know we had a visitor."

"Amy, this is my husband, Scott." Turning to her husband, she said, "Amy was just dropping off some things for me."

"Nice to meet you, Amy," Scott said.

"And you," Amy said, standing to face Scott. "I was just leaving. Deborah, please call me if I can be of any help. Any help at all."

An urgent meeting in Manhattan postponed the conversation about the future of their marriage, to Deborah's relief. After Scott left for his office, she opened the box. An envelope on top contained Amy's contact information. The young woman had made a strong, positive impression, and Deborah was glad to have her as an ally. She smiled and set it aside. The box contained about thirty manila file folders. Some were focused on the older men, Claude's friends. Others held summaries for each of the children. Deborah had met many of them, but not all. The remaining folders had detailed notes on each child. The tabs showed their names, dates-of-birth, and current places of residence. It was far more than she could have hoped for.

Her next step was clear. Somehow, they needed to collect DNA from these children to

KEVIN BOREEN

look for genetic modifications, and the sooner, the better. Deborah sorted the folders of the children into two piles: local and distant. Fortunately, while most lived hundreds or even thousands of miles away, four were close by.

Deborah called Dr. Slater. "I've made progress. We need to talk."

"I've got appointments until 5, but I'm free after that."

"I'll meet you at the hospital, and I'm bringing friends."

While Deborah now had a lot of information about the other children, that was a far cry from having DNA samples. Simply asking for genetic material was out of the question. The families would refuse, and Scott would be furious if learned of it. She was going to need help.

She dialed Amy.

"I was hoping you'd call," Amy answered.

"I'm sorry our meeting here was cut short. My husband's very suspicious."

"I sensed that."

"Where are you now?"

"I'm at the train station."

"In Greenwich?"

"Yes. I just missed the last one."

"We've learned some things that could deeply affect the families you were investigating. I can't talk about it over the phone. I'm meeting with someone, an expert, at 5 p.m. at McAllister Hospital today. Is there any chance you could stay in town and join us?"

"Absolutely. I'll be there. Do you mind if I bring Britt? I've told her everything I know, and she has a name for us, someone Tom was trying to find in Kentucky."

"That would be fine. What was the name?"

Deborah heard some paper shuffling.

"Renard Bergeron."

Deborah caught her breath. Why was that name so familiar? "Does Britt know anything about him?"

"Just that a breeding specialist told Tom that Bergeron was his point of contact on the Dumont farm."

Deborah strained to remember. It had been almost twenty years ago, but the doctor had had a French accent. Could it be the same man?

Deborah gave Amy the hospital's address. "We need to know more about the daily movements of the sons and daughters who live nearby. Do you have any suggestions?"

"The first thought that comes to mind is that we could hire private detectives. We've used them on other stories. I know some that I trust."

"Could you please reach out to them? When we meet, I'll give you the names that I think we should start with."

"It'll be expensive."

"Amy, sometimes I feel like I don't have much, but the one thing I do have a lot of is money. And since we're hiring detectives, do you think they could help us find Tom?"

"No guarantees, but they might." Amy paused for a moment. "If you don't mind, though, let's use separate agencies. I don't think we want to connect these two lines of inquiry. At least, not yet."

"I am so glad I called you, Amy. I'll see you and Britt at five. And thank you."

48

Claude stopped at the entrance to Nadine's dressing room and leaned against the door jamb, watching her. The cream-colored room was fifteen feet wide and thirty long, the high walls lined with clothes on hangers, drawers, shelves, mirrors, and shoe racks. A long couch ran down the center on the left, a white marble counter on the right. They terminated together at her vanity. Behind it the wall supported her considerable collection of purses, scarves, and jewelry, not including some valuable pieces they kept secure in the safe in his study. But the greatest treasure in the room, he knew, was his wife, who was selecting outfits and accessories with her typical focus and concentration.

"Packing already?" he said.

She looked up at him and smiled. She was holding a long blue dress that he hadn't seen before, no doubt a recent purchase. "It's hard to believe we're leaving so soon."

They were spending their Christmas at Vaux-le-Vicomte again this year. When the children were young, they had always enjoyed the holidays at the Kentucky farm, but when Chase and Audrey started school in Switzerland it became more convenient to meet at the chateau. Now it was a cherished family tradition.

"I assume Chase and Audrey are bringing friends?" Claude said.

"Yes," Nadine replied as she picked up another dress and examined it. "You remember Denisa?"

"From two years ago. Yes, a lovely girl. Czech, if I recall."

"Right. She and Audrey are flying back tomorrow for a wedding, so we'll have an evening with them."

"Wonderful."

"And Chase has invited Eric and his mother. You know that his father passed last year?"

"Yes, I remember. Poor man. I'm glad they can join us."

"Chef is preparing the menus if you want to check them."

"I'm more than happy to enjoy whatever he prepares for us. One doesn't question genius."

"I sometimes do," she said, grinning at him. "I got a call from Marie yesterday. She and Etienne will spend the Monday night after Christmas with us, and Johann and Elsa come on Tuesday."

Claude nodded, pleased with the news. Etienne Bardin was the current President of France. They had become close when Etienne was the Minister of Agriculture. Johann Lenz, one of Claude's protégés, was the lead conductor for the Berlin Philharmonic Orchestra, and his wife, Elsa, was the recently elected leader of Germany's Christian Democratic Party.

"I'd better freshen up my chess game," Claude said, still lingering in the doorway.

"You're always welcome to visit my dressing room, but is something on your mind?" She sat on the couch and patted the leather beside her.

He sat. "I just got a call from the police department in Lexington. They're trying to locate that reporter, Tom Wright."

"Why would you know where he is?"

"Exactly."

"Why call you in the first place?"

"I asked them that. Apparently, the morning he went missing he'd told a friend of his, a woman named Nielsen, that he was working on a story about the farm. When she couldn't reach him later, she contacted the police. They found his rental car. Evidently he'd been in some sort of minor collision."

"You told them what happened?"

"Not every detail, but enough to allay their concerns. They were very professional. It was a friendly call."

"I'm sure he's lying on a beach somewhere."

"I said that was my guess. I'm sure that's the end of it as far as we're concerned."

She rested her hand on his. "You did the right thing paying him off, Claude. Everyone's grateful to be rid of him. That story could have been so awkward."

Claude patted her hand and stooped to give her a kiss as he stood. "We'll have a beautiful Christmas, won't we?"

"The best ever." She smiled up at him, so beautiful that it almost hurt.

He smiled at her from the doorway. "I'm the luckiest man alive, darling."

49

Deborah went into her husband's study, entered the ten-digit combination to their safe, and pulled open the heavy steel door. The interior space was about the size of a standard home dishwasher, divided by shelves, sliding drawers, and cubbies. Behind a box of jewelry and their wills, she found and removed a small leather chest. It was filled with bound stacks of one-hundred-dollar bills. Deborah guessed there were a hundred in each stack. She took five of them and slipped them into her purse. She closed the safe and went straight to her waiting car.

It was a short drive to the hospital. She was at once determined, nervous, and excited. After years of doubt, suspicion, and the pain that only a mother can feel at the suffering of her child, she finally felt she was getting traction.

She arrived a few minutes early, eager to meet with Dr. Slater. She collected her purse and a leather briefcase and entered the lobby.

The receptionist told her that Dr. Slater would be right down. As Deborah turned toward the waiting area, Amy bounded through the

KEVIN BOREEN

door, followed by a tall blonde that Deborah vaguely recognized from fashion magazines.

"Deborah," Amy said, her eyes bright. "This is Britt Nielsen, Tom's friend."

"You look familiar to me," Deborah said to the tall blonde.

"Fewer and fewer people tell me that nowadays," Britt said with a modest grin. Then she touched Deborah's arm. "Thank you for letting me join you."

Deborah patted Britt's hand and turned to Amy. "Any luck with your investigators?"

"Yes, with both firms. I told the first everything we know about Tom's trip." She winced slightly. "They're asking for a ten-thousand-dollar retainer."

"That's no problem. And the children?"

"All they need are the names, addresses, and phone numbers. They can start first thing in the morning. They want five thousand upfront. I hope that's okay."

"That's fine." Deborah reached into her purse and took out four of the bundles. "That's forty K. Whatever happens, I want you to keep pursuing this to the very end. That means finding Tom Wright and following up with these kids. Use this to pay for detectives, travel, and any other expenses you might incur. Don't worry about receipts. Spend whatever you need."

Amy looked at the bound stacks, looked to

285

Britt, and then back at Deborah. "I'm sorry. I've never seen this much money! You don't want to keep the other twenty-five? Spend it if and when we need to?"

"Please take it now. I'll feel a lot better knowing you have it."

As Amy slipped the bills into her backpack, Dr. Slater appeared in the hallway and waved them forward. Deborah made introductions and they returned to the same conference room where she and Slater had met the day before. A fourth chair had been added.

"Amy has provided detailed files on the children that Claude Dumont may have genetically altered," Deborah began as they sat around the table.

"Wait just a minute." Britt leaned forward. "Genetically altered?"

"What's that supposed to mean?" Amy asked, looking at Deborah and then Dr. Slater.

Deborah removed a thin file from her briefcase. "Dr. Slater discovered recently that an entire chromosome in the DNA of each of my sons is not from me, my husband, or any combination of the two of us."

Britt and Amy exchanged glances.

"That means," Deborah continued, "that someone put it there before the embryo was implanted."

"Oh my God," Amy said. "We suspected some kind of secret in vitro clinic for the ultra-rich, but this is horrific. Mrs. Fiske…Deborah, I am so sorry. I can't imagine how you feel."

"From the expression on your face, I think you understand exactly how I feel."

Britt said, "So, is this connected to Tom's interest in Roger Bergeron? Is he some kind of genetics expert?"

"I've never heard of him," Dr. Slater said. "Anyone doing this level of work would be widely known in our field."

"That name is so familiar to me," Deborah said, "but I can't quite place it. Could it be the same man that I met at *Les Champs* eighteen years ago?"

"You said you'd made progress on a list," Slater said.

Deborah took a single sheet of paper from a file and slid it across the table. "These four are local. I thought they'd be our best opportunities to get samples."

"And the others?" Britt asked.

"I have some thoughts on that," Deborah replied, "but with these we can at least test our hypothesis."

"I agree." Slater glanced down the list. "This is a great start. Two females, two males. Ages fifteen to seventeen. All in Fairfield or Westchester counties."

"The problem is," Deborah said, "I have no idea how to get a DNA sample."

"I can help there," Slater said, sitting

back. "When I was doing my post-grad work in Stockholm, I assisted local detectives in cases that involved DNA-based evidence. This isn't going to be as hard as you think."

"So, we need hair samples, that kind of thing?" Britt asked.

"Well, not broken hair, but hair follicles are rich in DNA. Skin, blood, saliva, and semen are also good sources."

"How about fingernails or toenails?" Amy asked. "We could pay a salon worker to save them for us."

"That could work. The nails themselves are dead keratin, a protein, but they start as living cells. DNA extraction is more complex, but I can use special reagents to tease out what we need. So, yes, salons and spas are good options, at least for the girls. If any of them smoke, a cigarette butt could have traces of their saliva. So would a popsicle stick or a straw. You get the idea."

"Okay," Deborah said, "We'll have to be opportunistic." She turned to Amy. "Give these four names to your detectives. Tell them this is important and that we need information about their routines as quickly as they can get it."

"Do you want them to collect the samples too?"

"No." Deborah sighed. "I don't even know if this is legal. We can't take the risk of getting turned in before we even start."

"It probably won't be admissible as evidence," Slater said, "but at least we'll know what we're dealing with."

"Which means that we may need to collect them ourselves," Deborah said. "Based on what the detectives tell us, we can decide which of us is the best position to get them."

"Count me in," said Britt.

"Me too," Amy quickly added.

Deborah's cell phone started to ring. Concerned that it might be about her son, she apologized as she rifled through her purse. The screen said: NADINE DUMONT. Eyebrows raised, she showed it to the others, then answered.

"Deborah Fiske."

"Hi, Deborah. It's Nadine Dumont. I hope I'm not interrupting anything."

"What can I do for you?"

"Well, it's not anything like that. In fact, it's quite the opposite. Claude and I were talking just now and wondered how things are going with the twins."

"We've had some problems recently," Deborah said, wondering where this was going. "I'm sorry, but this isn't a good time to go into that."

"Look, Deborah, I'll get right to the point. We'd like to help. Claude and I were hoping that we could come out and see you. We have some ideas we'd like to share."

Deborah covered the phone and mouthed

they want to meet with me to the others. As suspicious as she was of their true motives, perhaps she could learn more about Tom's visit to the farm, or even ask about Bergeron. She assumed that if they wanted to come out to see her, they must already be in Manhattan. "How about if I come to you?"

"Well, sure," Nadine readily agreed. "We're here all week. Yes, that would be great."

"What's a good time?"

"We'll be home Wednesday evening, if that works for you. You've been here before, right?"

"Well, actually, I don't think I have, but I know the building. I'll stop by around 8 p.m."

"Wonderful. Penthouse 95. It's been too long, Deborah. See you soon!"

50

Amy had thought long and hard about what to tell the detectives about their project. She had settled on a scenario very close to the truth: a complex paternity suit that might require DNA samples from four young adults. She told them there were many uncertainties, that some of the subjects were suspected but not confirmed, and that millions of dollars could be at stake. She had asked them to identify the best collection opportunities. They had done their work, and she was not disappointed.

The following morning, they convened at Deborah's house to make their plans. Of the four local offspring, one of the boys, Ahmet Darwish, was home for the next two weeks. The other was skiing in Switzerland, so he was out of this round. Because Deborah had met both girls, she would try to get a sample from Ahmet, while Amy picked Arya Mukerjee and Britt took Olivia Hastings.

Amy didn't know how the detectives had managed it, but they had obtained, perhaps from her phone or through social media, Arya's schedule for the next three days. Most promising was a hair appointment that afternoon at a salon called Sonya & Company in Scarsdale. A quick Google search showed that it has been voted "best in Westchester County." It was just a few miles from the Mukerjee estate. The website listed the full staff of the salon. Amy copied the photo of an attractive middle-aged woman named Greta, the stylist scheduled to blow-dry Olivia's hair.

Amy stopped at a gift shop in Scarsdale and selected a small crystal flower vase, which the owner was happy to gift wrap for her.

"Would you like a card for this?" the woman asked.

"Yes, please. And could I borrow a pen?"

"Of course."

Amy wrote Greta's name on the envelope but didn't fill out the card. She paid the owner in cash and continued to the hair salon. It was easy to find, its name printed in bold white letters on a black awning. She parked on the street and entered the premises. The receptionist, seated behind a white marble counter beneath a bright chandelier, held up her hand in greeting and quickly wrapped up her phone call.

"Hi! Do you have an appointment?"

"No. I have something for Greta. Is she here today?"

"She certainly is. Can I pass it along for you?"

KEVIN BOREEN

"It's a gift. I'd like to give it to her myself. Would that be okay?"

"I'm sure it would be. Who turns down a gift?" The receptionist laughed. "I'll let her know you're here."

Amy recognized Greta working a few chairs away. She looked a little older than in her photo. She was busily chatting with her client as she finished up. She seemed to be a friendly, talkative sort of woman. Amy noticed that she didn't wear anything on her ring finger. She took a seat by the reception desk.

The receptionist returned and said, "She's almost done. It'll just be a minute or two. Can I get you some coffee? Espresso? Mineral water?"

"No, but thank you. Very kind."

The customer rose from her chair, handed Greta some bills, and left the salon with goodbyes to all. Greta followed her to the door, smiling warmly, and then looked to the receptionist who, in turn, nodded toward Amy.

Greta held her smile. "Hi. Can I do something for you?"

"No," Amy said, standing. "I have something for you, though." She held up the wrapped box. "It's from a mutual friend. She asked me to give you a message."

Greta extended her hands. "Who is it?"

"It's personal. Could we speak privately? It'll just take a minute."

Greta checked her watch. "I have a few

293

minutes before my next appointment. Come on back. We can use the office."

Amy followed her to the back of the shop. No one seemed to take any notice. They stepped into a windowless room made pleasant by a few fresh flower displays and a large Monet print on one of the walls. Amy closed the door and handed Greta the box.

"This is all very mysterious," Greta said with a grin. "Should I open it now?"

"Please."

Greta started with the card. Inside were twenty hundred dollar bills. Greta's mouth opened in silent surprise. She looked up at Amy. "What's all this?"

Amy had rehearsed her approach many times. "I'm a private investigator. I'm working for Arya's mother, Anika Mukerjee."

"I know Anika. Arya's my next client."

"I know. Mrs. Mukerjee told us. That's why I'm here."

"I don't understand."

"Mrs. Mukerjee is being blackmailed. They're claiming that her husband, Pratul, is not Arya's true father."

"That poor woman," Greta gasped, a look of horror on her face.

"Our hope is that we can prove that he *is* her father. Then we can go to the authorities and try to catch these criminals."

"What has this got to do with me?"

KEVIN BOREEN

"We need a sample of Arya's hair. If we can test it, we may be able to make all of this go away. We're offering to pay you $2000 for that sample."

"Just for a strand of hair?"

"It has to be a complete strand, with the follicle attached."

"You're talking about a...small piece of scalp?"

"Yes. That's all we need. I'll wait outside. When you're done, just put the hair back into that envelope and bring it out to me. I'm in a white Jeep just to the left of the entrance."

Greta looked at the money and then back at Amy. "I think I should call Mrs. Mukerjee about this before I say yes."

"You could certainly do that, Greta, but I imagine that would be very embarrassing for her, particularly since we don't know the answer."

"What answer?"

"Whether her husband is indeed the father of their daughter..." Amy paused to let that sink in.

Greta raised her hand to her mouth. "Is that even a possibility?"

Amy cast down her eyes briefly before looking back up at her. "She hired us for a reason, Greta."

"Couldn't Anika just give you a DNA sample directly? I mean, why me?"

295

"I'm sure you can understand that we're shielding her for now from any direct involvement. This may or may not end up in court, and she doesn't want to have to tell her daughter someday that she gave her DNA to investigators. Again, our hope is that we can just make all of this go away. She asked us to take care of this phase with the utmost discretion. She doesn't know that I'm here or what I'm asking you to do, but you'll be doing her an enormous favor. No one will ever know about your involvement."

Greta nodded her head slowly. "Yes, I guess I understand. That poor, kind lady. All right. I'll help you."

The salon manager stuck her head into the office. "Greta, your appointment's here."

"I'm on my way," Greta said.

"I'll be just outside," Amy reminded her.

"I'll be out in thirty minutes."

"Thank you."

Amy walked toward the front entrance and passed shoulder to shoulder with Arya as she waved to Greta. Arya was a stunning young Indian woman with gorgeous black hair, large brown eyes, and full lips. As Amy thanked the receptionist for her help and stepped onto the sidewalk, she recalled Pratul Mukerjee's photos from the dossier she'd created days earlier. Arya looked just like him.

51

Britt Nielsen made a 2 p.m. pedicure appointment at Elegance Nail & Spa. Olivia Hastings was booked for a mani-pedi at 3 o'clock, allowing Britt some time to check out the salon before Olivia arrived.

The front of the building faced Garth Street. The entrance was set back in an alcove between brick buildings, its glass front framed in dark green. All the parking spots were taken so she drove behind the building and parked on Grayrock. She walked back around the block and climbed the steps to the entrance.

The large facility was tastefully appointed. She was greeted and led to one of several faux leather chairs mounted on white, wave-like platforms. The foot basins were of a translucent amber material. It was every bit as nice as the nail salons she frequented in Manhattan and Miami, and she always chose the best.

Her pedicurist was an older Asian woman named Namjoo. The woman seemed shy and withdrawn, not making eye contact, but she clearly knew what she was doing. Britt leaned back in her chair, observing the shop and enjoying her session. The time passed quickly. At 1:45 p.m., Olivia Hastings walked into the salon speaking animatedly with another teenaged girl. They were directed to a comfortable sitting area clearly visible from Britt's chair. The friend with Olivia looked familiar. Where had she seen her before? The she remembered. Britt pulled out her phone and discreetly took a photo, which she texted to Amy with the note: IS THIS AUDREY DUMONT?!!

A moment later, her phone vibrated in her hand.

YES!!!

Britt felt her pulse quicken. They had assumed that Audrey was still at Oxford, but she must have flown home for some reason. This was the best possible stroke of luck. If Audrey had the same mutation on chromosome 7, it would not only tie her to the other children but also potentially tie all the children one or both of her parents. It was hard to imagine that a man like Dumont would substitute the chromosomes of someone else in his own child.

As Namjoo removed cotton from between Britt's freshly painted toes, Britt leaned forward and whispered, "Excuse me."

The woman stopped what she was doing and looked up. "Yes?"

Britt smiled warmly and said, "Look, I

need your help with something." Britt looked side to side. No one was seated within hearing distance. "I'm prepared to pay you a great deal of money for something that you'll otherwise just end up throwing away."

Namjoo looked back at her with a blank expression.

"I'm a...pharmaceutical representative. Don't look just yet, but there are two young women sitting by the window. I've been watching them, and I'm concerned they may be suffering from a genetically based disease that's one of my specialties."

"Really?" Namjoo's eyes slid to the girls and then back to Britt, her face still expressionless.

"I don't want to alarm them unnecessarily."

Namjoo continued to stare at her.

"I need to conduct some tests first. To do it, I just need the waste from their pedicure: any skin or nail clippings you can provide. I need it for each of them, and I'll need to know who each is from. Do you understand?"

"This is very strange. No one has ever asked me this before."

"I understand. I sincerely hope this amounts to nothing, but if I'm right, you'll be doing those girls a big favor. Here," Slater said, taking her wallet from her purse to let the woman see that her wallet was stuffed with bills.

"How much?" Namjoo asked.

"One hundred dollars each, so two hundred together."

Namjoo lowered her voice. "I could get fired for this."

"It's stuff you'd just throw away. No one will ever know."

Namjoo met Britt's gaze and leaned closer, lowering her voice. "I know who you are, and I don't believe your story, but…I'll do it for five hundred each. A thousand for both."

Britt had been prepared to pay far more than that. "Okay. Half now, half when you give me the samples."

"Where will you be?"

"I'm parked right behind this building."

Namjoo nodded in silence. Britt could almost see her mind working. The pedicurist whispered, "I have a better idea. When you leave, take your wallet but leave your purse behind the chair. Come back in one hour and tell the receptionist you left your bag. They'll return it to you. The samples will be inside. The blonde girl will be in plastic, and the brown-haired one will be in a brown paper towel."

Britt was impressed.

"Then you'll give me the rest of the money as a thank you gift for finding your Louis Vuitton." Namjoo smiled for the first time and gave a small bow. "Most generous of you."

52

Deborah found Ahmet Darwish on the tennis court at the Old Greenwich Tennis Academy. He was taller than she'd imagined, broad-shouldered and lean. He was at the net, volleying against an instructor who was holding nothing back, a cart of tennis balls at his elbow. She would have been terrified to have balls coming at her at that velocity, but Ahmet moved with a powerful, fluid grace, returning each shot with precision. Occasionally his instructor would lunge for one of them, but while she was watching none were returned.

She was wearing a tennis outfit she hadn't worn in years. She'd once enjoyed the game but hadn't had time since the boys got sick. She noticed a few men casting glances at her. She wasn't sure how she was going to get a sample from Ahmet. As he raced around the court, he sometimes seemed almost close enough for her to reach out and touch him. Could you get a DNA sample from a tennis ball? From a towel?

The two players approached each other at the net and walked to a bench between the courts. Ahmet opened his tennis bag and took out a water bottle. Dr. Slater had said something about saliva. That might be her best option. Would she have to steal his entire bag? Could she reach inside it and take out the bottle without being noticed?

Her heart sank when Ahmet threw his empty water bottle into a mesh metal garbage can by the net. It was full of identical bottles. She'd never know if she had the right one. The two men returned to the court and started slamming ground shots back and forth. She started to panic. Could she grab him by the hair and run out of the building? Scratch him, drawing blood? She shook her head. As much as she wanted his sample there was no way she was going to hurt that young man.

She felt her phone vibrate in her pocket and saw that it was from Amy. She answered, turning away from the courts.

"Any luck on your end?" Amy asked.

"No. I'm at my wits end. How about you?"

"Bingo. I got follicles and Britt scored at the nail salon."

"That's great!"

"It's better than that. Guess who was with Olivia at the salon?"

"Just tell me."

"Audrey Dumont!"

"And we've got her sample too?"

302

"We did."

Deborah immediately grasped the significance, pumping her fist as if she were at Wimbledon. "Where are you now?"

"I'm meeting Dr. Slater at the hospital to deliver our samples. She'll run the tests tonight."

"I'm sorry I don't have anything for you yet."

"I think we have enough. Why don't you get some sleep? We can meet in the morning when Slater has the results. I'll call you as soon as I hear anything."

"Thanks, Amy." Deborah felt a wave of relief. "You're terrific."

"So are you, Deborah. See you tomorrow."

Deborah ended the call, her mind racing. Audrey's DNA could be the key to everything. She walked away from the tennis courts and didn't look back.

53

The three of them met in the lobby of McAllister Hospital the following morning. Dr. Slater looked tired, but Deborah could tell immediately that she had important news.

"I've examined all three samples," Slater said as soon as she closed the door of the conference room. "All three have the same chromosome 7, the same as your boys."

Deborah realized she had been holding her breath. "That proves that Dumont and his scientists have been editing genes."

"Absolutely," Slater agreed.

"And it tells us that at least some of the genetic material came from a common donor," Amy added.

"That's right," said Slater. "There's no possibility that anyone could synthesize an entire chromosome. It was taken from a particular human's genome."

"Does it matter whose it was?" Amy asked. "We now know who's responsible. We know what they've done."

"The families should be told," Slater said.

"Will they want to know?" Britt asked. "Some might not."

"I don't think we have a choice," Dr. Slater said. "We simply don't know what this will mean for the affected children as they age, and for the generations that will follow them. They have to be warned. Whether they want to know or not, they *need* to know."

"Which means we have to tell Claude Dumont," Britt added.

Deborah was already relishing the prospect of confronting him after all these years, but she knew her enemy. "Of course, he'll claim he didn't know what his clinic was actually doing."

"Audrey and her brother, Chase, are the oldest of the offspring that we've identified," Slater said, thinking aloud. "Both twins have the uniparental chromosome. I'm speculating here, but if Claude and Nadine turned to science for help with their conception, and in the process found that one of them had a fortuitous mutation on that chromosome—"

Amy said, "We still don't know whether the genetic material came from Claude or his wife."

Slater paused. "There are several possibilities. First, they could have taken either Claude's or his wife's chromosome 7 chromatid, cloned it, and combined them to create the uniparental chromosome common to all the children. Or it could be that either Mr. or Mrs. Dumont already has this mutation, and, because it worked, they used that version to create subsequent embryos."

"Or," Britt said, "it's still possible that the genetic material came from someone else."

"I wonder if Sue Miller's baby has the same modification," said Deborah.

"Are we going to tell her too?" Amy asked.

"I wish there was some way to know without involving her at this point," Deborah said. "It's her precious baby. We have no proof that it's affected."

"Could you live with yourself if you kept this from her?" Britt asked.

Deborah lowered her gaze. It was a terrible decision to have to make, but the future mother had a right to know. She nodded.

"It won't be safe to test her baby until eight weeks," Slater cautioned.

Deborah rested her chin on her hand. "If we could get DNA samples from Claude and Nadine and tie one of them directly to these children, it would be almost impossible to argue that neither of them knew anything about it. We'd have a more powerful case."

"Both legally and in the court of public opinion," Slater agreed.

"You're going to their house tonight, right?" Amy said.

"Yes, after dinner."

"If you could take a hairbrush, a toothbrush…"

"I've been thinking the same thing." Deborah made her decision. Whatever the Dumonts had in mind for their meeting, she would get DNA samples from them, no matter what it took.

But first, she would see Sue Miller.

54

Sue Miller stared back at Deborah, both of their faces wet with tears. They were sitting side-by-side on a couch before the fireplace in their Park Avenue home, their hands intertwined, two glasses of mineral water resting untouched on the coffee table.

"Sue, I don't know if any of this affects your baby, but I thought you would want to know."

Sue reflexively touched her abdomen. "It's just too horrible to even think about. I never dreamed that they'd…add someone else's genes to ours." She winced.

Deborah nodded. "I feel the same way about the twins. It's a profound violation. I'm furious about it. I hope it doesn't apply to you, I really do."

"How do I find out if my baby is affected? Is there a test for this?"

"I asked the doctor who's helping us. You've got options. Amniocentesis can create complications if done before fifteen weeks. She recommended against it."

KEVIN BOREEN

"I'm not doing anything that could harm this child."

"I completely understand. She did say there's a non-invasive prenatal test you can have as soon as eight weeks after fertilization. If you want to talk to her, I'm sure she'll help you privately. I imagine you'll want to keep this to yourselves."

Sue's eyes opened wide and she seized Deborah's hand. "You can't tell Rick."

"That's completely your decision to make, but..."

"But what?"

"Don't you think he'd want to know?"

"That's not the question. He...we knew that modifications were going to be made. When you get right down to it, does it really matter if it's just a tweak or a whole section? Maybe we were naïve to think that small adjustments could make meaningful differences. Maybe whole chapters of the instruction manual needed to be replaced. I don't know anything about this." Sue tightened her grip on Deborah's hand. "I just want to have this child. The baby's going to be mine because I'm going to love it. People don't love their children any less if they are adopted. Why should this be any different?"

"It's different because adoption is a choice. You weren't given a choice."

"I can live with it." Sue closed her eyes. "Rick's a proud man. I don't know how he'd react to this. Eight weeks is well within the first trimester and...I don't even want to think about what he'd tell me to do."

Deborah leaned forward and hugged her, sad that this man had so much sway over her friend's life, sadly realizing that until very recently it had been something they had shared in common. "I'll respect your choice. I won't say a word."

"What are you going to do now?" Sue asked.

"I'm going to try to find the source of the foreign DNA."

"What's the point, Deb? What difference will it make?"

"Like I said, I hope none of this affects you and your baby. Maybe they figured it all out, found a better way. But these people need to be held accountable for what they've done. It's not just about my twins. Who knows how many families have been affected? These children have been *permanently* changed. They'll pass along these genes to their children and their grandchildren. They have a right to know what was done – what was *really* done – and what the effects may be in the long run. Claude Dumont can't be allowed to play God."

"Do you think he's the source?"

"It's a strong possibility, but I can't prove it. Not yet."

Sue turned to the cold fireplace. Quietly,

she said, "Rick would kill him."
        "He'd have to get in line."

55

When Deborah got back to her car, she checked per phone. Amy had called three times and left a voice-mail message. The detectives had information regarding Tom Wright. Deborah immediately called Amy back.

"Did they find him?"

"Not yet."

"What have they got?"

"Do you mind if I put you on speaker? I'm here with Britt."

"Sure. Of course."

"Hi, Deborah," Britt said as she joined.

"Well," Amy began, "they confirmed that Tom flew to Lexington. He rented a car and checked into a hotel called the Griffin Gate. They followed up on the Millers' hotel, a place called The Castle. Tom did show up on the security cameras, but he didn't appear to have any contact with them. Tom made a reservation at The Castle, but later called to cancel it. Now, get this: the hotel manager called Dumont to tell him about the private investigators, and Dumont contacted our PI's directly."

"That was pretty bold," Deborah said.

Amy continued, "Dumont admitted that Tom came to the horse farm, where Tom did meet very briefly with Sue and Rick. Dumont told the investigators that he felt his privacy, and that of his close friends, was being violated. He claims he paid Tom to drop the story. Dumont provided documentation showing a $10 million wire transfer going to a numbered account in Cayman. They're still trying to establish whether that account belongs to Tom, but I expect the records, if we can get them, will show that it does."

"I don't believe it," Britt said. "That just isn't Tom."

"Is there more?"

"A little. The afternoon Tom disappeared, he flew from Lexington to Miami on a chartered jet. He paid for the flight with his corporate credit card. The pilot didn't get a good look at his face, but the detective said that's not unusual. There were a few private credit card charges in his name in Miami. Then it looks like Tom chartered a boat. Late the next day the charter company got a call, supposedly from Tom, saying that he'd had a family emergency and had to leave the boat in Nassau. He left $5,000 in cash to pay the charter and recovery costs. That night $300,000 was withdrawn from the Cayman account. The trail goes cold there."

"So, the detectives think he's alive?"

"Or someone's going to a lot of trouble to make it look that way."

"I just met the man and barely know him," Deborah said, "but does this sound like something he'd do?"

"No, not at all," Amy said.

"Tom was financially well-off," Britt said. "He didn't need the money. Journalism was his life and passion. I don't believe for a second that he accepted any number of millions to drop this story. He was sure he was onto something big. And one more thing: a family emergency? Tom doesn't *have* any family."

"So, it's all a bunch of lies," Deborah said.

"It is," Britt said, "but who's telling it?"

Deborah squeezed the leather grip of her steering wheel as headlights passed in both directions. "I'm more worried about him now than ever."

"I agree," Britt said. "But if we don't believe that Tom disappeared with ten million…"

"Do we really think Claude Dumont would be willing to kill to keep his secret?" Amy asked, finishing the thought.

"I'm going up to see him now," Deborah said.

"Please be careful," Britt warned.

"I'm wondering if this meeting is such a good idea after all," said Amy.

"He's not stupid," Deborah said. "He's not going to do anything in his own home. Nadine will be there."

"Do you want us to wait for you outside the Dumont's building?" Amy asked. "We can be there in twenty minutes. 56th Street side?"

Deborah thought about that for a moment. How much risk was she really taking? She noted the time. "I think that might be a good idea. And Amy?"

"Yes?"

"If I'm not down within an hour, call the police."

56

Deborah pulled into the off-street apron at the 56th Street entrance to 432 Park Avenue and parked beside a Bentley.

An attendant quickly approached. "Sorry, you can't park there."

"I'm here to see Claude Dumont," she said coldly. "He's expecting me." She handed the attendant the keys and left him standing open-mouthed beside her car. *Good*, she thought. He would be a witness to her entering the building.

She announced herself to the concierge, a handsome Latino with steel gray hair and a crisp suit. Another witness. He directed her to the Dumont's elevator. The door slid open as she arrived. She stepped inside and felt the smooth acceleration of her ascent. She wasn't sure what to expect from the Dumonts tonight, but she knew their attempts to manipulate her would begin with the first words they spoke. Her plan was simple. She would put them at ease, then find an excuse to use their bathroom.

The elevator slowed almost imperceptibly, and the door opened. Both Claude

KEVIN BOREEN

and Nadine awaited her in the entryway, both smiling warmly.

"Deborah," Nadine said, advancing to her, "we're so glad you could stop by." She was wearing a black pantsuit, Claude gray slacks, a crisp white shirt, and a blue blazer. Nadine took her by the hand and led her to Claude, who touched her arm and kissed her check.

"You look fabulous," he said.

They led her into a spacious living room with a dazzling view of the Manhattan skyline. The last vestiges of twilight had almost faded from the horizon and the cityscape was alive with countless points of light. Deborah had the feeling that she was flying over the city.

"Would you like something to drink?" Claude asked.

"A glass of champagne would be nice," Deborah said, her mind on samples.

Claude raised his index finger and smiled. "I just might have some of that." He hastened from the room, moving with the ease of a man half his age.

Nadine led Deborah to two facing couches. They sat together, side by side.

"How are the twins?" Nadine asked, her eyes fixed on Deborah's.

Whatever this is about, Deborah thought, *it's starting*. Looking at Nadine, you'd think she'd thought of nothing over the past month but the fate of Deborah's boys.

"I don't know if you heard about Paul's last incident."

Nadine tilted her head. "No. What happened?"

Deborah gave her the short version of recent events: the change in medication, the self-attack at the hospital, the loss of his eye.

Nadine's hand rose spontaneously to her open mouth. "Oh my God! Deborah! How absolutely awful for you and Scott."

"Scott just got back from London."

"I know he's doing some important work for Claude—"

"More important than his family?"

Before Nadine could react, Claude entered the room with three flutes and a chilled bottle of Krug Clos du Mesnil. "Here we go. It's our last bottle of the 1990 vintage. I hope you'll love it as much as we do."

"Claude, Deborah just told me the most horrifying news."

Claude stopped, looking first to Deborah and then back at Nadine. "What is it? What's happened?"

"Paul had a bad reaction to his medication. He's lost an eye."

Claude sat slowly on the facing couch, placing the glasses and the bottle on the low table between them. "When did this happen? Why weren't we told?"

Deborah chose not to answer the second

question. "Two weeks ago."

"I assume he's getting the best possible care," Claude said, "but it there's anything we can do, anything at all…. but, the eye? What happened to it?"

"It was destroyed." Deborah lowered her eyes briefly and took a deep breath. "He tore it out with his own hand."

Claude reached out to touch Deborah. "I am so sorry. If I'd had any idea, I wouldn't have asked Scott to, well…"

"To what?" Deborah asked.

"He's selling some land for me in Australia. Vineyards."

"I'm sure he's grateful for the business."

"I'm the one that's grateful, Deb. He's the best there is."

Deborah didn't want to talk about Scott. Somehow, all the events of the past two weeks had to be connected. She'd met with Tom Wright. He'd either quit or been fired, and then disappeared. She'd been completely ostracized. Scott had filed for divorce, then changed his mind. Was it a coincidence he had done so after Claude offered a lucrative real estate deal? Was Scott supposed to control her? Keep her quiet? And now the Dumont's had invited her to their home. Why?

"You know, Deb," Claude was saying as he opened the champagne and poured, "they are doing amazing work with artificial eyes now. It's revolutionary, really. You just say the word and I'll make sure your son gets the highest priority, the best of the best."

"Thank you, Claude, but we need to get his meds right first."

Claude handed a flute to each of them and raised his. "To Paul's full and speedy recovery."

Nadine said, "We're your friends, and we're here for you. We heard that you and Scott were going through some things. We know how hard it must be with the boys, although we knew nothing about this latest…challenge. You shouldn't be going through this alone, and you won't if you'll let us help."

"I appreciate that." Deborah forced a thin smile. "One thing I could certainly use at the moment is the restroom."

"Oh, of course," Nadine said, rising as she pointed down the hallway. "Just past the elevator, first door on the left."

"Thank you." Deborah put her flute on the table and walked in the direction Nadine had indicated. She was grateful that they remained at the couches, talking in hushed tones. She passed the elevator and opened the next door. It was a spacious powder room richly appointed with plush towels, soaps, and moisturizers. Even at first glance, Deborah knew that they never used this room themselves. And even if they did, it was probably thoroughly cleaned every day. She waited a moment and flushed the toilet.

KEVIN BOREEN

There was no medicine cabinet. She lifted the cover of a small waste container: empty. She turned off the light and opened the door a crack. She could hear them talking in the living room, more animatedly than when she'd left. If she opened the door, they might not see her if they weren't looking in this direction. She pushed the door open more, and then fully. She stepped into the shadow of the hallway. They hadn't noticed her. The hall extended behind her and then turned left. She imagined that their bedroom suite was that way. She took a slow step back, then another, and turned the corner. She took off her shoes and rushed soundlessly down the hall.

She'd never been to their condo before. It was enormous. She passed a full kitchen, a dining room, some guest rooms, and a gigantic space that appeared to be a study. Ahead were closed double doors. She twisted the doorknob and entered their bedroom. Nightstands, lamps, a king-sized bed. A subtle scent of lavender. Two passages opened on the right. She guessed that they'd each have their own bathroom. She crossed the carpet. The first entryway opened to two rooms, one a dressing room and the other a bathroom. Clearly it was Claude's. The marble counter was clean except for an electric toothbrush and a razor beside the sink. She'd taken one step toward it when a voice behind her said, "Ah, here you are. We were wondering what happened to you."

She turned abruptly. It was Claude, an amused expression on his handsome face.

"I've told Nadine countless times that we should have a map for our house guests."

She hoped her fear appeared merely as embarrassment. She tucked a strand of hair behind her ear. "Yes, it's like a labyrinth."

"Fortunately, there's no minotaur," he said with a chuckle. "Here, let me show you the powder room. You must have walked right past it."

"Sorry about that."

"No problem at all." He stood aside so she could walk past him, but she noticed him checking out the room for anything amiss. If he was concerned, his voice didn't betray him. "Please don't forget what I said about that eye specialist, Deb."

"Thank you. I'll let you know."

"And feel free to wear your shoes in the house," he said behind her. "You don't need to carry them around like that."

Deborah felt the blood rise in her cheeks. She'd been caught snooping through their home. She hoped they wouldn't guess why. Not yet.

They walked the rest of the way back in silence, Deborah remembering at the last minute to pretend she needed the powder room. When she returned to the living room, Claude and Nadine were standing before the window.

Nadine asked, "Is everything okay?"

"I took a wrong turn."

"Happens all the time," Nadine replied warmly, and then her tone changed to one of concern. "You know, there *is* something that we wanted to discuss with you."

"Aside from helping me," Deborah said.

"That's right," Nadine said. "Since you're here, we understand that you've been in contact with a reporter named Tom Wright."

Deborah froze. *So, this is about Tom after all.*

"It's nothing for you to worry about," Nadine continued. "We just wanted you to know that he decided to drop the story he was working on. I can't say I'm sorry. It would have been awkward for many of us, including Paul and Edward. We're hoping we can all just move on now." Nadine looked directly into Deborah's eyes. "Can you do that?"

"Tom has disappeared," Deborah said. "Do you have any idea what happened to him?"

"He said he was going to take some time off," Claude said, suppressing a cough. "I don't blame him. He's sure to get that Pulitzer. He's single, and now he's got a few extra dollars. I'm sure he'll turn up eventually. The man has a great talent."

Deborah said, "Some people think something might have happened to him."

Nadine frowned. "What do you mean?"

"Some people think he was killed."

"Why would anyone think that?" Nadine protested, looking to Claude and then back again at Deborah.

"To protect secrets," Deborah said.

"What secrets?" Nadine scoffed.

Deborah glared at Nadine as she struggled to keep her composure. *What secrets?* Who did she think she was talking to? Nadine and Claude knew very well that Deborah herself had been to their so-called clinic, the one that no one could ever mention, the same clinic that Sue Miller had just visited. If they were willing to lie about *that*, they could very well be lying about Tom, and that meant that Deborah herself was partly responsible for his murder. She looked to Claude, who stood stone-faced, a flute of champagne lightly held in his long, manicured fingers. Yes, she had had enough. "You know very well *what secrets*. The hidden things you do for your *friends*, the things that you and Renard Bergeron did to my *boys*. What you did to *Tom*."

"Now, you...wait...just...one...minute!" Nadine seethed, jabbing her finger with each word. "You have no right to come into our home and make accusations like that. We asked you here to offer our *help*. This is how you repay us?"

"You asked me here to tell me Tom was out of the picture and that we should – how did you put it? – move on? Well, no one's moving on from Tom's murder! And we're not moving on while you continue to play God down in

324

Kentucky." Of course, she had suspected this for years. Now that she had the answers she had been seeking, she felt powerful. It felt good to be saying these things, things Deborah now knew to be true. She was so sick of the deception, the hubris, the payoffs, and now, tragically, a murder. "We know a lot more about your little side business than you think. Soon a lot more people are going to know."

"Deborah," Claude said from beside her, surprising her as he firmly clasped her upper arm. "Please be—"

Deborah tried to pull free, but his grip was strong. She'd never been restrained by a man before, and it infuriated her. She slapped him hard across the face, her fingernails catching his cheek. Three thin scrapes started to bleed. Claude stepped back, touching his face, seeing the blood on his fingers. Nadine lunged forward, pushing Deborah away from her husband.

"What are you doing!" Nadine screamed at her. "Get out of my house! I'm calling the police!"

"No," Claude said, taking a handkerchief from his breast pocket and holding it to his face. "No police. She's just upset. Let her go."

Deborah met his clear blue eyes. She couldn't tell if they held pity or menace.

"I'll get something for your face," Nadine said between clenched teeth, muttering angrily

LEGACY

under her breath as she went to the kitchen.

"She's very protective of me," Claude said evenly, continuing to watch Deborah. A moment passed in silence. "I think you know the way out." He turned and followed his wife.

Deborah got her breathing under control. Her head was surprisingly clear. She saw Nadine's empty champagne flute on the side table, picked it up, and put it in her purse. Then she went straight to the elevator and hit the down button.

She had a nervous moment passing the concierge on the ground floor, but the man just smiled and waved. So much for calling the police. Outside, she felt a wave of relief when she saw Britt and Amy waiting in a taxi. Britt got out and opened the door for her as she approached.

"Any luck?" Amy asked as Deborah slid into the back seat, followed by Britt.

Deborah didn't trust her voice yet, and she was too shaky to even think about driving. She opened her purse and handed Amy the flute. Amy held it up to the light and saw traces of lipstick. "Mrs. Dumont?"

Deborah nodded.

"I think it might be enough. What about him?"

Deborah held her left hand up to the light.

Amy saw the blood beneath her nails and gasped. "My God, Deborah, what have you done?"

57

The following morning, Maxim Fedorov sipped coffee on the steps of the Apple store on Fifth Avenue. The streets were crowded with cars, taxis, and pedestrians, a combination of people going to work and last-minute Christmas shoppers. Winter had finally arrived. Exhalations froze in the frigid air. Amidst the crowd he found who he was looking for, the tall man's silver hair visible before his face emerged and broke into a thin smile below his pencil-thin mustache. Claude was wearing a thick black scarf and a well-cut camel colored overcoat. Maxim noticed red scratches on his left cheek, partly hidden by a bandage.

"Mr. Dumont," Maxim said in greeting, "would you like a new razor for Christmas?"

Claude gave him a sideways glance as he guided him by the arm. "I'm hoping for something more than that. Come, let's walk in the park."

They crossed Grand Army Plaza and followed a narrow, paved path toward The Pond. When they were alone, Claude said, "That woman I told you about, Deborah Fiske, needs to be dealt with."

"She attacked you?"

"Yes, in our condo last night. But it's not that. She didn't mean to do it. It was an accident. But it's clear that she now knows far more than she should."

"Is there anything I should know?"

"Well, she has Renard's name. I have no idea how she got it. We just treated a woman, Sue Miller. Maybe she heard it from her. Obviously, Deborah knows what we do at the farm. I thought we had her under control, but last night convinced me that she's determined to expose us, as irrational as that is in terms of what's best for her and her family. I found her poking around the house last night. I don't know what she was trying to find."

"I'll have the house swept for bugs."

"I think that would be wise."

"Any thoughts on how and when?"

"I remember Scott telling me once that she drives like a demon. A collision with a heavy truck on the Merritt Parkway might be a simple solution. A hit and run, perhaps? But that's your department and I'll leave it to your discretion. As to when, I'd say sooner rather than later. Nadine and I leave for France in five days, so maybe wait until after we're gone?"

"That's next Wednesday."

"Yes, the 21st."

KEVIN BOREEN

"Consider it done. Is there anyone else to worry about?"

"Well, there's her husband, Scott, but he won't lift a finger. He might even be relieved. And then there are the boys, poor creatures, but in their reduced capacities, I don't think they'll be too affected. I'll make sure they are well cared for."

"I'm sorry, I meant to ask if the Fiske woman has been working with anyone other than Wright."

"I've had someone watching McAllister Hospital and the Fiskes' house in Connecticut. Recently she's been spending time with a socialite named Britt Neilson, a former model, and an intern at *Future* magazine named Amy Klar. Britt was a friend of Wright's, and Klar was working with him on a story about us."

They walked in silence for several paces.

"But let's restrict this to Fiske for now," Claude decided. "I hate the idea of taking someone's life unless it's absolutely necessary. The Fiske woman is a ticking time-bomb. The others have far less skin in the game. With her out of the way, I think they'll drop this."

"And if they don't?"

"We can deal with that if the time comes, but remember one thing."

"What's that?"

"They don't have a shred of evidence."

58

Renard Bergeron was completing some notes in his lab. He'd placed the enhanced horse embryo in a healthy young mare that afternoon. The procedure had gone flawlessly. Now they would wait for from 320 to 380 days for the foal to be born. It still struck him as odd that horses had such variable gestation periods. Then they would have to wait about eighteen months before they could start to train the young horse to race. Only then would they truly know whether they had succeeded. It was a long time to wait, but Claude had uncommon patience, one of many differences between him and Renard.

Ten years earlier, Renard had fully tested the limits of that patience. In fact, their partnership had almost come to an abrupt and final end. Renard remembered it as vividly as the night when Claude had proposed that they form Chromos.

Claude had always praised Renard's brilliance, but he sometimes chided Renard for being too easily distracted, of using valuable time unproductively on tangential projects.

That source of tension had marked their relationship from the beginning, and time had not lessened it.

Claude knew a lot about many things, but a particular area of expertise was horse-breeding, particularly of Thoroughbreds. During the war, he had grown up in the heart of horse-racing country. When his family was reunited after the Allied victory, they closely followed the most prestigious middle-distance flat races: the Prix de l'Arc de Triomphe, the Melbourne Cup, the Japan Cup, the Epsom Derby, and Dubai World Cup, and, of course, the Kentucky Derby. From an early age, Claude had been obsessed with the "Sport of Kings."

Middle-distance racing demanded both speed and stamina from the equine athletes, and these qualities had been fine-tuned through centuries of careful breeding. In fact, of the five hundred thousand Thoroughbred racehorses in the world, 95% were descended from just one stallion, the Darley Arabian, which had been bred with The Royal Mares owned by King James I and King Charles I in England in the 1700s.

Proper training and nutrition were critical to the performance of a racehorse, but genes played a foundational role. The greatest champions typically had enlarged hearts, often two or three times the size of a normal horse's. Secretariat's heart weighed twenty-two pounds while Sham, its Triple Crown rival, had a heart that weighed eighteen. An average adult horse heart weighed eight. But perhaps the most important genetic determinant was the same myostatin gene that controls the muscular development of both humans and horses. A specific non-coding portion of that gene controls myostatin protein production, which in turn dictates the muscle mass of the adult animal.

Claude had been breeding horses for decades, but with Renard he dreamed that he could alter DNA to create the greatest champions in history.

"What you're suggesting is impossible," Renard remembered complaining. "Yes, I can use zinc finger nucleases to create double strand breaks and then insert new material, but we don't know enough yet to be able to build what you're asking for. It's not just the gene. You've got all kinds of non-coding genetic material in the spaces between the genes, and single genes can be spread along a long length of a chromosome. Someday, yes. New techniques could be revolutionary if they work out, but that's years away."

"Renard," Claude had replied dismissively, "be serious. You're telling me that we can edit human genes, but you can't do the same with horses?"

Renard remembered shaking his head, looking back at Claude and getting flustered over the man's almost messianic zeal. Claude wasn't a scientist. There was so much that Renard had never bothered to explain to him. What would have been the point?

Claude had put his hand firmly on the younger man's shoulder. "I believe in you. I know you can do this. I think you *will* do this."

"You don't understand."

"What don't I understand?"

"You really want to know?"

"Yes, I do."

"Now, tonight, after all of these years?"

Claude frowned, confused. "What haven't you told me? I've always been available to you. If there's anything I need to know, tell me. I insist."

There were things he hadn't shared with Claude because he thought the man wouldn't understand. There were other secrets that covered his own embarrassments. In this case, he'd been protecting Claude's peace of mind as much as his own. The two men stared at each other, Claude clearly intent on getting his way. Just then, Renard felt…an overwhelming wave of relief. He could finally unburden himself. In a voice barely above a whisper, he said, "The truth is that you don't fully understand what I'm doing to those embryos."

"Of course, I do. You identify precise points along the chromosome, you cut them with restriction enzymes—"

"There are diseases that are caused by well-known single base pair mutations. Yes, I can do that. But the augmentations?"

"That's what I'm talking about—"

"Claude, there's only one real augmentation that means anything."

"That's absurd. The capabilities you've enhanced involve hundreds of genes—"

"They're *your* genes!"

Claude froze. "*What?*"

Renard hadn't been sure how Claude would react to this revelation, but the look of profound shock on the man's face made Renard deeply uncomfortable. He started pacing, speaking quickly, avoiding eye contact. "When you and Nadine wanted to have children, I collected and cloned your genome. I eliminated some defects and did some minor repairs to correct for your age. Nadine had some serious risk factors on her chromosome 7, so I combined two of your chromatids to form a healthy chromosome. You had beautiful children. I thought that was the end of it. But then you came back to me and wanted me to do the same for your friends."

Claude took a halting step backward. "What are you trying to say?"

"You're a very unusual man, Claude. Very special. The people you wanted me to work miracles for...weren't. They aren't you. I ran into problems I couldn't fix. When I tried to tell you about it all I got was pep talks, just like the one you were giving me just now. You never take no for an answer."

"So, what did you do?" Claude asked weakly.

"I couldn't fix their DNA, so I used pieces of yours. In fact, I used one of your chromosomes in its entirety."

"But these children all resemble their parents," Claude said, clearly stunned. "They don't look like me at all."

"Why would they?" Renard sighed. "There's just so much that you don't understand."

"I'm standing here! Explain it to me!"

"It's so simple, really. There are specific genes that dictate the shape of the face. Facial morphology is controlled by the C5orf50 gene on chromosome 5. The SCHIP gene on chromosome 3 sets face height and width. ASPM on chromosome 1 determines chin prominence. WDR27 on chromosome 6 establishes eye tail length. Hair, eye, skin color is dictated by PAX3 on chromosome 2—"

"Get to the point," Claude growled.

"I didn't touch any of those. The children got those from their parents. But your intelligence? Your focus? Your attention to detail? Your wide range of abilities? I used your entire chromosome 7, plus some regions of your X chromosome. That's why those kids are so special. You're like that Darley Arabian you always talk about. These children are the new human Thoroughbreds. They're *your* legacy."

"But…" Claude stretched out his arms. "How could you do this without *telling* me?" He closed his eyes, raising his hands to his face, bending forward as if he were in pain. "How can I go to my closest friends and tell them their children are partly *mine*?"

"I did it because you kept coming to me when I was busy with *real* research. I did it to get you off my back. You can be an incredible nag, Claude, and I don't like it. Plus, it worked! Everyone was happy: you, the parents, the children. As to your second question, you'd be a *fool* to tell them. They're happy with their offspring. They're proud. They're immeasurably grateful to you. Why would you throw all of that away?"

"We'll be sued. Ruined. Disgraced."

Renard looked up at his benefactor. "Not if this stays strictly between us."

59

"It's a perfect match," Dr. Slater announced, looking up from the colorful printout from the synthesizer. The four women were seated around the doctor's desk at her Manhattan office. "There's no question about it: Claude Dumont is the source of the seventh chromosome in each of the children we've sampled thus far."

"Is there any other possible explanation?" Deborah asked, her sense of triumph mixed with anger.

Slater shook her head. "Not regarding his being the source. The remaining questions are: How did this come to pass, and what did he know about it?"

"We know that Dumont works with that scientist in Lexington," Britt said.

"Sue Miller told me he performed the procedure while she was down there," Deborah said. "I think it's the same man Tom asked you about. You should have seen the expressions on the Dumonts' faces when I said Bergeron's name. It's got to be him."

"He may have performed the implantations," Slater said, "but is he the one who's editing the genes? That's a lot more complicated."

"I don't know," Deborah said, "but he's the only other person we know about."

"Well, Dumont isn't a scientist," said Britt, "so he's not doing it himself. We need to track down his accomplice."

"Claude's a control freak, I can tell you that," Deborah agreed. "Whatever's happening, he's on top of every detail."

Slater leaned back in her chair and laced her fingers behind her head. "At this point, we know that couples went to Claude with dreams of children. He guaranteed them successful pregnancies and the ability to control some of the genetic features of their offspring."

"That's right."

"How did he ensure that the pregnancies would go to full term?"

"He doesn't say each and every fetus will succeed," Deborah replied. "He just promises they'll keep implanting fertilized eggs until one does."

"So, the real secret to his so-called success lies in the embryos themselves. What they seem to have been doing two decades ago would be cutting-edge *now*."

"Maybe not," Deborah said.

"What do you mean?"

KEVIN BOREEN

"You told me it's only recently that scientists have been able to adjust particular base pairs."

"Generally, yes."

"It seems to me that what's happening here is not gene editing so much as wholesale genetic substitution," Deborah said. "Instead of cutting DNA and making insertions, they were just taking out entire chromosomes and putting in substitutes, in these cases, from Claude himself."

"It's a massive fraud," Amy said, her voice shaking. "They're telling prospective parents that they are fixing dents in their DNA, when in reality they're adding a second father."

"Perhaps their initial success with their own twins gave them the idea." Slater sat up straight. "I just thought of something."

"What?" Deborah asked as Slater started to type furiously on her keyboard.

Images flashed up on the screen and reflected from Slater's glasses. As she worked, she said, "I'm just wondering..." She stopped and nodded. "Yep. It's right here."

"What is it?"

"Nadine Dumont has significant irregularities on her chromosome 7. That's why they doubled Claude's. That's the secret sauce. That's what they've been selling to their friends in the name of revolutionary science."

"This isn't science," Deborah said. "It's a

339

crime."

"I couldn't agree with you more." Slater sighed, pushing back from her desk. "So, what are we going to do about it?"

They all looked to Deborah.

She said, "I think it's time for us to talk to a really good lawyer."

60

As he usually did when he was in New York, Claude spent his Sunday morning in the comfort of his study. The sky to the west was ominous, a line of high, dark, billowing clouds, but he was in high spirits. Spending the holidays at Vaux was always one of the highlights of his year, and it had been an outstanding year in nearly every respect.

He relished the time he would spend with his two children in just four more days. He knew he was biased, but he thought Audrey was the most beautiful young woman he'd ever met. They'd enjoyed her all-too-brief stop in New York. Now the prospect of a few weeks with his family at the chateau filled him with joy. Audrey was a remarkable likeness to her mother and combined a sweet disposition with a laser-sharp mind. She'd first beaten him at chess at the age of thirteen and at Go at fifteen. They'd traded wins regularly for a time, and now he was proud to regularly lose to her. Chase was everything a father could want in a son: warm, determined, and excellent in the wide range of pursuits he set his mind to. The chateau would be alive with music, and Chase would be delighted by their special musical guest from Berlin.

Nadine was his queen in every sense of the word: his partner, lover, muse, and counselor. She would attend to every detail to make this a perfect vacation, and she would do so with apparently effortless grace.

Claude had selected several books to enjoy, and he'd set aside sheet music for some Chopin pieces that had gotten away from him, but that he was confident he would soon remaster.

Davos would follow, a full week with friends and global leaders that always left him inspired. He was pleased that Hank Summers would be able to join. He still felt a little badly about having to temporarily dash Summers' hopes, but that was well behind them now.

His only real regret for the past year had been over Tom Wright. Claude had been too confident about his own ability to persuade the journalist to cease his investigations. What if Claude hadn't brought him to the lab in the first place? Claude had firmly believed that if Tom understood what was at stake, he would make the right decision. Claude's judgement had been wrong, so he'd had no choice but to defend his family and those that he had helped. But that, too, was behind them now, a lesson learned, a mistake not to be repeated.

His gaze turned to the portrait of their Kentucky home. After Switzerland, he would return to the farm for the birth of several foals that Renard had been working on. Creating these magnificent horses filled Claude with a sense of power and excitement unlike any other. Watching them grow, train, and win was deeply satisfying to him, and would be for many years to come.

At his last annual physical, just a month ago, his doctor of twenty years had declared him in perfect physical condition even for a much younger man. He felt strong, clear-headed, energetic, and happy. He had his family, his wealth, his passionate interests, and the loyalty and best wishes of countless friends.

Claude felt that he was truly on top of the world, with every prospect of remaining there.

61

The law offices of Black Stromm occupied the top three stories of 277 Park Avenue. Founded in 1960 by Justin Black and Felix Stromm, the firm had grown to more than six hundred attorneys and had a worldwide reputation for civil litigation. Black's son, Charles, had joined the firm in 1996 and was now one of its three managing partners. Deborah was ushered into his office at precisely 10:00 a.m.

"Thank you for seeing me at such short notice, Charles."

The managing partner grinned as they sat on two overstuffed leather chairs. "It's not often that someone claims to be offering me the biggest civil case in the history of the law. I figured it would be a fun way to start the week."

"You think I'm exaggerating?"

"I think you must be, but I'll confess to being extremely curious. How can I help you, Mrs. Fiske?"

"How much do you know about DNA?"

"I'm not a scientist by any means, but

it increasingly comes up in our casework. We
certainly know experts. We retain them often.
Why?"

"What I'm about to tell you is extremely
sensitive. It potentially affects many prominent
families, people you may know. They may even
be clients."

"Everything you tell me here is strictly
confidential." The lawyer leaned forward and
rested his elbows on his knees. "What's this all
about?"

Deborah started to tell her story. Within
minutes, the lawyer, wide-eyed, was furiously
taking notes.

A buzzer sounded on his desk and a voice
said, "Mr. Black, your 10:15 is here."

Without looking up or stopping his
writing, he said, "Cancel all of my appointments
for the rest of the day and hold all calls."

"Yes, Mr. Black."

Charles looked up at Deborah. "I may not
have believed you earlier, but I do now."

Deborah spoke for almost two hours,
Charles stopping her only to ask clarifying
questions, filling an entire legal pad with his
notes.

"So, what do you think?" she asked after
feeling she'd covered everything.

"It's monstrous. I've never encountered

such a profound violation of people's trust."

"I couldn't agree more."

"And it's much bigger than that. This is a threat to humanity. These alterations will be passed along to future generations. Who knows where this might lead? Has he unwittingly created a new species?"

"We have to stop him."

"Do you think there's a provable connection between your boys' condition and Dumont's chromosome substitution?"

"We know they have segments of DNA that came from Claude Dumont. I can't tell you conclusively that their illnesses were directly caused by genetic manipulation, but how can Dumont prove they didn't? Shouldn't that burden be on them? I have to believe a jury would give us the benefit of any doubt."

"Maybe you should have been a lawyer." Charles smiled, but then grew serious. "Which brings me to the core question: What do you want out of this? What do you want to accomplish?"

"Three things," Deborah quickly replied. "I want to stop Claude Dumont, I want to expose him, and I want to punish him."

Charles nodded. "I'll need to see the actual evidence and talk to Dr. Slater, but I'm confident that we can obtain a court order to stop his genetic tampering."

"I'm not so sure. With his resources and

KEVIN BOREEN

contacts, he could drag this on for the rest of his life."

The lawyer sat back, his arm extended along the back of the black leather couch. "People don't generally understand the extraordinary power that our courts have to stop dangerous activities. This is clearly a situation where irreparable harm is being done."

"He'll fight it."

"He can fight it after the fact, but he'll be bound by the order. It's what we call an *ex parte* injunction. They're used when the threatened harm is so extreme and severe that giving the other party an opportunity to oppose the motion is not practical. This clearly fits. I'll meet with a judge in her chambers, present the evidence you've collected, and obtain the order."

"I'll be very grateful for that."

"As to punishment, we have some options. This is clearly a case of medical fraud. Under the law, we can bring both criminal and civil charges."

"What's the difference? Is one worse than the other?"

"Well, when you think criminal, you think jail time. You're not going to see Dumont led off to prison in chains in a civil case. On the other hand, the civil penalties in this situation could be enormous."

"So, do we take this to the authorities?"

"Parallel proceedings can get tricky when

the government is bringing both a civil and criminal case for the same alleged conduct." Charles paused for a moment. "We can discuss this further, but my initial thought is that we could report this to the government as a criminal matter but pursue the civil case privately."

"The more we can do the better, as far as I'm concerned."

"Then I suggest that as our plan. I'll meet with your Dr. Slater and document the crimes that Dumont and his people have committed. We can submit that to the United States Attorney's office and let them take it from there. They'll obtain warrants for admissible samples. I'll use Dr. Slater's evidence to get that injunction I mentioned. At the same time, we should have a confidential meeting with the families in Wright's photograph. We can explain our fears and offer each family the opportunity to have their children tested. Those that wish to do so can join in the civil suit. Under the circumstances, I'm confident Dumont will want to settle quietly and quickly."

"Will that be enough to truly punish a man with his wealth? I don't want this to get swept under the carpet."

"Oh, it won't be, I assure you. If what you've told me is true, he's permanently contaminated the germ lines of some of the most powerful families in *the world*. Those parents are going to take him for everything he's worth. And if he fights it, he'll be crucified by juries."

"I'd like to see that. When do we start?"

"We already have," he said. "Now, tell me how to reach your Dr. Slater."

62

Two days later, Deborah was shown into Charles Black's office. He looked both excited and exhausted. The hair that he had been so perfectly combed on their first meeting was mussed and he looked like he hadn't shaved since they'd met. His tie was loose around his neck and his suit jacket was thrown carelessly over the back of his office couch.

"You look like you've been busy," she said, taking a chair in front of his desk.

"Getting all those families to come or call into a short-notice meeting with no announced topic is one of the hardest things I've ever done," he said. "But we've made progress on several fronts. I met with the US Attorney last night. She's going to be all over this."

"And the injunction?"

"I spoke with Judge Abrams yesterday. She wasn't happy with how the DNA samples were obtained, but based on statements from you and Sue Miller it's clear to her that Dumont is a danger to the public and must be stopped. She'll issue her order by the end of the day today."

KEVIN BOREEN

"I don't know if Dumont has other families in his pipeline."

"After today, you can consider that pipe permanently closed. Are you ready for this meeting?"

She nodded. As an affected parent, she'd felt that the painful message would be better received coming from her. Black had agreed but would be standing by to answer any legal questions.

"What time do you expect everyone?"

"We said 8 p.m., but they're all here now," he said, looking at his watch.

"Maybe you'd like to freshen up," she said. "This crowd is used to a certain look in their lawyers."

He smiled. "In five minutes, you'll hardly recognize me." He stood and disappeared through a door she hadn't noticed before. Alone in his large office, she stood and walked nervously across rich Persian carpets. Details momentarily distracted her. A few Harvard diplomas hung in frames on the paneled walls. Black also appeared to have a taste for bronzes and oriental porcelain. Fine specimens were displayed throughout the room.

Her mind returned to the terrible chore before her. She was about to tell a dozen families that their children, their most precious treasures, were not exactly who they thought they were. The horror of it was almost overwhelming. On the one hand, the people that they knew to be their offspring would not be changed by this revelation. On the other, the realization that someone had deliberately inserted a part of himself into their future families was the most personal and brutal betrayal imaginable.

The side door opened and Black reappeared in a fresh shirt and suit, shaved and combed. "All set?" he said.

"Yes."

"If you stick to the script we discussed, I think we'll get through this first meeting all right. Once this sinks in, though, we're going to have some very angry people."

She nodded. "I'm ready. I just keep telling myself, they have a right to know."

He opened his office door for her. "They're waiting in the conference room."

She followed him past his two assistants. They stopped in front of imposing double doors. She took a deep breath and nodded. He opened it.

The large, paneled room was filled with people. She recognized many of them. Some were surprised to see her, and many of those seemed displeased. Some had come as couples. Some had brought attorneys with them. Deborah locked eyes with Sue Miller, who had brought her husband after all. Sue nodded somberly. Rick, standing behind her, looked bored and impatient. Deborah was grateful to see

Dr. Slater standing at the back of the room. The light on the nearby speaker phone was bright green.

"Thank you all for coming," said Charles, immediately taking control of the room. "We have important information that may be of the greatest interest to some or perhaps many of you."

"What's this all about?" Lord Hastings asked. "What's all the mystery?"

"Once Mrs. Fiske has spoken, I'm sure you'll understand why we wanted to handle it in this way. Mrs. Fiske?"

Deborah stepped forward, placing her purse on the edge of the conference table. "First, I want to apologize to anyone here who isn't ultimately affected by what I'm about to share with you. I sincerely hope many of you are not." After some grumbles rose and fell around the room, she continued, "Eighteen years ago, my husband, Scott, and I went to Claude Dumont for medical help to have a child." The silence in the room was absolute. "The procedure was effective, and I gave birth to twin boys. As some of you know, my sons have had serious health issues. In the process of investigating the causes of that, I recently learned that both of my boys have foreign genetic material in their DNA."

Spouses looked to their partners, confusion written on their faces.

"You were invited here because we

thought that you might also have received assistance from Claude Dumont. I thought it was important to tell you this, because we have absolute proof that the foreign DNA in my boys came from Mr. Dumont himself."

After a moment of absolute silence, the room erupted. Half of the crowd seemed to be in shock. The other half seemed deeply offended that Deborah would make such an outrageous accusation.

"Settle down, everyone," Charles said. Then more loudly, "Let her finish!"

As the furor subsided, Deborah said, "We also have incontrovertible evidence that some of your children also have Mr. Dumont's DNA, in particular his seventh chromosome."

The room exploded again, a potent mix of anger and confusion.

"How could you possibly know this?" Khalil Darwish asked.

Slater stepped forward. "I'm a practicing medical doctor with a PhD in biochemistry. Mrs. Fiske came to me for help in analyzing her sons' DNA. Given the foreign DNA we found in their genome, and after careful consideration, Mrs. Fiske and I decided to collect samples from some of your children." She held out her hand to silence the angry parents. "We have protected their privacy, and yours. We were very discreet. This is my area of expertise and I conducted the analyses myself. As Mrs. Fiske said, we don't

KEVIN BOREEN

know if this affects all of you, but we do know it affects some of you."

"Who? Who's affected?" Khalil Darwish demanded. "Tell us what you know!"

"Is this what that reporter was after?" someone asked, creating a loud commotion in the audience.

Charles raised his hands to regain control over the meeting. "Each of you has an important decision to make. It's not one you need to make now. We believe – we know – that Claude Dumont's genetic material was inserted into the DNA of some of your children. You can choose to ignore that fact, or that possibility, if you wish. That's entirely up to you. But some of you may want to know. We don't know how this will affect your children in the long term. Because Mr. Dumont's DNA is now part of their germ line, it will affect their offspring for generations to come."

"But this is monstrous!" someone cried out. "How could he do something like this? *Why* would he do it?"

"I simply don't believe it," Rick said. "Claude would never violate our trust."

"Here is what we propose," Charles continued. "If you are concerned, have your children tested. Dr. Slater can help you or refer you to others. If your family hasn't been affected, we apologize but hope you'll understand why we needed to share our

355

concerns. If you decide you want to take legal action, we can be of assistance."

"Who else knows about this?" someone asked over the speaker phone.

"A judge today will issue an injunction stopping any future medical activities by Mr. Dumont and his associates," Charles said. "I've also referred this to the US Attorney as a criminal matter."

"So, the Feds have the names of our children?" a woman asked, her face red with fury.

"No," Deborah said, stepping forward, "just my boys." Several heads nodded approvingly around the table. "If you want to involve yourselves, we thought that should be your choice. I've made mine."

"You all have our contact information," Charles said. "I know this must come as a shock. We hope this isn't as widespread as we currently fear. Now, go home to your families. Talk it over. Search your hearts. Out of respect for your privacy, this is the last contact we'll have with you unless you reach out to us."

This was answered by an outbreak of furious, shouted conversation. Charles took Deborah by the arm, led her away from the angry crowd, and closed the heavy doors. In the quiet hallway, he said, "That went about as well as it could have."

"I feel like I just plunged a dagger into the

hearts of all of those people."

"Someone did," Charles said, "but it wasn't you."

63

Meanwhile, Claude and Nadine called their children from the limousine on their way to Teterboro Airport. Chase and Audrey were both in high spirits, enjoying showing their friends around the chateau and its grounds. Barring any delays, they would all be united in nine hours. Their jet was standing by to take them non-stop to Orly, an airport south of Paris, and then a short helicopter ride would bring them to Vaux and a resplendent brunch to start the holidays.

"It's been quite a year, hasn't it?" Nadine asked, streetlights flying by on the starless night.

"It has. Oh, and did I tell you? Scott called me this morning. He found a buyer for the vineyards in Australia."

"You're happy with the offer?"

"Very." He clasped her hand. "He managed to turn it into a bit of an auction, so we got twenty percent more than I'd planned. Can you think of anything we can do with an extra $200 million?"

"Hmmm. I thought I had everything I

KEVIN BOREEN

could ever want, but I'll give it some thought."

He smiled. "I'm sure you'll come up with something."

"I've been meaning to ask," she said. "Did that reporter ever resurface?"

He turned toward her. "What made you think of him? I hope Deborah's wild accusations didn't..."

"No, of course not, but the whole thing seems so strange to me."

"He took the money and ran. There's nothing strange about that. I see it all the time."

"It seems a shame that someone can profit so much from something like that. I would rather have sued him."

"What's that wise phrase? Always begin with the end in mind? Under the circumstances, I think we did the best we could. The problem's behind us."

"Behind *all* of us. Everyone is so grateful. I can tell you that."

Claude patted her hand as they pulled off the highway onto Industrial Avenue. Beyond a black metal fence, they saw runway lights and a long row of aircraft hangars. They passed through the airport gates and drove straight across the tarmac to their waiting jet.

As the car stopped and Claude opened the door, a row of blue lights began to flash. Three uniformed men approached the limo and motioned for the chauffer to lower the rear window. One of the officers shined a light into Claude's face.

"Are you Claude Dumont?" one of them asked.

Claude raised his hand to shield his eyes from the bright light. "Yes, I am. What's this all about?"

"Mr. Dumont, you are under arrest."

"Under arrest?" Nadine gasped. "What's going on? Who are these men?"

"I don't know," he said, shielding his eyes from the bright lights. "Obviously, there's been a mistake."

"Mr. Dumont," the officer said, "will you please step out of the car?"

"Claude," Nadine pleaded, "what are we going to do?"

Claude looked longingly at the aircraft awaiting them. "Get on the plane. Go to the children. I'll sort this out and join you as soon as I can."

"*Claude*," she said, touching his arm, confusion written across her face.

"Sir, get out of the car. Now."

Claude took Nadine's hand. "There's something you need to do for me right away, and it's very important."

"Yes, Claude?"

"Tell Maxim NOT to do what I asked him to do this morning."

"What did you ask him to do?"

He patted her hand. "There's just no point now." He stepped out onto the tarmac.

Nadine followed close behind. She watched helplessly as the officers handcuffed her husband and placed him in the back of a black SUV. She couldn't see Claude through the tinted windows, but she waved to him in case he could see her.

Then she bounded up the airstairs and took out her cell phone. She had their Lexington office assistant on the line before she reached her seat.

64

Renard Bergeron was tying up some loose ends in the lab when his cell phone rang. He knew that Claude was getting on a plane for France and wondered what last-minute errands he'd be tasked with, an all-too-common occurrence when Claude was set to travel. He glanced at his screen and saw that it wasn't from Claude but from Maxim. Renard couldn't remember the security chief ever calling him directly.

"Bergeron here."

"Dumont's been arrested."

"What?" Renard sat, stunned. "Why?"

"I don't have all of the details yet, but the charge is medical fraud."

"Shit."

"Yeah, it's shit all right. The court's issued an injunction against Chromos. You and Claude are listed as defendants."

"Am I listed by name?"

"Yes. Claude told me to be sure you know that."

"How did they…?"

KEVIN BOREEN

"It could have been the Fiske woman."

"Are you going to…"

"No." Maxim cut him off. "Claude changed his mind. He's right. It would be too dangerous now."

"So, what's next?"

"I imagine you'll be arrested before the night's out."

Renard had planned for this, hoping the day would never come. "Where is Claude now?"

"He's being held in jail. His lawyers are heading over now. Mr. Dumont wanted me to call you right away. He said you'd know what to do. He said it's urgently important."

"I understand. Anything else?"

"He said he's going to make sure everything's taken care of, including you. He wanted you to know that."

"I understand. Thanks for calling."

Renard stared at his phone for a moment before ending the call. He and Claude had never thought this day would come, but they'd talked about worst-case scenarios and what they would each need to do. Claude's conclusion had been that his situation would be precarious, but that Renard, if he played his cards carefully, should be able to navigate through it all safely.

He logged onto his computer and pulled up a master file containing all the genetic data they'd collected on human subjects over the past two decades. The file was enormous. It represented a lifetime of diligent, cutting-edge work...his work. He deleted it with a few keystrokes. He did the same with the backup files. He then ran a special program to overwrite the memory where the data had been stored, making it unrecoverable.

Next, he walked to the freezer and removed two trays containing hundreds of small test tubes. He placed them in an autoclave and turned it to its highest setting. He knew the heat wouldn't completely destroy the DNA samples, but the next step would be more thorough if the samples were thawed. He took a five-liter stainless steel pan, dumped the contents of the test tubes into it, and stirred in a beaker of hydrochloric acid, adding the empty glass tubes to eliminate any trace of organic matter.

He had just poured the acid-DNA mix down a hazardous waste sink when the laboratory phone rang. He guessed it came from the guardhouse. He was correct.

"Doctor, there's a federal agent out here at the gate who says he needs to see you in person."

"Tell him I'll be right there."

"Yes, sir."

Bergeron took one more look around the lab, logged off his computer, and grabbed a leather travel bag from under his desk. It contained his passport, cash, credit cards, bank account records, and two untraceable cell phones. He turned off the lights and locked the lab door.

"Have a good night, Doctor," the security guard said from his desk as Renard passed by.

"And you."

Renard climbed the stairs, crossed the dark lobby, and got into his car. Instead of heading to the guardhouse, however, he drove in the opposite direction. After about a mile of forest he came upon a tall gate held closed by heavy chains and a padlock. He used an app on his phone to shut off the electricity to the fence and the security cameras, and then a key from his glove compartment to open the padlock. He drove through, closed and relocked the gate, and reactivated the electric fence and cameras. Then he threw his cell phone into the 10,000-volt fence, where it disintegrated in a bright flash. Another mile of winding gravel road led him to a paved county road. An hour later, he was airborne on a privately chartered jet bound for Grand Cayman.

As he passed an altitude of ten thousand feet, one of his replacement phones rang. He didn't recognize the number. The country code was 86.

"Hello?"

"Am I speaking with Dr. Bergeron?" said a crisp male voice with a Chinese accent.

"Yes."

"We understand that you may looking for a fresh opportunity."

Renard smirked as he slowly shook his head. "I'm always open to new ideas."

"Mr. Dumont speaks highly of you, and we've long admired the work you've done at Chromos. As you know, some parts of the world are more open to new scientific thinking. Could we send a plane for you? Our terms will be most generous."

Renard smiled. Claude had indeed taken care of everything.

65

After her stressful meeting at Black Stromm, Deborah found her car and began the drive back to her Greenwich home. Along the way, she had an uncanny feeling that a heavy-duty pickup truck was tailing her, but it pulled off the parkway as she crossed the Connecticut state line. She admonished herself for imagining things. She parked in front of the house, dropped her purse on the entryway table, and stopped in the kitchen to pour herself a large glass of wine. She kicked off her shoes and sat by a window. Distant lights reflected off the dark surface of the lake behind the mansion.

Every family had asked to have their children tested. Dr. Slater had agreed to perform the tests and had signed iron-clad confidentiality agreements with each of the families. Charles Black had drafted the contracts personally. Only Slater and the respective parents would know whether the children had been inappropriately altered. Each family would then have to make its own decision about whether to seek damages.

Deborah had already made that choice.

She had worried about the statute of limitations for medical fraud, which is normally five years, but Black thought that under these circumstances a court would find it reasonable that the clock should start from the date that the harm was discovered and its cause known, which was today.

She left her empty glass by the sink and crossed the darkened great hall to the passage leading to her son's suite. She walked down the stairs and was surprised to see that the doors were open and unlocked. She rushed to Paul's room and stopped suddenly. Her irritation at seeing Scott sitting at his side was quickly overwhelmed by her joy at seeing that Paul was sitting up and awake, a smile of recognition on his face

"He woke up two hours ago, Mrs. Fiske," said the nurse at her side. "I think they've finally got the medicines right."

Deborah went to the bed and stroked her son's hair. The swelling on his face had subsided, and the bandage over his eye socket seemed less imposing now.

Paul reached for her hand. She grasped it, a lump forming in her throat. His grip was weak, but it had been so long since he'd responded to her. Her heart leapt.

"I owe you an apology," Scott said. He seemed so shrunken and old to her across the bed, his head and shoulders sagging. "I never dreamed…" He stopped and took a breath. "All these years I thought you were, well, just crazy. I thought…your wild suspicions were a threat to everything I was trying to do. And…it turns out you were right all along. All these years… I put my loyalty in the wrong place. Deborah, I'm sorry."

Deborah heard his words but was unmoved by them. She was Paul and Edward's mother. She'd known. Somehow, she'd known, and Scott had fought her every step of the way.

"Please say something," he said quietly.

"Thank you for apologizing. It doesn't change anything. You left us. While we were here struggling with these terrible demons you were playing on the French Riviera. The stories about you and your women reached me at the lowest points in my life. You can't imagine how humiliating that was for me. And now you want to come back to us? Be a part of our lives again?"

He lowered his head even more. "Yes, that's what I'm asking."

"That won't be possible. Not for me. So, here's what you should do. Give me the house and add two zeroes to that separation agreement you sent me, and I'll sign it. I won't stop you from visiting the boys, but you and I are done. I never want to see you again."

He looked even older now. "That's a lot of money."

"I think it's generous, under the

circumstances, and it's a drop in the bucket compared to what I'm going to get from your hero."

66

Claude Dumont was charged and, after handing over his passport, released in the early hours of the morning. His attorneys brought him home to his Park Avenue condo. He had been careful to say nothing to the police. The charges thus far were focused on medical fraud. His lawyers had been cautiously optimistic about the statute of limitations until Claude told them about the Millers. His attorneys would work throughout the night to plan his defense, but they advised him to prepare himself for the possibility that he would spend the rest of his life in prison.

The criminal charges were only the beginning of his problems. He knew what the genetic tests would reveal. His friends would never forgive him. Whether he settled or went to trial, the penalties would set records, perhaps amounting to many billions of dollars. The discovery of his DNA in the Fiske boys alone created an enormous liability. He knew that Renard and Maxim would do whatever needed to be done to eliminate as much incriminating evidence as possible, but the key and incontrovertible facts were embedded in the nuclei of his cells and those of the children who had inherited them unbeknownst to their parents.

Once the extent of his genetic research became publicly known, it would only be a matter of time before attention turned to his horses. While the relevant law was less clear, his lifetime of success would be irreparably tarnished, his reputation as a breeder destroyed.

He had always prided himself on seeing situations clearly, and he did so now. His world was falling apart before his eyes. The only good news was that there had been no mention of Tom Wright.

He thought of Renard and wondered if he was already on a plane to China. Claude had been so furious that day he'd learned Renard's secret. But he had forgiven him. In time, as Claude vicariously witnessed the achievements of the children that carried his genes, it had become a quiet source of pride. He would live on through all those gifted children long after he was gone. He hoped that one day they would take pride in their full ancestry.

It was lonely in his palatial home high above Manhattan. He poured himself a cognac and called Nadine in France.

"Where are you?" she asked, her voice thin and dry. She sounded like she hadn't slept.

"I'm home."

"I've been on the phone with the lawyers all night. Claude, it any of this true?"

Claude pressed the bridge of his nose with his thumb and index finger. "We should be careful about what we say on the phone, Nadine." After a long silence, he asked, "Are you there?"

Another moment passed. "Yes, I'm here. Audrey and Chase were disappointed you missed the plane. I haven't told them anything. It hasn't hit the media yet. I suppose it's just a matter of time."

"There will be stories. You can count on that. When can you come home?"

"I am home."

"I mean here. I need you."

After a long pause, she said, "Claude, I think it's best for everyone if I stay here with the children."

"Well, I can't come to you. They've taken my passport. Legal proceedings will take months, maybe longer."

"I know. These are really serious charges. I have to say, I'm stunned that you could have been part of…something like this."

"It's much more complicated than that."

"Well, someday I'm sure you'll explain it to us. You're so good at that."

"Nadine."

"Goodbye, Claude."

EPILOGUE

Two years later, Deborah Fiske invited Britt and Amy for lunch at her home in Wilton, Connecticut. After her divorce, she'd sold the Greenwich mansion and moved to a far more modest brick colonial on five acres of rolling, wooded hills. Scott had returned to his life in Europe, calling the boys more often that she had expected.

The three women had collaborated closely to find Tom Wright, without success, and in the process had become close friends. Law enforcement had taken matters more seriously when they saw a potential connection between his disappearance, the taxi incident near LaGuardia, and the damage found on his rental car in Lexington. After failing to find any evidence to challenge Dumont's explanations, however, their investigation was at a standstill.

"Thanks for coming," Deborah said, greeting them warmly at the door. Britt had flown up from Miami earlier that week for a New York gala, and Amy was now thriving at *The Atlantic*.

"It's so beautiful out here," Amy said. "You should ask us out more often."

"You know you both have open invitations," Deborah said as they walked through the house to get to the back patio. Edward was playing the piano in the living room while Paul read on a nearby couch.

Britt ruffled Paul's thick hair as she passed. "What're you reading?"

He looked up at her, a shy grin forming. "Voltaire. In French."

"But, of course," Britt smiled back.

Once the women were outside, Britt asked, "How's he doing?"

"So much better," Deborah replied. "This therapy really seems to be working. *Finally*. He's stable…sometimes even happy."

"I'm so glad," Amy said.

"It's an incredible relief, I can tell you."

Deborah had already laid out their lunch, a salad with grilled chicken and vegetables. A big vase of colorful flowers graced the center of the table, flowers she had grown herself. She'd enjoyed returning to a life more like the one she'd had growing up, one in which she made her own food, took care of her children, and enjoyed the luxury of a house cleaner just once a month.

They sat around a wrought iron table, maples and oaks extending down a slope to a reservoir below them. Deborah poured them iced tea and they ate and talked beneath a perfect summer sky. As always, their conversation eventually returned to the fate of Tom Wright.

Britt shook her head. "I hate to say it, but I've almost given up hope."

"Someone continues to withdraw funds from that Cayman account," Amy said. "I hope it's him."

"I don't understand why these banking secrecy laws are allowed to stand," Deborah said. "The account has to belong to someone, and someone at the bank must know who that is."

"It's not him," Britt said, "though deep down I wish it were."

"Well, it's certainly not Claude Dumont." Deborah had been at once gratified and fascinated by the man's catastrophic fall. He had shocked the world by pleading guilty to the medical fraud charges, and then refused to implicate anyone else in his genetic research. Claude's close friendship with Renard Bergeron's father had come to light, and it became clear that Renard had worked for Claude for the past twenty years, though there was no record of his activities. Whether out of fear or loyalty, Claude had protected him, then and now. Renard had disappeared nearly as completely as Tom had, although there were reasons to believe that the scientist had joined a research center in China. Claude was currently serving a ten-year sentence in a federal prison in upstate New York, a plea deal that took into consideration his age and settlements with the affected families.

The civil cases had never gone to trial. Dumont had proactively offered a billion dollars to each family, sums that were ultimately accepted. The forced asset sales and reputational damage ruined him financially.

KEVIN BOREEN

Nadine had quietly divorced him, sold the Kentucky farm, and now lived full time in France. By all accounts, her two children continued to excel, amaze, and impress.

The names of the affected offspring were never publicly disclosed, which did not stop pundits, social media, and conspiracy theorists from speculating about a new breed of superhumans now circulating in our midst. The implications for the future of the human species were now standard fare on blogs and talk shows across the political spectrum.

Deborah had used her settlement money to create a trust and two foundations. The trust would care for Edward and Paul for the rest of their lives, which thankfully now had brighter prospects than ever before. The Paul Fiske Foundation's mission was to conduct research on the treatment of schizophrenia and bipolar disorders, as well as to offer financial assistance to afflicted families in need. The Edward Fiske Foundation's focus was to raise awareness among the public, scientists, and legislators on the ethical challenges of genetic engineering.

Britt and Amy insisted on helping Deborah with the dishes, and then said their goodbyes amidst promises to return soon. Deborah walked them to Britt's car, embraced them once more, and waved as they drove down the driveway. Then she turned back to her home, took a deep breath beneath the bright, warm sun,

LEGACY

and climbed the steps to enjoy a quiet afternoon with her boys.

THE END

AUTHOR'S NOTE

This is a work of fiction. I made many assumptions about where genetic research may lead us, some of them highly speculative. I do believe, however, that we are on the verge of revolutionary developments in our ability to manipulate the human genome, and that progress should be thoughtfully and carefully guided and regulated.

I am very grateful to my wife, Catherine, my son, Steve, and son-in-law, Bela Wilde, to my sisters, Kathy and Mary, to my parents, Allen and Dorothy, and to friends Ralph Alderson, Andrey Belov, Morgan Harting, Denise Hughes, Rich Innes, and Alan Lui for their suggestions and encouragement. I would also like to thank Ed Stackler and Matt Bialer for all of their advice, instruction, and support.

ABOUT THE AUTHOR

Kevin Boreen

Kevin is a graduate of the US Naval Academy and Harvard's Kennedy School of Government. He served as a naval intelligence officer, management consultant, research analyst, and investment portfolio specialist. He now lives and writes in Florida.

Made in United States
Troutdale, OR
02/26/2024